T0265789

Peril
in
Pink

Peril in Pink

A HUDSON VALLEY B&B MYSTERY

Sydney Leigh

CROOKED LANE

NEW YORK

Copyright © 2024 by Sydney Leigh

Published in the United States by Crooked Lane Books, an imprint of The Quick Brown Fox & Company LLC.

Crooked Lane Books and its logo are trademarks of The Quick Brown Fox & Company LLC.

Library of Congress Catalog-in-Publication data available upon request.

ISBN (hardcover): 978-1-63910-639-4
ISBN (ebook): 978-1-63910-640-0

Cover design by Ana Hard

Printed in the United States.

www.crookedlanebooks.com

Crooked Lane Books
34 West 27th St., 10th Floor
New York, NY 10001

First Edition: March 2024

10 9 8 7 6 5 4 3 2 1

To Remy and Scarlett

Chapter One

"Pink flamingos make me sick."

My brother's easy smile edged toward a disapproving frown. "They're a symbol of joy and a cultural icon, not to mention the signature color of the Pearl B and B."

I cleared my throat. "The birds' legs are freakishly spindly, and the namesake cocktail is more Pepto Bismol pink than our soft-blush aesthetic."

Nate grabbed the bar towel from his shoulder and started polishing the already-clean beer glasses that separated us. "Don't you have a B and B to run, Jess?"

I feigned a pout. "Teasing you is much more fun."

He finished up the beer glasses and flicked the towel at me. "Aren't siblings supposed to have each other's backs?"

"You're my little brother. It's my job to give you a hard time. Besides, I wasn't insulting your bartending skills, just your choice of drink specials."

A voice came out of nowhere. "Maybe we should rename it the Nate Byrne Special. Then I'd drink it every day."

I spun around on my barstool and looked down. Sarah, my brother's new wife, was perfectly balanced on two hands in some sort of twisty yoga position.

"How long have you been doing that?" I asked.

She turned her face sideways and looked up at me. "I'm working up to ninety seconds. This would be a great one for you to learn. It's good for the detoxification of internal organs."

I pressed my lips together. Sarah didn't wear makeup, and she had a six-pack. I never left home without mascara and preferred rosé to exercise. But she was sweet, if a little too granola-like for my taste. "Let me work on the toxify part first and see how far I get."

"Speaking of toxic," Nate said, "Mr. Rock and Roll is here."

My stomach knotted. It had been a long time. I resisted the urge to dart around to the other side of the bar and check my hair for fear of ridicule by Nate, who'd never been a fan of my ex. "He's not that bad. I hope you were nice to him."

"I didn't actually see the guy. But a flashy SUV with a personalized license plate that reads *luvme* pulled in while I was passing through the lobby."

I fought back a smile. "Okay, might be him. Lars has been known to be a little self-involved."

Nate quirked an eyebrow. "Ya think? The gas guzzler had all its windows down, blasting eighties glam metal."

A snort slipped out. No denying it: that was Lars. Leave it to Nate to make my high school boyfriend sound like a complete idiot. Not that he wasn't. Still, I'd never quite rid myself of a soft spot I held for him. Plus, he'd won *Sing This!*, prime time's latest reality songwriting competition, six months ago. The media referred to him as TV's newest singing sensation. Nate could've given him some props.

"*Bing, bang, boom, babe.*" Nate sang his best Lars impression.

My top lip curled up. *Ugh. Babe.* Forgot about that.

Nate clapped my shoulder. "Don't stress about it, sis. You made it through almost a whole year of dating the creep. What's one more night of listening to a hit song he wrote about you?"

No way I'd admit a miniscule part of me actually looked forward to seeing him again. Maybe because I didn't really understand it myself. Either way, it was time to face the music maker.

"I never liked the guy much, but I have to admit him coming to play on opening night is awesome."

Nate was right. I knew the importance of a strong social media presence for a business's success. Being able to splash Lars's photo up on our Instagram feed was huge. Especially since it was on-brand. The goal was to turn a former boarding house, owned and operated by my grandmother back in the sixties and seventies, into a chic bed-and-breakfast. The behemoth Queen Anne–style building was set on a huge swath of land, complete with a big pool, sprawling deck, and adjacent garage-turned-bar. Nate and Sarah had recently opened the Cool Vibes Café, and it had quickly become a hot spot for locals and tourists alike. Me and my BFF slash business partner, Kat Miller, hoped to piggyback on their success with the B and B. Our dream was to make it the trendiest accommodation in the area for bachelorette parties, girls' weekends, date nights, and romantic getaways. Having the winner of a reality TV singing competition come and perform? It definitely got the attention of our target market.

My only question was why Lars had agreed to do it. Yes, this was his hometown, but we weren't boasting a large crowd. The B and B had only ten rooms. The capacity of the bar was well under a hundred people, a much smaller number than he'd normally get at a regular performance. He used to play for my grandmother's guests on the back deck with his high school band. Maybe he was feeling nostalgic. Did he miss home? Did he miss *me*?

Stop it. Big breath in. Big breath out.

I strolled through the California-inspired decor of the pool area. As I scanned the huge green leafy plants, natural wood furniture, and soft pink accents, everything looked perfect. Kudos to faux greenery.

I continued into the café, a transition made seamless thanks to the bar's floor-to-ceiling sliding glass doors. It was one of the few features Nate had chosen to keep when he overhauled the property's dilapidated garage. The wide doors were designed to be left open on nice days, allowing patrons a full view of the newly renovated pool and adjacent B and B.

A bark broke through my thoughts, and I glanced down to see Duke, my one-blue-eyed, one-brown-eyed husky, fresh from his nap. He wagged his tail as our eyes met, and I bent down to give him a pat. He flipped upside down, and his tongue flopped out onto the pool deck without a whiff of grace.

"I hope you don't try this move with our guests. Not everyone appreciates your talents."

He sat up and barked at me as if arguing with my reproval. Huskies were known to be chatty. Duke was a legendary motormouth.

"Zip it, furball. I have things to do."

Duke licked my bare knee, and we marched side by side toward reception. The back entrance into the bright and airy space was quiet. But the retractable front window was up, and I could see the shiny, blinged-out SUV Nate had been talking about parked nearby. Our full-time summer season receptionist, a local art student named Penny Rankin, was busy organizing the soap and essential oils we had on display. A last-minute addition, they were one of a few details left to attend to, like setting up the samples for guests to sniff and shelving the dozen or so bottles. We wanted them visible without taking center stage.

Penny glanced up and waved before turning her attention back to her task. A long mirror adorned with the Pearl's logo in hot-pink neon lights ran behind her. No doubt she was engrossed in our favorite podcast, *My Favorite Murder*. I didn't bother to interrupt. This week's episode was a nail-biter.

I caught my reflection as I turned my attention toward the door. I took the opportunity to fluff up my bangs with my fingers and smooth down my long brown wavy hair. It hadn't changed much since high school. Neither had the rest of me, really, although the casual black shirtdress I wore now was a little more sophisticated than my teen faves of bedazzled jeans and halter tops.

"I knew it," an invisible—and judgmental—voice said.

I whirled around to see my best friend and Pearl co-owner, Kat Miller. She was peering out from behind the collection of faux greenery as if auditioning for a low-budget version of *Tarzan*. Duke barked and wagged his tail in approval.

"What are you doing back there?" I demanded. "Didn't we already agree you weren't allowed to hide from guests?"

Kat harumphed as she rose to her full height of five foot ten, a fact she lorded over five-foot-nothing me whenever I was winning an argument. She shook out her shiny jet-black hair as she brushed off her scrawny knees. "I was plugging in the espresso machine so it would be ready when the guests arrive. How about you? Wait, don't tell me. I already know. Checking yourself out before the wannabe rock god gets here."

Not her too. I started to argue, but she cut me off.

"You were doing that weird scrunchy-eye thing you save for mirror checks. Admit it, you're busted." She folded her arms across her chest and waited for an explanation.

D'oh. Not fair. I wanted to make the point that she looked good too. But that would fall flat; she always looked good. With her lithe frame, intense brown eyes, and easy breezy style, she had an effortless beauty. It was one of my least favorite things about her.

Instead, I popped the collar of my dress and held my head high. "I'm representing our brand. I can't go around looking like a troll."

The side of her mouth twitched. "You're way too delicate and cute to be a troll. Much closer to an elf, in my opinion. And since we're talking opinions, do I need to remind you again to steer clear of Lars?"

I placed my fingers in my ears. "What? I can't hear you."

There were only so many times I could listen to her rants. *He's nothing but trouble. Having him here is a bad idea. Don't get sucked back in.* Blah, blah, blah. With Lars's number-one hit and a million followers on Insta, her arguments against him fell flat. And he'd offered to play for free. Besides, I wasn't interested in him anymore. Hot rock stars? So overrated.

Before Kat could say any more, the side entrance door swung open, and two women strode in. Duke sprang up and wagged his tail but remained behind the counter, as we'd practiced. I slid my fingers out of my ears and twirled my hoop earrings.

The two women were a mirror image of each other. Not only were they identical twins, but they were also on trend. A perfect pair of fashionistas. I couldn't have dreamed up a better example of our desired demographic. In their late twenties or early thirties, they were casually dressed, with hints of glam. The first wore wedge heels and black-and-white-striped paper-bag shorts with a sky-blue linen sleeveless blouse. Her long hair was pulled off her face in a messy bun, and she wore bright-red lipstick. Her sister wore strappy black sandals, a yellow cotton maxi dress with big side pockets, and an oversized straw beach hat that screamed fun. Matching smiles completed their looks.

"Welcome to the Pearl." I opened my arms and beamed at them. "You are our first official guests."

They exchanged a high five and approached the front desk. Penny stood up, but I gave her a dismissive wave. She shot me a thumbs-up and went back to the display.

The first woman spoke. "Hi, I'm Lila, and this is my sister Elle."

"So nice to meet you guys," I said. "I'm Jess, one of the owners here. If you need anything, just say my name. I'm here pretty much twenty-four seven."

Kat shuffled up to the desk. "Sorry to interrupt. I'm just going to steal Penny for a few minutes to finish toiletry checks in the rooms."

"Sounds good," I said.

Kat and Penny exited through the back. I turned back to the twins. "Sorry about that."

Lila dropped her bag at her feet. "Don't be. We're low maintenance. All we need is a place to chill."

Elle leaned forward, resting her elbows on the counter. Sparkling crystal bangles shimmered from her wrist. "And the Pearl is amazing. I was sold as soon as I saw the perfect pink doors. Look at this place! I'm ready to post a thousand Instas already, hashtag *glam girls weekend*."

I stood a little taller. "Thank you." The millennial-pink doors had been a risk, but they'd already paid off in spades, snagging the attention of style mags and influencers from coast to coast before we'd even opened.

"I'll leave that part to you," Lila said, reaching out and squeezing her sister's hand. "The only thing I want in my hand is a glass of chilled vino."

"You're in luck," I said. "Every room is equipped with two wineglasses along with a bottle of local sparkling rosé in the mini-fridge. All included with your stay. I just need a credit card for incidentals."

Elle turned to Lila. "You have my wallet, right?"

Lila passed her twin her oversized purse. "Good luck."

I did a double take, and my heart skipped a beat. "Is that from the new Stella McCartney collection?"

Lila flushed. "Vegan leather, with—"

7

"With the extra-wide logoed shoulder strap." I nodded. "Few things get me as excited as an iconic purse. This one gagged me. It looks even better in person."

Lila beamed. "I treated myself. Decided I couldn't work six months of twelve-hours days with nothing to show for it."

"Lila's a nurse," Elle explained. "Long hours." She unzipped the bag and peeked in. "As proven by her habit of keeping half her apartment in here. This might take a while." She began to sift through its contents. "Lipstick, phone, keys, corkscrew, protein bar, sunglasses, pen, hand sanitizer, and . . . aha." She pulled out a simple black wallet. "Here we are." She slid her credit card out and passed it to me. "My sister is nothing if not prepared."

I grinned. "My kinda gal." I started to enter the information. *Elle Katharine Hicky.* "Pretty name."

"It'll be even prettier soon," Lila said to her sister with a wink.

I tilted my head to the side. "Aw, you getting married, Elle?"

Elle's shoulders slumped and she shook her head, "Divorced."

My face warmed. "Gotcha. Sorry." Married and divorced by thirty. She and Kat had more in common than just a name.

Lila put a protective arm around her sister. "The lawyers are drawing up the papers even as we speak. Something to celebrate. Right, Elle?"

Elle gave her a wistful smile and nodded. Poor thing. No wonder she needed a weekend away with her twin. Time to change the subject to something more fun. "Will you two be hitting the beach?"

Overshadowed by bigger towns with bigger lakes on either side, Fletcher Lake wasn't known as a beach town. However, since overcrowding wasn't a problem here, our sandy shores were becoming more popular.

"We might pop over," Lila said.

"If you do, let us know. We can direct you to a locals-only secret spot just across the road."

"How about food? Any suggestions?" Lila asked.

"We have some great options in town worth checking out. I'll put together a list."

Our small hamlet had been heralded as the Hudson Valley hot spot of the season by several popular travel sites, in large part because of the opening of a slew of new eateries. In particular, there'd been rave reviews about Our Bistro, a casual fine-dining restaurant recently opened by a famed NYC chef who'd decided to trade in the city to open his own restaurant.

"Perfect," Lila said.

"There's also the show here later. Have you heard about it? It's going to be awesome."

Elle's body stiffened. "Not our thing."

"Lighten up, Elle. We're here to have fun, remember?" Lila said, then turning to me, asked, "What's happening tonight? I've been working a lot of overtime lately, so I haven't been keeping up on social."

My heart swelled with pride. It wasn't every day I could boast a visit from a certified rock star. "Lars Armstrong is playing an acoustic set for us to kick off opening weekend."

Lila's face drained of color. Her mouth dropped open, but no words came out.

Elle started fidgeting with a diamond heart-shaped pendant hanging from her gold necklace. "Didn't I mention that, Lila?"

Lila brushed her curtain bangs back savagely and glared at her sister. "Nope. Guess it slipped your mind."

Uh-oh. "Not a Lars Armstrong fan?"

Lila flinched. "His voice is like a bellowing moose."

Not the reaction I was hoping for. I flashed a smile, determined to set this right. "Don't worry. If it's not your scene, you can sit out back. We'll stoke up the firepit for you. I can even whip into town and grab the ingredients for s'mores."

The women ignored me.

Lila crossed her arms. "Why didn't you tell me?"

Elle rolled her eyes. "I thought a weekend away would be good for you. So what if there's a show? Like Jess said, we'll have a fire and chillax."

Lila put her hands on her hips. "You can't possibly think I'd be foolish enough to believe this is a coincidence?"

A ping alerted Elle to an incoming text. She pulled her phone from her purse and held up a finger. "One sec." She strolled away from the counter and began to text a reply.

"Saved by the bell," Lila said under her breath, before looking around with an uneasy frown.

I scrunched my nose. "Guess you won't be hitting up Lars for an autograph."

She scoffed. "Only if it was accompanied with a restraining order for him and his whole posse."

Sheesh. Was there such a thing as an anti-fan?

Elle returned to the counter. She held up the phone. Our Instagram page flashed before me. With a grin, she asked, "Is it true you paired with a local artisan to create your own toiletries?"

I grinned back, relieved we'd moved on. "Yup, and they all have a unique peach-vanilla scent only available at the Pearl."

Elle turned and faced her sister with a told-you-so smile. "C'mon, Lila. You have to admit it. This place is heaven. Pink doors? Rosé all day? It's our dream aesthetic."

Lila's shoulders relaxed, and she sighed. "Promise me you didn't plan this with Nico?"

Nico? Who's Nico? This girl had a hit list. I scanned the register. *Phew. No Nico.* The last thing I needed was to have to shuffle guests around to accommodate a high-maintenance drama queen.

"I swear," Elle said, holding out her pinkie finger. "I only found out after I'd made the reservation, and I'm tired of changing my life to accommodate him."

"Gah, fine." Lila briefly locked her sister's finger with her own. "What's the worst that could happen?"

You get into a fistfight and my B and B turns into a rerun of Jersey Shore? *No thanks.* I decided I'd better keep an eye on these two. I finished checking them in, directed them toward their room, and waved goodbye. Elle paused to take three selfies before floating through the lobby door, Lila close behind. I had the urge to go ask my aunt for instructions for a white-witch spell to cleanse the air. With bank loans and bills to pay, there was no time for negativity, and no room for anything else to go wrong.

Chapter Two

A car door slammed shut, alerting me to another newcomer. I walked around the desk and stepped outside. Emerging from the blinged-out Cadillac SUV was a face I knew well. My heart skipped a beat as I saw Lars Armstrong and his all-too-familiar coiffed blond hair bounce toward me. With his sunglasses up, tight leather pants, and a swagger that matched his big new life, he strutted up the sidewalk toward me with a brilliant toothy grin. In spite of myself, I couldn't help but grin back. Though I hadn't seen him in ages, Lars had been my first love. Idiot? Check. Self-involved? Definitely. Handsome and charismatic? Yes and yes.

"Jessie, my girl, how are you, babe?" his voice boomed.

Cringe. I'd forgotten how much more likable Lars was when he wasn't speaking. "Hi, Lars. It's been a long time. Good to see you."

"Come here, you," he said, pulling me into a big bear hug.

I had to laugh. Lars had a way of breaking through my natural reserve.

Duke appeared at my side and gave a bark.

"Hey, handsome." He patted the oversized furball on the head, triggering a wagging tail.

"This is Duke," I said. "My personal bodyguard."

"Duke may need to work on the intimidation factor."

The ninety-pound baby sat on my foot. "He's big enough to make someone think twice before messing with me."

The goofy grin spread even wider across Lars's face. "I told you, size does matter."

"I prefer what George Michael said: *The clothes don't make the man.*"

"Touché. Unless they look like this, huh? Hey, what do you think?" He did a spin in his designer duds with an Elvis hip thrust at the end.

I couldn't stifle a laugh. "It suits you." *Loud and obnoxious.*

"Thanks, babe. You know I never liked shopping at the Better Sweater." He'd always loved taking digs at a local shop frequented mainly by ladies of a certain age. "Had three signature hoodies made last week. Premium French terry."

"Okay, big shot." I held my hand up. "I suppose I should thank you for taking time out of your new life to pay us a visit and give local fans a show."

"You're sort of a homing device, Jess." His eyes lingered on mine.

I blinked, feeling heat rush to my cheeks. I'd forgotten what a smooth operator he was. *Don't fall for it. Not again.* "Like a pigeon?"

He grinned. "When I heard you were back in town and had revamped your grandma's house, I had to come see it for myself."

"C'mon, let's go inside." I swiveled around and strolled back toward the entrance. I turned to see him taking it all in. I could see he was impressed. Then again, he should be. We'd done an awesome job. "As you can see, we combined the front foyer and den to create one big lobby." I fanned out my hand. "On one side you have our reception desk, made from local repurposed wood, and just across the room, a place for guests to chill."

He strolled across the room and did a 360-degree turn. From the oversized palm to the rattan furniture with pastel-pink cushions to the black-and-white tile floor, he took it all in. "This place is unbelievable. You nailed it."

One thing Lars and I had in common was big dreams. He'd wanted to be a star, and I'd wanted to live on the West Coast with a fancy job and an even fancier corner office. His plan seemed to be working out better than mine.

"Thanks." On the far side of the room, I pushed open the patio entrance. He followed close behind. "And out here we have the social area, where guests can take a dip in the pool, chill out on the deck, or stroll across the patio to the Cool Vibes Café."

Lars's mouth dropped open. "God, Jess, this is incredible. I was surprised to hear you'd left California. I think I get it now."

My cheeks flushed with pride. "Pretty great, huh? The café serves complimentary breakfast to the B and B guests and light fare for guests and locals. Nate and his wife, Sarah, own the bar, and Kat and I split the B and B."

"He's not going to throw me out again, is he?"

"Not unless I ask him to," I teased.

He looked chagrined. "I'll keep that in mind. Honestly, though, I can't believe this is the same place our band used to play on Friday nights. Back then, this was nothing more than a dusty old house with a decrepit garage and a crumbling pool."

"Even then, you always had at least a handful of locals come out to see you play."

"Yeah, guess I did. Not so sure they'd be as welcoming now."

I tilted my head to the side. "Do you have any friends left around here?"

My words made him cringe.

"Hey." I gently elbowed his side. "I was kidding. Remember me—Jokey Jess? Ball-of-laughs Byrne?"

He blinked and gave me a wistful smile. "I feel you. But I burned a lot of bridges on my climb up, babe, starting right here in Fletcher Lake."

Uh-oh. I could see he was ready to unload.

"C'mon, it can't be that bad." My voice was chipper. I had no time for a segment of *Confess to Jess.*

His dogged expression suggested he needed more coaxing.

"Lars, I forgave your bad-boy antics years ago. If I can let go of the past, I'm sure everyone else can too."

"I hope you're right, 'cause if not, my whole life could get derailed."

A sense of unease filled me. What had he done? Dismissing the thought, I tugged at his elbow. "C'mon, let's get you checked in. You can tell me your troubles later on."

"Sure thing," he said. "Anyways, it's amazing, babe." He looked at me pointedly. "You're amazing."

I ignored the deepening flush in my cheeks and marched back toward the door. "So how did you find out about the Pearl?"

"I read it in the *New York Times.*"

I paused and narrowed my eyes. "Since when do you read the *New York Times?*"

He laughed. "I did a TV talk show last month. The green room banned mobile phones. The *NYT* travel section was sitting out. Almost fell out of my chair when I saw your pretty face smiling up at me. Wanna share the secret of how you scored that gig even before you opened your doors? Even *I* haven't gotten an interview in that paper yet."

"Helen McKay's cousin is the managing editor. She put a word in for me."

He snorted. "The Momfia strikes again, huh? Impressive."

The Momfia was the nickname we'd given my mom and her circle of friends, who seemed capable of accomplishing anything they put their minds to, from convincing a professor to expand his class for a few needy students to barring the building of a well-known hotel chain in our charming little town. It took a little nudging, but my mom's best friend, Helen, had managed to convince her cousin to include our new venture in an article on Hudson Valley's up-and-coming hot spots.

"The day after it ran, we sold out every weekend from June to August," I told him as I opened the door back to the lobby. "And when we announced on social you'd be here for an up-close-and-personal acoustic set? The phone rang off the hook for days."

"Sweet." He sauntered inside and dropped his bag. "The whole town looks great. I'm starting to wonder why I stayed away for so long." He looked around at the reception area again before letting his gaze settle on me. "There's so much to miss."

"Right." I gave his arm a pat. It was the same *settle down, boy* gesture I'd give Duke when he barked at a nearby squirrel.

At my touch, Lars leaned in and flexed his bicep muscles, blatantly ignoring personal-space etiquette. My nose itched at the onslaught of way too much cologne. "Ready to check in?"

"Let's do it. I'm excited."

I felt myself relax. So far, Lars had been nothing short of charming. Then again, he'd always had a strong start. It was his ability to maintain the good-guy persona that messed him up.

"Look who decided to finally come home," a voice said from behind the desk.

It was Aunt Marnie, with a most definite case of bedhead. A dead giveaway she'd been napping in the little nook we'd incorporated into the design of our new front desk. As the unofficial caretaker of the property even before my grandmother passed, Aunt Marnie had come with the B and B, almost like the furniture had. Except we liked her better, so she was allowed to stay, unlike practically everything else, which had needed replacing.

"Auntie M," Lars said, looking a little surprised. "I assumed you'd be sailing around the Galapagos or something."

"That would be a hoot." Her smile faltered a little. She brushed back a knotty cluster of hair from her eyes. "No, I'm sticking around to help the kids set up the B and B. Although I have been daydreaming about Ko Tao in Thailand."

"Nice. I'd love to spend a week there perfecting my tan." Lars winked at me.

An unexpected snort slipped out. I clapped a hand over my mouth.

Aunt Marnie shook her head. "A little snorkeling, sure, but I prefer going there to volunteer. Excellent turtle rehab programs on the island."

Aunt Marnie had never been able to hold down a job. She quit every time her request for a months-long break to wander the planet was denied. It never bothered her. Unlike my mom, the retired school principal, Aunt Marnie wasn't career minded and liked to live by the beat of her own bongo drum. Mom called it a failure to launch.

"Anyway, good to see you, kid." Aunt Marnie patted him on the arm. "Now I've got to go check the new cameras. I'll catch you two later."

Lars waved. "All right."

Aunt Marnie turned toward the mirror, trying to tame her unruly locks without much success. She gave up, then wandered through the side door. Duke followed her out, sniffing at her pocket, which was likely filled with snacks for both of them.

17

Lars turned back to me. "Cameras?"

"I know it sounds a little over-the-top, but the two outside cut down on our insurance premium by twenty-five percent, and the ones inside monitor the front desk and protect Mom's treasured first-edition romance novels from thievery, so she says. All *you* need to remember is that they're there. I hear the paparazzi pay good coin to catch young celebrities in compromising positions."

"Noted," he said with a grin.

"I've got to pop over to talk to Nate," I said. "Catch you later?"

"Why don't I come with you and say hi? You'll protect me, right?"

"As long as you behave," I warned.

"Deal's off," he joked. "I'll have to fend for myself."

With a stern look, I grabbed his bag and tucked it under the desk. "Anything valuable we need to worry about?"

"Just my deep dark secrets."

We made our way back along the hallway and through the patio doors. Before I had a chance to get details on his dirt, a scream pierced the air. I excused myself hastily and left Lars standing there. The sound came from behind the B and B.

Sarah.

I rushed through the pool area and into the bar. My head swung left and right, on the lookout for my brother. Nate was nowhere in sight. *Rats.* I sped up and passed through the far gate, which doubled as the bar's public entrance. The walkway up from the sidewalk was clear. I sprinted behind the building, where the B and B's cozy campfire area was arranged. Empty. *Where is she?* I craned my neck. *Aha.* Further back, just past the pond, I spotted Sarah in the gazebo, where she'd been teaching morning yoga classes. She was on her knees, her body bent forward.

I sprinted over. "Sarah!"

Nate arrived at the same time, emerging from the opposite direction, where the L-shaped parking lot was laid out. His chest heaved as he tried to catch his breath. "Sarah, are you okay?"

She didn't answer.

Nate wiped sweat off his brow as he knelt to examine her. She was holding something in her hands. Her face was ashen and expressionless. She glanced from Nate to me, surprised by our sudden presence, as if we'd appeared out of nowhere. She held her hands out to show us what she was holding.

It was an old metal horseshoe, rusty and battered. "Did that drop on you?" Nate asked. "Are you hurt?"

She shook her head slowly and allowed him to help her up.

Seeing no visible wounds, I felt a jolt of irritation. "Sarah, what happened? You scared the nuts out of us."

My sharp tone seemed to snap her back to attention, and her cheeks reddened. She blinked a few times before answering. "Sorry."

"*Sorry?*" I repeated. "Our goal is to create a comfortable space for people to relax, not an atmosphere for panic attacks."

Nate frowned at me but didn't step in. He wanted to know as much as I did what had brought on Sarah's sudden outburst.

"It's this." She thrust out her hand to give me a better look at the horseshoe. "I had it attached to the wall for good luck. While I was doing a dolphin pose, it shifted upside down, as if someone had taken all our good luck and dumped it out. Then it ripped off the wall and crashed down."

I clucked my tongue as my mother would've done and threw my hands up. "You nearly gave us a heart attack because you're a lousy carpenter?"

Her eyes lifted slowly to meet mine. "No, Jess, this is a bad omen. If I didn't know better, I'd swear someone—or something—did it on purpose."

Like gravity?

"Cool," a voice said. I whipped around to see Lars with a wide grin on his face. He must've strolled over to see what was going on just in time to hear Sarah's ridiculous explanation.

Everyone ignored him.

Nate looked at Sarah as if she'd just asked him to smell an old sock. "Sarah, this isn't like you. You're not superstitious."

Sensing the beginning of a conversation that was none of my business, I considered excusing myself to let the newlyweds sort it out. But my feet didn't move. Curiosity beat out social protocol.

Sarah swallowed before meeting Nate's gaze. "When I was a kid, my grandfather gave my mom his lucky horseshoe the day before he died. He'd brought it to Canada from Ireland. She displayed it prominently on the kitchen wall. Every time something bad happened, we'd come home to find it upside down, starting with his death. She passed it down to me when we got married. Nate, I put it up thinking it would continue our good luck. But now I think I may have brought ruin to all of us."

Huh? I wasn't sure what to say. *You've lost your marbles* sounded a little harsh, even in my head. Nate had to be thinking the same thing. He turned to me and Lars slowly. It was the first time he'd taken notice of my old boyfriend, and he gave Lars a subtle nod of acknowledgment.

"Guys, can you give us a little privacy?"

"Sure," I said.

"Bro," Lars added. "You do you." He winked at Nate as if the two were old friends.

Nate shot me a look, and I grabbed Lars's sleeve and pulled.

"Nice girl," Lars whispered into my ear as we scuttled away.

"Don't get me started," I muttered back.

Nate was in a tough position. What was he going to say? Calling your new wife a nutjob was probably a no-no. On the other hand, if the straitjacket fits . . .

There was just one catch: superstition and ghost stories weren't new to the house. It wasn't exactly my thing, but there'd been rumblings about strange occurrences here since before I was born. In the early days of my grandmother's time as a landlord, there'd been some sort of dispute between guests, resulting in one of them ending up at the bottom of the pond out back. Was it possible that Sarah had tapped into some unsettled spirits? *Nah.* Sarah was just being melodramatic. Maybe Nate was too focused on work and she was making a play for his attention. Much more plausible. Bad omens didn't exist.

So why did I feel so shook?

Chapter Three

Lars and I made our way back to the reception area without another word. I tried to calm my nerves as he took in the surroundings. It was still early, and I hadn't anticipated more guests showing up for a few hours, so maybe that's why I jumped when I saw a figure sitting with his back to us. He turned, and I recognized the balding man instantly. Squeezed into beige skinny jeans and a tight red button-up shirt was Lars's stepfather/manager, Bob Strapp. He reminded me of a hot dog in a bun with too much ketchup.

"Well, well, well, Jessica Byrne. Look who's all grown up. Come over here and give me a big ol' hug."

"Hi, Mr. Strapp." I took a step back to make sure I wasn't within reach of his thick, meaty hands.

He leered at me. "You can call me Bob now that you're a full-grown woman, and what a woman you are."

Lars stood in front of me in a protective stance. "Bob, cut it out."

A grunt of acknowledgment was all Lars got. Bob had been Lars's stepfather since he was seven years old, yet Lars had never taken to calling Bob by anything but his first name. It still puzzled me why he'd agreed to let Bob manage him in the first place, other than some sort of loyalty to his mom, who'd passed away while he was a fresh-man in high school.

"I didn't realize you were coming too, Bob," I said. He still owned a property in town, as far as I knew. I'd just assumed he'd stay there, if he made an appearance at all.

"Where Lars goes, I go." He loomed closer. "I assume that won't be a problem?"

"No problem at all." I refused to let him get to me. "We always have an open room in case of emergencies like this one."

Lars reached out and touched my elbow. "Thanks, babe." He looked at Bob. "Can you grab my stuff out of the truck? I'm going to check in, then have a look at the stage area."

Bob grumbled a few words of complaint but did as he was told, trudging back outside to fetch the luggage.

When he was out of earshot, Lars leaned toward me. "Sorry. You know Bob. He is what he is."

A creep? A gross old man? Yeah, I know.

"Let me grab the keys for yours and Bob's rooms. Then I'll show you where we've set up for you to play tonight. Since it's a solo acous-tic performance, we have a cozy nook tucked in near the pool."

"Sweet." He pulled a phone from his pocket and checked the time. "I think I saw it when we passed through earlier. Enough space for people to watch and my roadie to grab some stills with his cam-era, so I'm good."

I raised an eyebrow. "You have an assistant?"

He made a clicking sound with the side of his mouth. "Dropped him off on Main Street to pick up a few things. Handy, right?"

I frowned. "Does he need a room too?"

"Nah, he and Bob can share."

Poor guy. I would've chosen the dumpster out back over sharing a room with Bob. I popped behind the desk and started filling out the guest intake form on the computer. "Am I allowed to ask why you chose your stepdad to be your manager?"

Lars propped up his elbows on the counter. "I know you were never a big fan, but Mom stuck by him, so I gave him a shot. And before you ask, it was before I got the nod to appear on *Sing This!*"

"So it's been a while."

"Two years ago he showed up on my doorstep with a suitcase; said he'd had a dream about me. As corny as that sounds, he was right. He hustled to get me gigs and worked as hard as I did to score my big TV win."

An uneasy feeling set in. Bob had burned through what was supposed to be Lars's college fund before we finished high school. He blamed grief. I wasn't convinced. I finished typing and grabbed two rooms keys. "Just make sure he's looking out for you."

Lars stiffened. The easy breezy grin slid off his face. "Where was all your friendly concern when I was flat broke, eating instant noodles, and having doors slammed in my face?"

"Ouch."

He rubbed his hand over his face, as if he was trying to stop what he was really feeling from peeking out. "I'm sorry, okay? Let's just get through tonight," he said, giving me a fixed smile.

What did that mean? What was going on with him? Before I could ask, a gust of wind made its way through the sunny space, bringing with it a shaggy-haired hipster in tight jeans and an oversized hoodie. Dripping with sweat, he still managed to retain his boyish good looks.

He heaved an audible breath and dropped two grocery bags on the floor next to Lars, who looked him over and chuckled. "Nicky, you look awful. You need to work on your stamina, bud. And maybe get yourself some shorts."

I came around the front of the desk. "Can I get you a glass of water?"

"Nah," Nicky managed to get out between gasps. "I'm fine."

Lars clapped him on the shoulder, then cringed as he looked at his sweat-soaked palm. "This guy needs to grow a little hair on his chest."

I pointed to the sofa. "Until then, why don't you have a seat and catch your breath? I don't want anyone collapsing on opening weekend."

Light-blue eyes peered out from behind stringy bangs. Nicky hesitated.

Lars waved him over. "Go on, do as the lady says."

"Hold on a sec." I reached over the desk and grabbed a handheld mini-fan Aunt Marnie used for hot flashes. I held it out with a friendly smile. "It doesn't look like much, but my aunt swears by it."

Nicky studied me for a minute before accepting the device. "Thanks," he said quietly before the high-pitched hum kicked in.

He shuffled over to the sofa and sank down, then leaned back and shut his eyes as the fan did its thing, micro gusts of cool air gliding over his sweaty face.

Bob waltzed back in with a few suitcases in hand. He glimpsed at Nicky and frowned.

"We paying this guy to put his feet up?"

"Relax, Bob," Lars said. "I don't need arm juice dripping on my gear. Give him a minute to stop the flow."

Nicky's eyes were still shut, but I thought I detected a hardening of his jaw.

Lars grabbed a pen from the reception desk and wrote something on the back of one of our business cards. He passed it to me.

"What's this for?"

"Just in case." He winked.

I shoved the business card in my pocket, then passed each of them a room key. Relief set in as I watched all three disappear out the back door. Once they were out of sight, I took a long sip from one of the fancy water bottles I'd nicked from Lars's grocery bag when he wasn't looking. Cold and refreshing. I enjoyed every last glug.

The door swung open and two more women glided in, each with a weekend bag slung over her shoulder. A few years older, a few shades blonder than I remembered, but I recognized the pair as if I were roaming the corridor of Fletcher High. It was Queen Bee Britt Sanders and her loyal sidekick, Paula Davis.

Is this some sort of joke?

When Britt caught my eye, her jaw dropped and her arms flung open as if we were long-lost sisters. I looked behind me to see if I'd missed someone she actually liked, or at least someone she hadn't actively targeted in senior year. Nope, just me. The girl she knew only as—

"Jess the Mess," Britt announced.

There it was. She said the words as if the moniker had been a source of pride rather than a hallmark of humiliation. I could practically hear her high school minions titter with delight at the words.

"Britt," I said flatly. "This is an unexpected surprise."

"You're welcome," she cooed.

I frowned. Last I heard, her whole family had left Fletcher Lake, with the exception of her brother. How was this place even on her radar? And why? I refrained from asking. What would be the point?

Best to take the high road. Bygones be bygones. "Thanks for coming."

"Of course, doll. Hashtag *workhardplayhard*, hashtag *girlsweekend*. Am I right?"

My spirits lifted at her words. We'd branded ourselves on social media with girls' weekends in mind. Maybe we'd both matured. Time for a truce?

Paula cocked her head and gave me the same sourpuss expression she'd had since freshmen year. *Ugh, nope, not with you.* I focused back on Britt, who was still talking.

"The vibe speaks to me. You wasted no time honing your big-city styling skills to make this place gorg. And what better timing? Opening weekend with our very own rock god playing an intimate set? Definitely worth a trip home from New York."

My cheeks flushed. *Now I get it.* Britt was still hung up on Lars. She hadn't given him the time of day until his band started making headway on the radio. By then, he'd had his sights elsewhere. Not on me, not on her.

I logged in to the reservation page on my computer and saw two people registered under the name Hawthorne.

Britt peered around the lobby as if looking for something.

"Can I help you with anything, Britt?" I asked. "A bottle of water?"

"You're sweet, Jess the Mess."

I gritted my teeth, all thoughts of a truce trampled. "It's just Jess now."

"Just Jess. How modest. You always did love to play that part, didn't you?"

The heat rose in my cheeks, but I refrained from taking the bait. "If you need water, food, or a beverage, the Cool Vibes Café is out the side door."

"Cute," Britt purred. "Actually, we couldn't help but notice the big shiny truck out front. The license plate says *luvme.* We thought Lars might have arrived early."

Paula nodded like an obedient lapdog. "It has to be his."

So predictable. I sighed. "He just checked in. I'm sure you'll run into him sooner or later."

Britt preened in front of the mirror, turning left and right, adoring herself from every angle. "That's the plan." She paused briefly and shot me a quick glance. "You two aren't back together, are you?"

"No," I said firmly. Not that Britt had ever let a little thing like a girlfriend stop her from going after what or whom she wanted.

"Good." She dragged herself away from the mirror. "We'll take our key now, Just Jess. I want to freshen up before taking a dip in that beautiful pool I saw featured on social."

"Sure." I finished checking them in, then held out their two room key cards.

Britt was about to take them out of my hand when she paused. "Was that Nate I saw in the bar photos?"

My eye twitched. "Yeah, he runs it."

"Interesting." She gave Paula a not-so-subtle jab with her elbow.

This moment was hands down the most appreciative of Sarah I'd ever felt.

Before another ugly word could come out of Britt's pretty mouth, I thrust the two sets of keys at them. The pair wandered out the door, taking one last look around as if I might be stashing Lars away, trying to keep him all for myself.

I'd been warned to expect the unexpected when running a bed-and-breakfast. I'd thought I'd been prepared for that. The one thing I hadn't seen coming? A high school reunion I couldn't escape.

Chapter Four

The rest of the day went smoothly. Guests checked in, Penny shone behind the reception desk, and everything felt back on track. I heard tidbits of praise in passing conversations and grinned at the sound of laughter echoing from the pool.

At seven o'clock, Aunt Marnie shuffled up next to me and squeezed my arm. "You've worked your tail off today. Go get dolled up and show Lars Armstrong what he's missing."

I leaned into her and rested my head on her arm. "Thanks, Auntie M."

"Of course, Jess. Now scoot." She gave me a kiss on the forehead and shooed me away.

All dolled up for me wasn't that complicated: a little glimmer, a lot of gloss, and an extra layer of mascara. I swapped out my work clothes for a simple teal sundress that showed off my tan and made the green flecks in my hazel eyes pop. I paired it with a pair of black ankle-strap heels. I had no interest in rekindling anything with Lars, but I had to admit I wanted to look good while he was here.

I went back out to the reception area and did a twirl for Marnie.

"You look beautiful, Jess," she said. "Now, don't move. I'm going to grab a burger from Eddie's Place; I've got a sudden hankering. Then the night is yours."

I glanced around. "Where's Penny?"

"I told her she could go."

I frowned. "Why? I had her scheduled until eleven."

Auntie M shrugged. "The girl was tired. I don't mind."

But I did. What next—would she cancel the morning cleaning service in case they felt like sleeping in? Maybe that wasn't fair. Either way, this was a conversation for another time. She was trying to be helpful. My irritation eased as I noticed the strain in her face. "Get your burger and come on back. Not a big deal."

Odd. Things didn't usually register with her, never mind upset her. Then again, it was a big weekend for everyone who worked here, and that included her.

She reached over and gave me a squeeze. "Back in a jiff."

She hurried out before I could ask for an order of fries. I'd call her if she had a phone; one of these days, I'd insist on it. I'd bet that Stevie Nicks—even Joni Mitchell—had given in by now.

Eddie's Place was just down the road. If I was that desperate, there was still time for me to go grab something when my aunt returned. Lars wouldn't be on for almost an hour, which gave me loads of time beforehand. For now, I would just decompress and let the success of the day wash over me.

Opening day had gone even better than I'd hoped. Everything felt right and in its place. Now, with all the guests checked in, locals began to filter through the door, excited to see the hometown celebrity play. Familiar faces wandered in and shot me a wave or a quick hello before heading to the bar.

Even Mom and her bestie, Helen, showed up. I beamed as Mom pointed out all the changes we'd made in the lobby, and I could tell she was proud of me. It was a feeling that never got old. The chic vintage aesthetic practically glowed in the sunset.

Like Thelma and Louise, these two were not to be trifled with. On the outside, you wouldn't know it. Mom had never given up the understated high school principal look, even after retirement, and wore a fitted black pantsuit over a blush-colored blouse paired with three-inch heels. Helen, the semi-retired Fletcher Lake Police Department office manager, was in a pencil skirt and flats. I watched as they leaned in to examine a floor-to-ceiling faux plant. With satisfied smiles, they gave me a double thumbs-up. We exchanged a look of genuine affection, and—

Wait a second!

Was it me, or had Mom's top dipped down, showing a glimpse of cleavage? And was that a black leather choker around her neck? I frowned. When had Helen's skirt gotten so short?

"The place looks marvelous, Jessica," Helen said. "You and Nate really outdid yourselves."

"Thanks, Helen," I said. Were those Jimmy Choos on her feet? *Stay focused, girl. Eyes up.* I tried to match her grin. "We're happy how it turned out."

Mom, in her not-so-mom-like-top, agreed. "I love that you, Nate, and Kat are in business together. Although Nate would've made a wonderful philosophy professor."

"He can philosophize with customers as they tell him their troubles," Helen said.

Did she know her lacy bra was visible through the nearly sheer top? Maybe it was the lighting. "How about me, Mom? Sad I left the retail industry?"

She clucked her tongue. "You know how I feel about that, Jess. I never understood what it was even about. A career focused on trying to manipulate people to spend their hard-earned dollars on stuff they don't need? No, I never worried that you'd made the wrong choice to come home and do something meaningful."

"Thanks, Mom," I said, ignoring the backhanded nature of the compliment.

Helen lowered her voice. "We stopped by the Coffee Haus, and Mona said there'd been a sighting of Lars driving into town. Has he arrived?"

The Coffee Haus was Fletcher Lake's oldest coffee shop, and its owner, Mona Dumbleries, had run it for as long as anyone could remember. I wasn't surprised people were excited about Lars's return. He hadn't been home since he'd hit the big time. "I assume he's getting ready in his room."

Mom studied my face. "How is the boy?"

"The boy's a man, Mom, and he seems just fine."

Helen did a shimmy shake with her shoulder. "A man, huh?"

She and my mom exchanged a look and burst out laughing.

"Cut it out, you two," I said.

Mom elbowed Helen. "I hope you didn't mention to that *man* you're homeless."

Helen snorted and swatted at her. I rolled my eyes. "I'm not homeless, Mom. I'm staying in Grandma's old room. It's easier for me to be on-site for the first few months."

"Mm-hmm." Mom gave me *the look*. "Just don't get any ideas from your aunt. She lives in a shoebox."

"Mom, it's called a tiny house, and they're super trendy right now. Besides, I sold my condo in San Francisco so I could afford to buy Grandma's old place from you and Aunt Marnie, remember?"

"I suppose. But don't get too comfy there, okay?"

"Yes, ma'am. For now, if I get lonely, Lars is just down the hall." I gave her my cheekiest grin. One of my favorite pastimes was trying to get under my mom's skin.

Mom's expression flattened. "Don't chew your cabbage twice, Jess. And don't tease your mother."

She'd been using the cabbage line since I'd done back-to-back book reports on Sweet Valley High novels in fifth grade. It didn't make sense then, and it didn't make sense now.

Helen wandered over to the door that led to the fun zone, then waved excitedly to someone in the distance. "C'mon, Val. Nate spotted me. He's holding up a bottle of Jack Daniels and calling me over. I think he's making us a signature drink."

Good Lord.

No sooner had they exited than my aunt came sweeping back in. Her face was flushed.

"Back already?"

She frowned. "Back?"

"From Eddie's Place?"

"Oh, right." She tapped her macrame bag. "I found a sandwich in my purse. I'm all set. You go ahead."

Something was up. Her aura was off. "Are you okay, Auntie M?"

"I'm fine," she snapped. "Just go before you're late."

I hesitated. It wasn't like her to be grumpy. But she was right. Time was not on my side. I tapped my hand on the desk. "Okay, I'll head back there. Will I see you after the show?"

"If it doesn't go past eleven. I'll lock up if it does, and you can direct traffic around the far side of the inn."

A shot of guilt went through me. "You sure that's not too late?"

She huffed in a show of defiance. "I've stayed awake long enough to watch the sunrise more times than I can count. I may not be dancing by moonlight these days, but you can bet I can manage midnight on occasion."

I held my hands up. "Fair enough. Thanks, Auntie M."

She shooed me toward the door. "Go enjoy yourself. You've earned it."

I leaned over the desk and give her a peck on the cheek. "Thanks." I headed out without another glance back.

The evening air was thick with the scent of sweet wine and an energetic crowd. Nate moved in time with the beat of the music from behind the bar. He poured drinks and chatted up a group of women, who were hanging on to his every word. The pool was closed, but the lights were on, making the tables closest to the wide opening that connected the bar to the pool deck glow in the mixture of patio lanterns, candlelight, and glistening stars. A crowd hovered around the small stage. The place was hopping.

I checked my watch. Eight-oh-five. Where was Lars? I scanned the area. Not here. My pulse quickened. *Settle down, Jess.* A few minutes late was no big deal.

I made my way to the small stage area, where a microphone had been set up. I switched it on and gave the crowd an exaggerated wave.

"Hi, everyone! Welcome to the grand opening of the Pearl!"

There was a round of cheers and applause from the audience.

"We're just waiting for our hometown singing sensation, Lars Armstrong, to grace us with his presence and sing a few songs."

"Where is he?" a voice shouted from the crowd.

"He's late," someone replied.

I held up a hand. "Don't worry, everyone. I'm sure he'll be here soon."

My old "pal" Britt's voice carried above the murmurs. "Is history repeating itself? Is Jess the Mess going to be stood up a second time? First prom and now this!"

My face flushed, and I began to feel hot all over as the crowd broke into a laugh. I forced a smile. "Not tonight. If he doesn't show up this time, I'll kill him."

More lighthearted titters wafted up from the crowd. Prom night was not something I remembered fondly. Leave it to Britt to open up an old wound.

After one more call out to thank people for coming, I gave a wave and bounced off the stage.

The bar area was packed as people waited for Lars to show. I caught Nate's eye, and he motioned for me to come over. I fought through three layers of ladies to reach him.

He leaned close. "Everything okay?"

"It will be, once Lars shows up."

He frowned. "Where is he?"

I shrugged. "No idea. I haven't seen him around."

Nate's eyes flicked to the far exit. "If he's not in his room, maybe check in the back? From what I remember, he was never particularly concerned with being on time."

Probably one of the reasons he had an assistant/roadie. But I hadn't seen Nicky either. Or Bob, for that matter. A wave of anxiety hit, and I began to run my hand through my bangs. "You're right. I'll go now."

Nate returned to chatting up the customers while I slipped out the back. I kicked a patch of grass and left a clump of mud on the toe of my new stiletto. Great. Now, instead of sophisticated innkeeper leaving her stamp on the world, I'd be Mudfoot leaving her tracks on the tiles.

A glorious sunset stained the skyline. Any other time, I would've taken a moment to appreciate it. But not right now. I was way too angry. Instead, I kept my eyes down and marched the long way around the house, slipping past reception and straight down the hall.

I knocked on the last door, the room assigned to Lars. No answer.

35

I pulled out my phone along with the piece of paper he'd jotted his number on earlier. Good thing I'd brought it with me. I pulled up the message app, copied the number, and started typing.

Me: *It's Jess. Where R U?*

I heard a ping from inside the room. A minute later three dots appeared in the text.

Lars: *Sorry babe. Have to cancel.*

Anger bubbled up inside me. Britt's voice echoed in my ear: *Welcome to prom night 2.0.*

He can't do this to me. I hammered my fist on the door. Still nothing. With shaking fingers, I dialed his number. The phone rang twice before a message told me the caller was unavailable.

Rage pulsed through me like wildfire. "Lars!"

An older couple peered down the hallway and eyed me curiously. I waved at them. They looked at me warily before disappearing through the side exit.

I shut my eyes and collapsed against the door. It took every ounce of restraint not to run back to reception and grab the master key. But what would be the point? I couldn't exactly pick Lars up and force him onstage.

With no other options, I left. I trudged back around to the quiet of the gazebo. The sun had dipped below the horizon, dragging with it the remainder of the light. I stood for a minute while darkness engulfed me.

As a visual merchandising coordinator, I'd always been flexible, changing the landscape of window displays at the beck and call of each fickle trend. But tonight, I had nowhere else to turn, no new option to capture the audience's attention. I had trusted Lars. Again. And I had been burned. Again. Kat was right. Lars was nothing but trouble. He was exactly the same guy he'd always been: unreliable and selfish.

I fought the urge to cry. I was not done yet.

Shaking off the anger, I took a deep breath and headed back to the bar. Time to come up with plan B. I couldn't let Lars's no-show ruin the night. It was opening weekend for my new business. Now wasn't the time to give up.

I spotted my brother and waved him over. "How fast can you pour?"

Nate's eyebrows shot up. "I'm the Doc Holliday of bartenders." He demonstrated his speed by grabbing two bottles of booze from the bar as if they were pistols in a side holster from the Old West, holding them up in front of me with an air of pride. "Why are you asking?"

"Get ready" was all I said. Before he could press me for details, I spun on my heel and made my way onto the stage. I flicked a switch on the microphone, then tapped it twice to make sure it was on. Two booming thumps filled the air, and the crowd turned toward me.

Game time.

I rolled my shoulders back and lifted my chin. "Hi, everyone . . . again. Like I said a few minutes ago, we're so grateful you've come to celebrate our opening tonight."

I paused as a spatter of applause and a few "woot, woots" came bursting from a back corner. I didn't need to look to know it was Mom and Helen. I forced a grin onto my face, attempting to crinkle my eyes for full effect. "Thank you. Unfortunately, I'm afraid Lars won't be able to perform for us tonight."

There was a collective groan and a few random boos. I held my hand up to acknowledge the communal disappointment. "I'm really sorry." Before I continued, I braced myself for another snarky comment from Britt. Would she bring up the prom again? I scanned the crowd for the blonde beast and imagined myself stage-diving and tackling her to the ground. Miraculously, she was nowhere in sight.

One point for me. Time to press on. "Although Lars can't be here, we want to make sure you have an unforgettable time tonight, so we're offering everyone complimentary cocktails for the next hour. And for all of our designated drivers out there? I'm here to tell you Nate's mocktails will blow your mind."

Lukewarm applause met my ears. Better than boos. Was the deal enough to salvage good reviews and return customers? I hoped so.

Before I could thank the crowd and leave the stage, a figure approached, waving his hand to get my attention. It wasn't necessary; he would've had it either way. Standing in front of me was George Havers, the swoon-worthy country rebel from Lars's season of *Sing This!*.

"Hi there." His voice was rich and smooth, like my favorite brand of ice cream. "If it would help, I could step in and play a few songs."

I stared for a minute, unable to speak. Nate, from out of nowhere, hopped up beside me. He tactfully pushed my chin up to stop me from gaping like a stray dog looking at the display window of a butcher shop.

He gave George a double thumbs-up and reached his hand out to pull the singer up onstage. "Hey, everyone," he said into the microphone. "Did anyone see who was hiding out in the audience? We've got a surprise guest for you."

When George stood up to his full height of six foot something and tipped his cowboy hat as a way of greeting the onlookers, there was a collective gasp. Then the crowd went ballistic.

The rest of the evening could be summed up in two words: Lars who?

George played more than a dozen songs, and the crowd ate it up. It was like a dream.

If only I didn't wake up to a living nightmare.

Chapter Five

George Havers stood before me shirtless, with a big grin on his face and an even bigger doughnut in his hand. It was double chocolate and calorie-free. He held out his hand to pass me the sweet treat. I reached forward and almost had it in my grasp when I heard the scream.

I opened my eyes. George was gone, and it was barely dawn. The best dream I'd had in years had been interrupted by the now-familiar sound of my sister-in-law's call for help. Lars was off the top of my hit list. Sarah was officially my number-one target.

I rolled out of bed with a grunt and grabbed one of a dozen pairs of black yoga pants I had on hand. I exchanged my sleep shirt for a T-shirt and a hoodie and grabbed my phone.

Duke was already up and raring to go. I gave him a pat on the head, then stomped out the door, Duke running ahead toward the sound. One of the drawbacks of staying at the B and B was the possibility of interruptions. It had never occurred to me that it would be the early-rising, yoga-loving Sarah who would be the one to start the trend.

Duke rushed out the back door of reception, past the pool and bar area, then reared up, placing his front paws on the back gate.

He barked repeatedly until I reached him. I shushed him, and he whined. I peered into the dark, grassy area behind the B and B. "Sarah?"

If her cursed family horseshoe had dropped again, I would probably pick it up and whack her with it, proving that it was, in fact, bad luck. I cleared my throat and with a louder voice tried again. "Sarah?"

"Jess? Hurry!" Sarah's voice sounded shaky and panicked.

Uh-oh. I unlatched the gate. Duke shot forward, barking again as the gazebo came into view. With a creeping feeling of dread, I picked up my pace and followed.

Cold, slick grass brushed my toes as the predawn dew soaked my flip-flops. An earthy raw scent hit my nose, and I shrank into my hoodie even as I rushed toward my sister-in-law's voice. It took me a minute to spot Sarah and Duke in the dark. Sarah was crouched down between the dense cattails and tall grass in the small clearing at the edge of the pond. Duke was next to her, staying put but still barking. It wasn't a friendly *found you* sound; it was a call for help.

My stomach churned. Something was wrong. Really wrong. Duke quieted once I got close. He moved back a few steps to let me approach. Sarah whipped her head toward me. Her eyes were huge, and she was trembling. I looked away from her, shifting my focus to the dark mass at her feet.

I edged closer, my flip-flops sinking into the spongy ground. I bent down and craned my neck to get a better look in the murky light. Then I saw it. No, saw *him*. I gasped.

Lying just ahead was a motionless body. I looked closer, and my whole body began to shake. It was Bob Strapp, Lars's stepfather. Even in this twilight state between the darkness and the light, I knew he was dead.

Bob's body lay sprawled along the edge of the water. There was a pool of blood near his head. He was so still, his eyes open and unfocused.

Nausea hit me like a tsunami, building slowly but growing stronger with each passing second. I fought the urge to scream. One of us had to remain calm, and seeing Sarah's ashen face, I knew she couldn't do it. I pushed aside the queasy feeling and grabbed her arm, pulling her away from the pond's edge onto drier ground.

"What happened?" I whispered.

"I don't know," Sarah cried.

I searched her face. "You just found him here?"

She nodded. "Uh-huh. I got up this morning and rode my bike here like always. When I rolled out my mat to do my morning mantra, I noticed something lying near the edge of the pond. I went over to see what it was." She gulped, taking a breath before continuing. "He was on his stomach facedown in the water. I pulled him out and turned him around. His face . . ." She stopped then and shuddered.

Before I could ask her anything else, the shudder morphed into a full-body tremor. *She's going to pass out.* I seized hold of her with both hands and tried to make eye contact. Her pupils were dilated like a cat's in the dark. She wouldn't—or couldn't—look me in the eye.

"Steady," I said. Goosebumps enveloped her bare arms. I whipped off my hoodie and shoved it into her hands. "Here. Put this on."

She did as I said, but the shaking persisted. I grabbed her right arm firmly under the thick layer of fleece and led her back to the gazebo, where she could sit down. She collapsed onto the hard wooden seat of one of the built-in benches.

"I'm going to call the police," I told her. Sarah's sagging head gave a small nod. She waited, motionless, while I placed the call.

After I hung up, I sat next to Sarah and put my arm around her. It felt a little awkward, since we hadn't yet reached that level of closeness, but the girl needed comfort and I could do that. After all, Nate was my little brother and this was his wife. I wouldn't let him down.

"Help is on the way, Sarah."

The reassurance seemed to revive her a little, and she looked at me with more focus. "Okay," she said, then let her head fall on my shoulder. We sat like that in silence for a few minutes until the distant shrill of sirens roused me to my feet.

I turned and grabbed both of Sarah's hands. "I need you to walk to the entrance of the B and B and wait for the police. When they arrive, bring them back here."

She nodded.

"You okay with that?" I mimicked the tone my mother used when speaking to an upset student.

"Yes," she said in a clearer voice. She stood up and took a big breath.

Duke stood at attention. He'd been quietly watching from a few feet away as if monitoring the area for any lurking danger. "Go with Sarah," I told him. Instead of walking toward her, however, he moved closer to me and sat on my foot. In any other circumstance, I would've laughed. But not today.

I pointed to Sarah. "Go." This time I spoke in a more commanding voice.

He slunk over to Sarah and stood at her side but kept his eyes on me.

Duke's support seemed to comfort her. She glanced down at him, then shuffled toward the entrance. Duke kept pace by her side. They moved more quickly than I thought was safe, given her unsteady state, but the desire to get away, I guessed, gave her a good reason to motor.

I pulled out my phone and sent a text to Nate.

Me: *Need u here. 911.*

A minute later three dots appeared.

Nate: *You OK?*

Me: *Yes fine. Just hurry.*

Nate: *K.*

I tucked my phone away and tiptoed back over to where Bob lay. It didn't seem right to leave him alone. My breathing sped up as I glimpsed his lifeless face, which was now blotchy and gray. Looking closer, I thought I could see some sort of open wound near the back of his head. I didn't dare move him to see the extent of it. It didn't really matter now. He was still fully clothed in the same outfit he'd been wearing when I saw him yesterday.

I turned away, fighting off a sudden wave of nausea.

Time for more backup. I dialed Kat's number. It took three rings before she answered.

"Hello?" her groggy voice croaked out.

"Hey, sorry to wake you."

"What's up?"

"Bob Strapp is dead," I blurted out.

There was a shuffling sound. "Say that again?" Her voice was more alert now.

"Lars's stepfather. He's dead."

"What happened?"

Good question. How could he have ended up here like this? With the initial shock wearing off, my head spun with confusion. "I have no idea. Sarah found him by the pond. The police are on their way."

"Give me ten minutes."

"Take your time. Have a shower and eat something before you come. It's going to be a long day."

She asked me ten more times if I was okay before hanging up.

Once I was off the phone and staring down at Bob, all sorts of gruesome scenarios began to flood my imagination, an unfortunate side effect of listening to true crime podcasts. I trudged back to the gazebo through the darkness and plunked myself down on the bench. Taking a deep breath, I shut my eyes and began to rub my temples. I had to slow my thoughts before my mind went off the rails.

In the eerie stillness, I realized there might be a much simpler explanation that I hadn't yet considered. Under the night sky, in an unfamiliar place, the most likely explanation was that Bob had either slipped on a wet patch of grass or tripped over a wayward branch, then fallen in the pond and drowned. Nothing sinister at all. Yes, that had to be it. As bizarre as it seemed, a freak accident made the most sense.

Only a few minutes passed before Sarah and Duke were back. Duke kept his eyes on me and bounded forward, followed by Sarah, who was accompanied by two EMTs with a stretcher in tow. What were they going to do? Had I not mentioned Bob was dead when I called? They hustled forward.

I hopped off the step of the gazebo. "He's there." I pointed to where Bob's body lay.

The paramedics nodded and wordlessly moved toward the body. They first checked his throat for a pulse. Sarah watched them, transfixed. Did she feel guilty she hadn't been able to save him?

One of the attendants pulled her radio from a chest attachment. White noise broke the silence as she called what I guessed was the nearest hospital in the adjacent town.

While she contacted the care team, the second attendant, a guy, opened Bob's shirt and attached what looked like suction cups to his chest. I realized that the monitor must be linked to a hospital machine.

The female attendant looked at her partner. He gave her an almost undetectable shake of the head. I didn't need to guess what it meant. No signs of life.

The police arrived on the scene as the paramedics were packing up their stuff. They used their own radio units to make more calls and cordoned off the area using yellow police tape. Sarah and I were told to move back and stay put.

I was so engrossed in what was in front of me that I didn't hear the sound of approaching steps until the snap of a twig a few feet away nearly did me in. Even Duke seemed surprised, jumping back at the sound. I spun on my heel and was met with a hooded angular figure. He gave me a start, and it took me a minute to recognize Nicky, Lars's assistant. I could just make out light stubble on his chin, which emerged from under an oversized hood that reminded me more of a traditional monk's robe than a modern sweatshirt.

"Nicky?" I glared at him. "You scared me."

"Sorry." He pulled back the hood to reveal his light-blue eyes and flushed cheeks.

Standing this close to him made me realize he wasn't as young as I had first guessed. His stubble had flecks of gray, and he had shallow wrinkles at the outer corners of his eyes.

"Where did you come from?" I demanded. Guarded by an officer, the rear pathway was blocked; no one could get in or out. I looked to the other side. It was fully fenced along the parking lot, although I had to admit that anyone taller than a Smurf could easily hop it.

Nicky was staring past me, and I didn't need to wonder what he was looking at. "Couldn't sleep. I was out for a walk." He jutted his pointy chin up into the air. "That Bob?"

Nicky hadn't answered my question to my satisfaction, so I wasn't in the mood to answer his either. Tit for tat. I didn't like the way he was looking at Bob's body, like it was a slab of meat ready to be put on display at the butcher's. Anger surged inside me and I wanted to press him further, make him tell me where he'd been walking and what he'd been doing. I didn't like this guy, and suddenly he felt like a pretty good place to aim all of my bad feelings.

Any conversation we might have had was cut off by the arrival of a plainclothes officer dressed in a typical khakis–polo shirt combo with his badge attached to his belt. He crouched near the body and jotted a few notes. A minute later he was back on his feet, looking around.

He approached the area where Sarah and I had been told to wait. Sarah hadn't made a peep since the arrival of the paramedics, other than to give basic answers. She'd pulled the hood of my sweater forward over her face, so it was hidden in shadows, and she stood stoically, her fists balled by her side.

The detective peered at us. "Sarah Jones?"

I waved a hand. "Yes, that's us."

The officer's deep-brown eyes met my gaze. Heat filled my cheeks. What a mug. I hadn't been around a lot of hot men since I'd left San Francisco. Now they were popping up like weeds.

"Jessica Byrne," he said.

"Yes. That's me."

He held my gaze for a minute. He looked vaguely familiar. Was he waiting to see if I'd recognize him? *Nah.* I'd remember a face like his.

"I'm Detective Holloway."

"Hi. I'm Jess, and this is Sarah." I took a step closer to my sister-in-law, who'd folded into herself like an underweight hedgehog. She said nothing but peeked out from below the shadowy hood, her perfect button nose the only feature clearly visible.

"Good. Jess, Sarah," he said. "I'd like to talk to you two somewhere private, if possible. Someone told me you live here?"

"I do, uh, sort of," I said. "It's temporary." Mom's mortification that I lived here seemed to be rubbing off.

He kept his eyes on me. "Can we go inside now to chat?"

"Of course." I was about to introduce Nicky, but when I glanced back to where he'd been standing, he was gone. That guy had some serious creeper skills.

Detective Holloway scanned the area. "Is there another way to your place other than through the bar? A crowd has formed, and I'd like to avoid them if possible. I need to ask the two of you a few questions before I can answer the ones that'll almost certainly be coming our way."

I pointed to the low white fence that separated the back field from the side parking lot. "We can hop over that, if you like."

His eyebrows rose in surprise. He held out his hand in a mock gesture of chivalry. "I'm up for it if you two are."

I stuck my thumb out and gestured to Sarah. "This one can bend like a pretzel."

"And you?" he asked.

I flushed for absolutely no reason at all. "I can manage the three feet."

"That would be helpful, thanks." He stood back to let me lead the way. I pried Sarah away from the unfolding scene and led her by the elbow toward the fence. Duke remained by my side.

"Nate's on his way," I told her.

"Okay." Her tone was robotic, and I felt a pang of worry. I slowed down and gently pulled back the hood that covered her face.

"Sarah?" I scoured her face. Had shock immobilized her brainpower? When she didn't answer, I pulled my phone out of the side pocket of my yoga pants and sent Nate a quick text.

Me: *Where are you?!*

Three dots told me he was sending back a reply.

Nate: *Car wouldn't start. I had to get a boost. Tell me what's going on.*

Me: *Sarah and I are OK but there's been an accident.*

Nate: *What do you mean?*
Me: *Just get here.*
Nate: *OK.*

I shoved the phone back in my pocket and looked behind me. Detective Holloway was watching me. "Sorry. I had to send my brother a text."

He nodded. "Sure."

We'd reached the fence. Detective Holloway gestured again in mock gallantry. "After you two."

I lightly grabbed Sarah's elbow. "Can you make it?"

Sarah blinked a few times, then glanced from me to the detective, as if seeing him for the first time. "What?"

"The fence. Can you make it over the fence?"

She glanced back at the detective again, then nodded and did as instructed. She balanced one hand on the fence, then glided over it with the grace of a deer. Easy peasy. I leaned my hand on a picket as Sarah had and tried to emulate her light hop. It would've worked if I'd had legs like hers. But I didn't. As it was, one flip-flop hooked the pointed tip, and I went over like a lump of soft dough.

The ground felt cold against my cheek as I lay there, winded. I hadn't thought the morning could get any worse. Guess I'd been wrong. *Swallow me, ground, and spit me up on a beach in Australia.* Duke sprung over and licked my face. Sarah, standing next to me, didn't seem to even notice I'd fallen. I glanced up to see Detective Holloway's outstretched hand reaching toward me. "Thanks. My shoe . . ." I flapped my hand around, then let it drop with a sigh.

A hint of a smile played on his lips as he helped me stand. "You all right?"

I brushed myself off. "Fine, thanks." I spit out a piece of grass as I turned to glare at the evil barricade, which taunted me with its perky white innocuousness. A small piece of black fabric caught my eye. It was stuck between two of the white posts. I was about to pull it out when a voice made me jump. "Don't touch that."

Detective Holloway reached inside his jacket, pulled out a pair of rubber gloves, then proceeded to place the fabric in a small clear bag. He looked at me.

With Sarah now a certified zombie, I had no one else to ask one all-important question. "Please tell me there isn't a rip in the rear of my pants." I straightened up with the tiny bit of dignity I had left and did a spin for him to check.

He cleared his throat. "You're still decent."

In an effort to move away from the subject, I leaned toward him and pointed to the bag containing the fabric. "Can I see that?"

"Sure." He held the bag up for me to see. "Look familiar?"

"It's French terry." A trendy fabric for upscale leisure wear. It also just happened to match the logoed hoodie that Lars had been wearing the day before. I kept that second bit of information to myself.

Detective Holloway studied my face before tucking the bag with its contents into his jacket.

I took one last look back. It was a mistake. Bob's body was being prepared to move. A mix of fear and anxiety set in, and a hard lump formed in my throat. *Not now.* I had to get a grip. *WWVBD?* The acronym came out of nowhere. *What would Victoria Beckham do?* Not panic, that's for sure. With that in mind, I linked my arm through Sarah's. Time to keep calm and carry on.

Chapter Six

We walked along the overflow parking area at the back of the B and B. It was quiet here, sheltered from the buzz of activity. The air was still cool and crisp, filled with the scent of lilacs. Detective Holloway took in the surroundings, seeming to also take note of the small camera fastened above. It had been hastily installed, with pull ties sticking out left and right and a lavender footstool decorated with rainbow unicorns tucked against the wall beneath. Not everything had to smell like patchouli for me to recognize it as the work of Aunt Marnie.

He paused, looking up. "You have security cameras?"

I perked up. "We do. Kat found a secondhand system online for fifty bucks. It's old but seems to work fine. If you want to watch the feed, it'll have to be on my computer."

"Sure. If you have time, that could prove helpful."

We rounded the corner, where we could hear a buzz from the EMS personnel milling about in the main parking lot. We continued on in silence until we reached the front. Detective Holloway nodded at the officer stationed at the B and B's entrance, then followed us inside.

Thankfully, no one was here yet demanding answers. Either guests were gathered by the bar, trying to sneak a peek out back, or they were lucky enough to be still sleeping. But it was nearing six AM. People would be out and about soon, and they would demand to know why their weekend holiday had turned into the set of *CSI*.

Past the front social area, beside the check-in desk, was a narrow hallway. It led to two guest suites, a small office next to a supply closet, and finally, my apartment. My place was at the very back and was the only one equipped with a small kitchen. I paused outside my door and turned around. Was it wrong that the first thought that popped into my head was whether I'd left my pink flannel cat pajamas draped over the sofa? I guess it didn't really matter; the hot cop was not here for me.

I unlocked the door. Sarah kept her head down but trudged inside. I followed her, then spun around and waved Detective Holloway in too. "Home sweet home."

Sarah, who hadn't said a word, dropped onto the corner of the sofa. She drew the hood back so her face was visible yet remained expressionless. Then she pulled her feet up onto the sofa and wrapped her arms around her knees. I wrapped a plush throw blanket around her before sitting next to her and inviting the detective to use the chair across from us. He did so, keeping his eyes on Sarah.

"I think my sister-in-law is struggling with what happened," I said.

The detective nodded. "Yeah, I can see that. It's not uncommon for people to shut down after experiencing trauma. I won't push her. Just a few questions if she's up for it."

Sarah was still visibly trembling under the blanket, but the mention of her name seemed to rouse her out of her fog. She began blinking repeatedly, as if trying to focus on us, but without much success. "I'm fine," she said to no one in particular.

Detective Holloway clasped his hands together and leaned forward. "Even if you feel physically okay, you may be experiencing some emotional backlash. But if you're able to, I'd like you to explain what happened as best you can. Do you think you can do that?"

Sarah nodded, still blinking excessively. "Okay."

The detective reached into his jacket pocket and pulled out a small black notebook and a pen. "Go ahead, I'm listening."

Sarah swallowed hard. She peered at the detective before looking down at the floor. "I arrived at the B and B and was just about to do my morning yoga."

"Outside?"

"At the gazebo." She pulled her knees in closer. "It was still mostly dark out. When I was setting up my mat, I noticed something near the water."

He jotted down a note. "What drew your attention to it?"

"Light colors against the dark." She rubbed her face. "I thought maybe one of the campfire blankets had been left out or blown away. I wanted to grab it before it got soiled. I'd almost reached it when I saw it was pants and realized it was . . . a person."

Another note. "What happened next?"

An involuntary gasp escaped from her. "Sorry."

He leaned back to give her some space. "Take your time. I'm in no hurry."

She closed her eyes and took several deep breaths. When she opened them again, the blinking had slowed and the shaking had subsided. Her eyes steadied on Detective Holloway. She rolled her shoulders back, let her knees fall into a crisscross position, and clasped her hands together, resting them in her lap. She took one more deep breath, then met the detective's gaze. "It was weird. I remember thinking it was weird. At first, when I saw someone was lying there, I assumed they'd passed out by the water."

He gave a quick nod. "Sure."

She squinted, her focus shifting toward the window. "I considered ignoring them. I worried if they were still drunk, they'd yell at me. But I knew it would be too distracting, so I moved closer toward where they lay. Once I reached the water's edge, I realized . . . I saw . . ."

Another gasp, and she couldn't finish her sentence. The tremble returned.

I wanted to help. "Sarah realized Bob's face was submerged," I said.

Sarah clutched her knees. "I pulled him out, but it was too late. His face . . ." She shook her head. "That's when I screamed. The next thing I remember, Jess was there."

The detective continued to take notes. "Okay." His focus shifted to me. "So you came outside from here and found Sarah with the body?"

"Exactly," I said. "I ran through the bar area out back. When I found her, Sarah was crouched down, rocking back and forth. I approached her and then saw Bob's body nearby. I pulled her back and called 911."

Before the interview could go any further, my door burst open and Nate rushed in, eyes wide, face ashen. "What's going on?"

Sarah stood up, the blanket dropping to her feet. She held her arms out toward him, then her face crumbled and she began to wail. He ran toward her and grabbed her just as she was about to collapse. He held her tight and looked over her shoulder from me to Detective Holloway.

"It's Lars's stepdad, Bob," I said. "He's dead. Sarah found the body."

Nate's eyes shut, and he drew Sarah even closer. "Is she okay? Are you okay? What happened?"

I swallowed a lump, fighting back tears. "I have no idea."

The detective stood up. "We can finish this later." He tucked his notebook away and turned toward me. "While these two catch up, can you show me Bob Strapp's room?"

Nate and Sarah moved onto the sofa. Nate pulled Sarah close, then gave me a wave with his free hand. I returned the gesture, then grabbed my phone. Detective Holloway followed me to the door, reaching past me to open it. I snuck a peek back at the newlyweds before slipping out of the room. Duke hovered nearby, but I told him to stay put. His tail drooped, but he followed instructions and lay down, shooting me a sad puppy-dog face, as if I didn't have enough to fret over.

When we reached the lobby, the detective paused. "Could I bother you for a cup of coffee? I haven't had my fix, and I'm starting to feel the effects."

Another java junkie. A point in his favor. He may have been stalling, wanting to ask me more questions, but I didn't mind. I was ready for a caffeine treat myself.

"Absolutely," I said.

While the aesthetic we were aiming for with the B and B was vintage Palm Springs, the perks, such as an express espresso maker, had been on my list of must-haves. The bar had a proper top-end machine, but for day-to-day pops of perk, the instant Nespresso hit the mark. I didn't mess around with coffee and kept one within arm's reach of the check-in desk. Whoever'd said *Coffee makes everything okayer* had it right in my books. I brewed two cups and brought them over to where he stood.

"Thank you." Detective Holloway accepted the coffee and took a seat on the sofa. "Now, can you walk me through what you know about the victim? I understand he was a guest here?"

"Yeah, he was, sort of."

He studied my face. "I don't understand."

"The room was comped . . . complimentary. Lars was supposed to play last night. Bob was his manager. He told me when they arrived that he went where Lars went."

"And this show has been in the works for a while?"

"A few months, maybe?" I began to chew on my thumbnail. "I'm sorry. I don't know how I can help other than giving you access to Bob's room. The guests are going to start getting up, and I've got a million things to do that I haven't even begun."

"We can walk and talk." He stood up and drank the remains of his coffee. I grabbed the master key from behind the desk while he fished out the notebook from his pocket. He followed me up the stairs en route to the second floor, where Bob's suite was located.

"I'm sorry," I said as I climbed up the steps. "It's awful what happened. Poor Bob . . . and Lars."

"Bob was Lars's father?"

"Stepfather." I informed him. "And Lars is a singer. He won a reality show called *Sing This!*."

Detective Holloway tapped his pen on his notebook. "Hometown hero."

I smiled. "Celebrity, yes; not sure about the hero part."

His eyebrow quirked. "Meaning?"

I shook my head. "Sorry, I meant that as a joke."

I wasn't about to unload Lars's past misdeeds. Time to zip it.

We reached the second floor. I stopped in front of Bob's room. "This is it." I paused before inserting the key in the lock, then turned to face the detective. "I need to know something. Was Bob's death an accident?" The question had been weighing on me. Guests would have questions, so I needed answers.

He tilted his head but looked at me with an expression I couldn't read. "I can't make that call yet. What do you think?"

If he'd asked me the question earlier, I would've said yes, but I was beginning to have my doubts. How could Bob hit the back of his head and then fall forward and drown? It didn't add up. "I don't know."

Detective Holloway's eyes locked on mine. "Can we pick this conversation up later?"

"Definitely." I put the key in the lock and opened the door.

Chapter Seven

The air was thick with steam, and the scent of citrus and bergamot hit my nose. Nicky was sitting on the edge of one of the two unmade beds with a towel wrapped around his waist and an acoustic guitar resting on his lap.

His face flushed, and his wide eyes looked from me to Detective Holloway. "Don't people knock around here?"

Oops. My cheeks went pink. "Sorry, Nicky. I completely forgot you were sharing the room with Bob."

Nicky eyed me as one side of his mouth lifted into a smirk. "Guess it's all mine now."

My body stiffened. *Did I hear that right?*

Detective Holloway cleared his throat. "And you are?"

Nicky's eyes shifted to the detective, narrowing as they went. "The guy whose room you just entered uninvited. Isn't that, like, a breach of the shield?"

Detective Holloway didn't seem to care he'd been made. "If a search is done in good faith, a judge usually has leniency. Heard of that one, friend? Or did you miss that episode of *Law & Order*?"

Nicky plucked at a guitar string but maintained eye contact with the detective. "I'll take your word for it, man."

The air was heavy with testosterone. Were they going to start bumping chests?

I cleared my throat. "Nicky, this is Detective Holloway. He wanted to take a look at Bob's room. I'm sorry we barged in. It's my fault."

He stared at me. "You're welcome anytime. Just don't bring a friend along next time. At least, not this one."

It seemed Nicky had picked up a few tips from Bob. Like how to be a creep.

Detective Holloway gave me the side-eye and stood up taller. "When you manage to get yourself dressed—Nicky, is it?—I'd like to ask you a few questions. I'm also going to need you to vacate the room for a while so I can take a look around."

Nicky shrugged. "Maybe later. I'm a little busy right now."

Detective Holloway stepped a few feet closer to Nicky. "Say that again?"

Nicky dropped his chin and chuckled quietly, as if in on a joke with himself. He plucked another string on his guitar. "Listen, I'm in the middle of writing a song."

I stepped to the side, looking from Nicky to Detective Holloway. There was a subtle twitch in Detective Holloway's jaw. Nicky began to hum.

"Inspired by the morning's events?" the detective asked.

Nicky raised his face, a wicked smile on his lips. "You got it, man. I'm calling it 'Celebration.'"

My head jerked back. I'd heard reactions to death could vary, but triumph and satisfaction didn't feel right. Did Nicky hate Bob that much? My throat was suddenly very dry. *Get me out of here.* I leaned forward and grabbed the door handle. "Detective?"

Detective Holloway kept his eyes on Nicky. "You've got fifteen minutes, kid." He looked at me. "We can go."

No need to chew his cabbage twice. I yanked open the door and followed him out, closing the door shut behind me without another glance back. Once we were back in the hallway, I let my breath out and looked up at Detective Holloway. "Sorry about that."

He gave me an inscrutable look. "Don't be."

Detective Holloway had what my mom would call bedroom eyes: dark and very broody. Just the thing to make my knees go weak under normal circumstances. We walked in silence for a minute.

When we reached the end of the corridor, Detective Holloway stopped to peruse the shelves of books we'd used to decorate our makeshift library. Nearby were two brown leather chairs and a small white table. "You a romance fan?"

Caught off guard, I felt my cheeks heat. "Depends who's doing the wooing."

"Ah, I see." A barely perceptible rise of his eyebrows made me realize he was talking about books, not courtship preferences.

Since it was impossible to hide my mortification, I tried to pretend I was referencing authors. "Mom's a big Austen fan. Me too, although I love Emily Henry and Tessa Bailey as well."

The eyebrows rose another microinch. "Spicy."

"Yes . . ." I swallowed. How did we get here?

He turned back to the books. "Who exactly is Nicky again?"

I let out a breath, with a promise to myself to never bring up the hot topic of reading again. "Lars's assistant slash roadie."

"Right," he said, as if somehow that explained Nicky's behavior. "Quite the charmer." He wrote something in his notebook, then clicked the pen closed. "Okay. I think we need to talk to the rest of the guests."

"We?" I echoed.

"It's time to let people know what's going on. I assumed you'd want to be involved. But if you'd rather I did it—"

"No, you're right. I'll do it." Never mind good service; guests would need some serious reassurance. It should come from me. I didn't usually balk at public speaking, but this was different. My palms began to itch.

Detective Holloway studied my face. "You okay?"

No, nope, absolutely not. "Yes."

He nodded at me. "If you're sure. I'll stand by in case there are questions. Keep the details sparse."

"Sure thing."

We went downstairs and out the side exit. There was no need to organize a chat. The guests had gathered in the bar area. Detective Holloway stepped onstage. Reaching out his hand to me, he pulled me up to stand next to him. Two police officers stood nearby. Judging by the concern and confusion on people's faces, my guess was the officers hadn't offered any information.

Britt spotted me. Her hair was piled on her head in a messy bun and she wasn't wearing makeup, exposing bad skin that matched her ugly expression.

"Look who finally decided to grace us with her presence," she said in a voice loud enough to shut everyone else up. "Have a nice sleep, princess?"

I gritted my teeth. "Good morning, everyone. I'm afraid I have some bad news."

"Cut the perky act and tell us what's going on," Britt demanded.

I swallowed the urge to bite back. "There's been an accident. One of the guests has passed away."

Gasps escaped, followed by a low buzz as onlookers whispered to each other.

"Who died?" a man near the back called out. I recognized his voice. It was George Havers. Without his signature cowboy hat, he looked older. And balder.

I hesitated and looked at Detective Holloway for permission to speak. He gave me a subtle shake of the head. "I can't share that information quite yet."

"Why not?" Britt demanded.

"We have a right to know," her sidekick, Paula, added.

A grumble of dissatisfaction coursed through the crowd. Detective Holloway held up his hand. "Until we've had a chance to notify the next of kin, we're not at liberty to disclose that information to the public."

"At least tell us what happened," Britt shouted above the noise. "We need to know if we're in danger too."

Paula pointed at the detective. "Who's the beefcake?"

He took a step forward. "My name is Detective James Holloway."

Another woman raised her hand. "Why is a detective here if it was an accident?"

Astute observation. The crowd went silent as the implication hit.

"Good question," Detective Holloway said. "The victim appears to have drowned in the pond out back. I'm here to determine what happened and how."

Gasps erupted. The detective held up his hand, and people quieted down to listen.

"I understand this is shocking and upsetting news. However, it's important that we have everyone's cooperation here. Our goal is to figure out exactly what happened in the shortest time possible. I'm going to need all of you to make a statement about your whereabouts last night."

"What does this have to do with us?" someone called out.

"Was he murdered?" another voice said over the buzz.

The detective shook his head. "We're not forming any conclusions until we gather more evidence. I'm looking for witnesses and trying to form a timeline. I need each of you to give a statement to one of the officers standing by. When you're done, feel free to go back to your room or, if you prefer, stick around here. But do not check out until you've been cleared by me."

"How long will we be stuck here in Hotel California?" George Havers called out. Paula, standing next to him, snickered, pressing her face into his shoulder. When had those two become an item?

"I understand your frustration. But I need you to stay put for now. I'll give you the green light ASAP, but I can't give you a specific time until I have a better idea of what happened, and the longer I'm standing here answering questions, the longer it will take. Got it?"

George growled something about amendment rights, but I couldn't quite catch what he said.

In spite of the dissatisfaction most faces displayed, people did as they were told and began filing into lines to get their statements taken. Even Britt seemed keen to get it over with and didn't argue.

Movement from behind caught my eye, and I turned to see what was going on. My heart lifted as I spotted a flash of a tall body topped with perfect, glossy black hair making a beeline in our direction. Kat. Her fierce brown eyes locked on to mine, and she rushed toward me.

I hopped off the stage to greet her. She engulfed me in a hug before holding me out at arm's length to inspect me.

With her hands on my shoulders, she twisted me back and forth, looking for damage. "Please don't say I told you so," I said, squirming in her grasp.

"I'll save it for later." Her sharp eyes looked me over. "Are you alright?"

"I'm fine." Her eyes narrowed; my voice was an octave higher than usual. A bad sign, and one only she would notice. I cleared my throat. "By the beard of Zeus," I pledged.

Maybe not the most appropriate time for quoting *Anchorman*, one of our favorite movies, but it worked. The corners of her mouth lifted, and she backed off. "Okay."

Detective Holloway cleared his throat. "Kat."

My eyebrows shot up. *Kat?* Since when did my best friend not mention a hot guy she was on a nickname basis with?

"Present," she said, giving him a salute.

"How did you get past the entrance?" he said, ignoring her cheek.

"Don't worry, James," Kat said. "A uniformed officer tried to stop me. But I told him I was with the FBI."

Detective Holloway shot her a look to let her know he wasn't amused.

She put her hands up. "Don't shoot." He frowned at her.

"I'm kidding." She gave him a jocular elbow tap. "I told him the truth."

"Which is?" he pressed.

A hint of a smile crossed her lips. "I'm Jess's partner. Co-owner of the B and B."

His eyes narrowed. "Really?"

"Yup." She stood up taller and anchored her hands on her hips. "Since Connor left, I decided to change things up a little."

"Nice," he said. "The place looks great."

A uniformed officer approached. "Detective, can I have a word?"

Detective Holloway acknowledged the officer with a nod, then turned his attention back to us. "Congratulations, Kat." His eyes flicked from Kat to me. "Excuse me, Jess. I'll catch up with you two later."

"Sure," Kat said to his back with a wave. When she looked back to face me, she flinched. "What?"

My head was tilted and my eyes were slits. "How do you know him?"

"Friend of Connor's, unfortunately. And speaking of losers, where is Mr. Rock Star anyway? Shouldn't he be out here signing autographs?"

"His stepdad just died, remember?"

"Sure, and if memory serves correctly, no one hated him more than Lars. Although I'll admit it was well deserved. Bob was gross."

"You won't hear an argument from me," I agreed. "But I haven't seen Lars yet this morning. I wonder if he even knows what happened."

We both looked over at the side entrance. As if on cue, it opened up and two uniformed officers stepped outside with Lars in tow. He glanced around before trudging past the gathering toward the back gate. Why were they taking him there? Did they want to show him where Bob was found? I didn't know what that would accomplish other than making him more upset. He was barely recognizable as it was—worlds apart from the cocky guy who'd strutted back into my life yesterday. His shiny hair was now flat, and mirrored sunglasses hid his eyes. Even his broad shoulders were slumped.

My stomach knotted. Poor guy.

"You okay?" Kat asked, following my gaze.

"Seeing him like this reminds me of when we met."

"In that youth grief group?"

"Uh-huh. I was grieving my dad, but I still remember the first day Lars walked in. It was right after his mom died. In spite of his drooping posture and red eyes, I thought he was the best-looking guy I'd ever seen."

"It took all of about two minutes before you two were inseparable."

"We bonded over grief before it turned romantic." Our relationship had felt like nothing I'd experienced before. "He was my first love. Back then, no one understood me the way he did."

"Don't get sucked back in," Kat warned.

I shook my head but kept my eyes on Lars. "Of course not."

"I mean it, Jess."

"Don't start that again."

She ran her hand through her silky hair and blew out a breath. "He's dragged you down too many times. I knew having him here was a bad idea."

"Stop," I said. "He just lost his stepdad, Kat. He needs a friend." An idea cropped up. "Maybe I should call Travis."

Her eyes widened. "Travis Sanders?"

"Yeah," I said. "Isn't there supposed to be some kind of lifelong bond between bandmates?"

"Not a good idea," she said, moving toward the patio. I followed. We began to open poolside umbrellas for the guests.

"Why not?"

Kat popped her face out from under one to answer me. "The band broke up years ago. So did their friendship."

"You're being melodramatic."

Once the umbrellas were all up, we made our way back to the side entrance. "Trust me on this one, Jess. Leave it alone."

She pulled open the door, gliding through. I followed her into the lobby, relieved no one else was around. I'd get it—whatever "it" was—out of her sooner or later. Obviously, I was missing something. But for now, I had to drop it. As soon as guests were done giving their statements, they'd need to be tended to. Part of our mission statement was to spoil our guests with top-tier service. While I couldn't control the police presence, it was in my power to make everyone more comfortable while they hung around.

Kat began puttering, picking up scattered magazines on the coffee table. The current issue of *Vogue* was open to the summer travel page, and she paused to look at the photos. There was a feature on boutique motels popping up along the California coastline, a big part of our inspiration for the Pearl's aesthetic.

"You good here?" I asked Kat. "Penny and Marnie should be in soon, but I want to check on Nate and Sarah."

"Power on, soldier," she said. "I've got your back."

Would Nate feel the same? I needed him on duty to set up the bar. Sarah, too, if she was feeling better. Poolside yoga sessions could certainly help calm guests' nerves, especially if chilled mimosas and comfort foods were waiting for them afterward.

I headed back to my room. Nate had never let me down before, but Sarah was his priority now, and I wasn't so sure I could count on her. Would she still be too shaken up to help out?

I knocked lightly. Nate's muffled voice told me to come in, and I opened the door to find him sitting on the sofa with Sarah lying down, resting her head in his lap. She sat up as I entered. Duke, who'd been napping at their feet, ran to greet me.

"Hey, you three."

Sarah's color was back, and Nate gave me a reassuring nod. "Hey, you okay?"

I nodded. "All good. You two?"

Sarah attempted a smile. "Better."

Phew. "Does that mean you're ready for duty? The police have just put everyone under house arrest, and I don't think it'll be long before people get restless and grouchy. You two are my best hope to stop a revolt."

"Why aren't they letting people leave?" Sarah asked.

I shrugged. "They want to figure out what happened first, I guess."

"The way you described it, Sarah, chances are the death wasn't from natural causes," Nate said.

Sarah straightened up. "So the bed-and-breakfast is now a prison and we're housing a murderer?"

Egad. I hadn't thought about it like that. Were we turning into the Bates Motel?

"Let's not jump ahead," Nate said. "We don't know what happened yet."

He was right. "All I can say for sure is that I have a B and B full of unhappy people. I need to change that so our opening weekend isn't also our closing weekend."

Nate stood up. "What can we do?"

Time to think on my feet. I'd been prepared for rain. A power failure. A rowdy guest. Death was unexpected. I went with the obvious. "I need Sarah to yoga the bad away. While she's lifting inner spirits, I need you preparing the liquid kind. Grab the rosé and fill champagne glasses with sunshine and happy thoughts. Maybe you can get your kitchen staff to prep some homestyle breakfast dishes at the same time. What do you think?"

Nates brows lifted. "I like it." He turned to his better half. "Sarah?"

Sarah closed her eyes and began to rub her temples. Was she humming? I looked at Nate.

"Is she—"

Nate shushed me. I recoiled, giving him the stink eye. He tapped his finger on his lip and pointed to Sarah. I watched as her fingers detached from her temples and each digit splayed out. Her arms shot straight up, then her wiry fingers forged together. She held the pose, still as a statue of a laughing Buddha. Finally, she took in a deep breath, then formed her mouth into a perfect circle. She unclasped her hands and lowered her outstretched arms while exhaling with a loud "ahhh" that would make any decent dentist giddy with delight.

Nate looked at me and nodded, his eyes shining with pride. "Meditative breathing helps her get into the zone."

I pressed my tongue into my cheek and felt my eyebrows lower. "Are we talking, like, a yoga zone?"

"You want our help, right?" he said slowly.

Point taken. But I didn't *want* their help. I needed their help. I tried to emulate Duke's saddest puppy-dog face and nodded. Nate's face softened, and he gave me a double thumbs-up. I put my hands together and gave him a slight bow. *Namaste, bro.* Then, with Duke at my side, I left the room.

With those two on board and Kat at the front desk, there was only one more thing to take care of. I had to provide an experience that would make everyone here forget they weren't allowed to leave. We had food, drinks, and a patio to chill on. There was only one thing to do. It was time to call the local goddess of goodness. I pulled out my phone and dialed Easy Bakery. I needed to order a triple batch of everything.

Chapter Eight

There was one rule for the Pearl: *Cool Vibes Only.* That was our motto, and it was under fire on opening weekend.

"Can you remind me why we decided to risk everything to open a bed-and-breakfast?" I propped my elbows onto the front desk and began rubbing my temples. Duke had settled into a spot near the window, ready for a nap.

Kat looked up from the computer screen to give me a stern look. "We were both miserable and desperate for a change, remember? How about creatively stifled and burnt out at the tender age of twenty-eight? Any of this sounding familiar?"

She was right. Like always. "Is it wrong that I'm questioning our decision?"

"A dead body and police presence can do that to a girl." Kat piled her smooth black hair on top of her head and secured it with the scrunchie she'd pulled off her wrist. "You're allowed a moment of doubt."

The image of Bob Strapp lying by the pond flooded back, front and center. I shut my eyes, hoping to will it away. "What do you think happened to him?"

Kat wandered toward the back patio entrance and gazed at the pool. "It doesn't make any sense. The max depth of the pond is barely two feet. How can someone drown in that?"

I shuffled over to the sofa and collapsed onto it. "Preposterous."

She turned to face me. "I don't like to jump to the bottom line without doing the math, but in this case, something's not adding up."

Our eyes met. Before I lost the courage, I needed to get it out. "I think he was murdered."

Kat tucked a few wispy strands of hair behind her ear. "I want to say you're wrong—that you've been listening to too much *My Favorite Murder*."

That was it. At last, a voice of reason. Tension oozed from my shoulders. "Go for it."

She looked back at me. "I can't." Another pause. "Because I think you're right."

A jolt of nausea hit me. *Say what?* Kat was the logical one. How could any of this make sense?

As if reading my mind, she shook her head. "I know. This is next-level bizarre."

I swallowed. "Uh-huh. And it brings us to the inevitable next question."

Her face was grim. "Who killed him?"

"Bingo."

She raised an eyebrow. "Well . . . ?"

"Well, what?" I asked with a frown.

She put her hand on her hip and gave me a stern look. "Are you serious right now? Since day one of listening to true crime podcasts, you've had an opinion about who did what and why."

I shrugged. "This is different."

Her eyes narrowed. "Liar. You know something."

"I don't, not really. I just have a weird feeling. You know, spidey-sense stuff."

Her eyes widened. "Spill it."

Big breath. "Okay, it's Nicky. Lars's assistant. I saw him lurking around the back before the cops arrived this morning. Something about it didn't sit right with me."

Her voice dropped to a near whisper. "So you think he's our guy?"

I clasped my hands together and cradled the back of my head. "I don't know—maybe? Who else could it be? I mean, if yesterday was any indication, Bob treated Nicky like crap."

Kat frowned. "Like he did everyone else."

She had a point. "Does that mean the entire population of Fletcher Lake should be under suspicion?"

"Let's exclude those under the age of twelve."

I groaned. "Kat, practically the whole town was here last night."

"Makes for a pretty big list, doesn't it?"

"Can I shift into panic mode now and run back to San Francisco?"

"Not a chance. You quit your job and I gave up my accounting practice. Besides, you're a people pleaser and I don't like humankind enough to deal with grumpy guests. I'm the money gal. You're on the front line, remember? Time to pull up your big-girl pants and make some plans for our guests."

I buried my face in my hands. "What are we going to do?"

She strode over to the sofa and dropped down beside me, draping her arm over my shoulders. "Things will be okay."

I wasn't so sure. "How can we keep everyone distracted? *Rosé the day away* only goes so far unless we get into blotto territory. And that's not good for anyone."

She tapped her lip. "Hmm . . . what about hula?"

"Who?"

"Hula dancing."

"Huh?"

"No, seriously. Remember when Aunt Marnie spent a few months at that Hawaiian spiritual retreat a few years ago? She came back dancing like a pro."

She stood up and started gyrating like an overambitious Elvis impersonator.

I waved my hands. "Please stop that right now."

"Why? I'm demonstrating. You always say you're a visual learner."

A giggle crept up my throat. "Kat, you're assaulting my eyes. It's supposed to be side to side, representing the endless waves of the ocean, not back and forth like an unfixed puppy on a homemade quilt."

She stopped moving and scrunched up her nose. "Ew."

I grinned. "My thoughts exactly. Besides, cultural appropriation shouldn't be our go-to in times of crisis."

"Ah, right. See? That's why I should stick to finance."

Kat's execution needed work, but it gave me an idea. I pushed aside my doubts. Maybe we could pull this off after all. "What do you think about bike riding? The police said they wanted the guests to stick around. I don't see why they'd object to a guided cycling tour. We could rent some bikes, and Aunt Marnie could take interested guests for a short ride to Fletcher Point."

Kat thought for a moment. "You know, that might work. Maybe send them out with picnic baskets too?"

I clapped my hands together. "Good idea. I've already called the bakery and ordered some cupcakes. I'll call back to make sure they have bikes available."

"They don't call it Easy Bakery and Bikes for nothing." The owner was a former city cyclist who'd traded in her road bike for a mountain bike and her marketing job to become a career baker and bicycle specialist.

"In the meantime, Nate could have the kitchen whip up a bunch of complimentary apps and put them on the bar for guests to share."

"Sounds perfect. As long as Detective Holloway agrees to all this."

I started to call the bakery, then paused. "How come you've never mentioned the detective? You two seem pretty chummy."

Kat grinned. "I was waiting for that question. I saw your thirsty eyes on him."

My mouth dropped open as my face heated up.

"Oh yes, girlfriend. I caught that," she continued. "No worries. He's all yours."

"That's not what I was asking." My voice was once again an octave higher than I intended. "Just curious. Always curious. Like a monkey."

She threw her hands up defensively. "No judgment here. And back to your question, he and Connor played ice hockey together in a beer league Thursday nights. Well, at least before Connor took up tongue hockey with Delia Young."

Cringe. "Gotcha."

"Make your call. And check the closet for the picnic baskets."

I did as instructed, calling to tentatively book a dozen bikes with the promise to confirm back within a half hour. First, however, I needed to find Detective Holloway—James?—and ask if that was allowed. Kat promised to call Aunt Marnie.

Next, picnic baskets. I walked to the supply closet, opened the door, and jumped back. Lars was standing there. He put his finger to his lips and pulled me inside, closing the door behind me.

He looked awful, much worse close up than he had when I'd noticed him stalking out of his room earlier this morning. His face was scratched and swollen on one side, his complexion pale and clammy.

I took a closer peek. "Are you okay?"

73

He drew back. "Fine. Shh."

I looked around. "What are you doing in here?"

He tried to brush his bangs down to cover his wound. Were his hands trembling? "I'm in trouble."

I squeezed his arm and spoke in a soft voice as I held his gaze. "I heard about Bob. I'm sorry."

He swatted my hand away. "You don't understand. I need your help, Jess."

I frowned. Here's the thing: Lars calling me Jess was like a mom including their child's middle name when summoning them. Not a good sign. "What is it?"

His breaths grew shallow, his features tight with strain.

"Lars, what's going on?" I tried to stand back to get a better look at him in the unflattering white fluorescent light in the closet, but there wasn't enough room. The small space wasn't meant for two. I started to reach for the door, and Lars shifted sideways, giving away what I hadn't noticed before. He was hiding something behind his back. I craned my neck to see what it was, but he put his free hand up to stop me. "Don't."

"What is it, Lars?" I demanded. "Show me."

He rubbed his face. "Do you have any bleach?"

I pulled back as far as I could and took a deep breath. "You're scaring me, Lars." My soft tone now had an edge.

"I'm sorry." He shut his eyes, then slowly pulled out his right hand from behind his back, revealing a T-shirt. It was soiled and had a metallic scent. There was a smudge of dark red on his palm from the shirt. "I need to clean this."

My heart almost stopped. *Oh no, oh no, oh no.* My mouth opened and shut. I held both hands up as if to ward him off.

"Babe, relax. It's not what it looks like." His tone was clipped. "Bob and I got into it last night. If the cops find out . . ."

"What did you do, Lars?"

Before he could answer, the door swung open. I turned to see Kat standing there, looking confused. Duke was by her side, and behind them stood Detective Holloway. His face was stony and cold.

My stomach lurched.

Kat broke the silence. "Jess?"

I swallowed hard. "Hey, you two. Look who I found." I moved a few inches back, making me bump into Lars. He put his left hand on my shoulder.

Lars stood up taller and stuck his chin out. "Hey."

Detective Holloway looked from me to Lars to me again. "What's going on in here?"

Lars pulled me closer. "Jess was helping me find some extra soap. I like to be scrubby clean."

Detective Holloway gave him an icy glare. "I told you to stick to your room."

"James . . . ," Lars started.

It was Detective Holloway's turn to stand a little taller. He cleared his throat. "It's Detective Holloway."

"Sure, boss," Lars said. "Here's the thing. Jess and I have history. I think you knew that, right?" He looked at Detective Holloway, the left side of his mouth lifting into a cocky smile.

The detective's face remained stony. "So?"

"We thought it might be fun to try and rekindle the magic a little. This closet may not look like much to some, but to Jess and me, it's sentimental. See where I'm headed?"

I would've shoved him across the tiny room if I hadn't been shocked into silence and humiliation.

"You'll be headed to the station if you don't follow my instructions," Detective Holloway said. "You can't wander at your leisure. Keep it in your pants until I've concluded the on-site search."

"Okay," Lars said. "I'll go back to my room. Just one question: Why am I not allowed to leave it?"

"I'm trying to piece together the events of the day leading up to your stepfather's death. You need to stay out of my way and out of trouble."

Kat interrupted, her face as cold and formal as the detective's. "FYI, Jess, a news van just showed up."

"The *Fletcher Lake Chronicle* has a news van?" I blurted out.

She shook her head, now meeting my gaze head on. "No, they don't. But *Spill the Tea* does."

Lars swore under his breath. Just what we needed. *STT* was the biggest tabloid in celebrity gossip.

"They're not the only recent arrival." Kat said. "Jess, your mom's here too."

It was hard to say whose arrival I dreaded more.

Chapter Nine

"Jessica?" a familiar voice rang out. "Kat? Hello? I need someone to verify my relationship to the owner. Now."

I exited the closet and pushed past the group to greet my mother. Duke had abandoned Kat to sit at her feet. "Mom, what are you doing here?"

It was impossible to tell whether the hassle of the police request or my curt tone had her on edge, but one look at her hard-set jaw and I knew to stand down. "Mom?" I said again. "You okay?"

She surveyed the scene before responding. "I heard there was trouble down here, and the boys in blue out front tried to prevent me from entering. Would one of you go and vouch for me while my daughter fills me in?" It was more of an order than a request.

Kat nodded. "I'll go." She turned and left without another word.

Lucky duck. I wanted to escape this scene too.

Before I could plan an exit, Mom's eyes narrowed. She looked at the closet before homing in on Lars. "What happened to you?"

He hesitated, his good eye shifting from one person to the next. No one stepped in to help.

"Lars," Mom said in a clipped tone. "Do you know what I used to tell my students when they were about to lie to me? You are delaying the inevitable." She paused. "But you have a pass for now. I don't have time for shenanigans."

Lars's shoulders drooped. Narrow escape. Next in line was Detective Holloway. "James," my mother began, her voice now decidedly softer. "Helen McKay tells me you haven't had a lot of experience with homicide investigations. She's worked at the Fletcher Lake police station since your only weapon was a Nerf gun. She wanted me to tell you she's standing by in case you need her help. That goes double for me. Getting to the bottom of things is my specialty."

Detective Holloway's face flushed. No one was immune to the embarrassment suffered at Mom's attention. He gave her a stiff smile. "Thanks. And speaking of help, I should probably go check on the scene out back." He paused, taking one more long look at Lars. "It's time for you to get back to your room. Wait for me there."

"Sure, boss." Lars shot me a pleading look, then slunk out.

Detective Holloway watched him go, as if ensuring he wasn't making any pit stops along the way. He then turned to me. "I'll be back in a few minutes to go over the video."

I nodded. "Sounds good."

Once alone, Mom and I walked back to the lobby. She sat down on the sofa and patted the seat next to her. "Please sit down and fill me in."

"What have you heard?" I sank down beside her. I didn't really have time to spare, but there was no way I could brush Mom off.

She leaned forward. "Only that someone drowned in the pond out back under suspicious circumstances."

Good grief. "How did you know that, Mom? He was only found a few hours ago."

Mom cleared her throat and sat up as if she were in the witness box trying to justify some unsavory behavior. Sticking her nose where it didn't belong, in her case. "I was doing my morning cross-word on the porch when two police cars zoomed by the house."

I waited for a beat. "And?"

"*And*," she said, twirling her pearl earring and avoiding my gaze, "I knew it meant trouble, so I called Helen to find out more."

I frowned. "Helen? I thought she was semiretired."

"Oh, please. That didn't last a month. They couldn't manage without her, as I'd predicted." She grinned slyly. "The chief lured her back with a pay raise and the promise of part-time morning shifts."

Mom had said law and order would fall apart without Helen. Maybe she was right. Her bestie kept the police station running as tight as a Delta Force task team.

"Good to know." I tucked that nugget in the back of my mind.

"Now it's your turn, Jessica." Mom's sharp blue eyes studied my face. "And don't spare the details."

I hadn't planned to spill it all, but once I started talking, I couldn't stop. Mom was a good listener. And she was always there for me, even when uninvited.

I'd barely finished talking when Kat stomped back in, her eyes narrowed and her lips pursed.

Ay, caramba! "What now?" I asked.

"The reporters' cameras are out." She flailed her arm toward the front door. "And rumors are flying. Almost the whole time I was out there, some aggro reporter was waving his mike around, demanding details."

A feeling of dread washed over me. "This isn't exactly the sort of press I was hoping for."

Kat threw her hands up. "What should we do?"

Mom stood up and peeked out the front window. "A few years ago, at the school, a violent assault occurred during recess, sending a student to the hospital. Parents stormed the school demanding details. To protect the privacy of the affected students, I couldn't give specifics, but I knew they were worried that their child would be next, so they wouldn't leave without some sort of answer."

"How did you handle it?" I asked.

"I told them enough to get them off my back," Mom said. "What they really wanted was reassurance it wouldn't happen to their kids."

Kat looked from Mom to me. "So what are you saying? We should throw them a bone?"

"Find out exactly what they need to get them off your backs. If you give them enough to report a story, maybe they'll give you some breathing room."

Not a bad idea. "They're here because of Lars. Maybe we could reassure them he's all right."

"With the promise of a more detailed update in the not-too-distant future," Kat suggested.

An idea came to mind. "Mom, can you do it?" If I could give her a task, it would give me time to sort out other things while keeping her out of my hair.

Her eyes flashed, and she gave me a wicked grin. "Absolutely. What exactly would you like me to tell them?"

I pointed at her. "Let them know Lars is okay and has asked for a little space. Say he'll be out to see them soon enough."

"Brilliant." She stood up, straightened her shirt, and strode out the door.

"Are you sure that was a good idea?" Kat asked. "No offense to your mom, but once you accept the Momfia's help, there's no going back."

She was right. But at this point it was a risk worth taking. Besides, a little help from well-connected friends might come in handy.

"Kat, we need to stay on top of this so we're in control of the narrative. Not the press or even the police. The Pearl is our business baby. We must protect it. Can you hold the fort down here until Penny arrives? She might be delayed coming in, and I want to go find out what's going on with the investigation. Guests will have questions, and I want answers."

"You're not going to answer my questions about Lars and the closet?" Her voice was tinged with irritation.

I stood up. "Don't read too much into it. You think if I had something hot and juicy, I'd keep it from you?"

Her mouth slid into a smirk. "I can read you like a book."

"All I know for sure is he's a hot mess." *And wanted me to help him clean a bloody T-shirt.* This last detail was something I'd save for later when we had more time.

The back door flew open, and Britt stormed in. My cue to leave. I tried to hide behind the artificial palm tree—with no success. With hands on hips, she cornered me. "What are we expected to do in this no-tell motel? We're shut in, yet shut out. I'm ready to bring this whole place down with one devastating review on TripAdvisor."

Before I could answer or take a swing, a shadowy figure emerged from the back hallway. "Would a custom mimosa ease the pain?"

Britt's head snapped up. Nate stood there, offering his signature smile.

The sour expression morphed into a coquettish grin and she batted her way-too-long lashes, eyeing him like a fresh grilled steak at a five-star chophouse. "Nate Byrne," she purred. "What do you have in mind? I have a headache the size of Manhattan."

The Pied Piper of desperate women, Nate led Britt away with the sound of his voice. He turned back long enough to give me a wink before they disappeared, prattling on about the virtues of using rosé instead of champagne in his signature drinks.

Kat and I waited a beat, then followed the pair outside. Kat huffed as we watched them stroll past the pool toward the bar. "Should I offer Britt a straw to suck up the drool?"

I scrunched up my nose. "I don't know how I feel about him using his masculine guile while poor Sarah is back there suffering."

"I'm touched," a voice said from behind us. I turned to see Sarah appear from the doorway, looking about a zillion times better.

My eyes widened. "Sarah!" Relief set in. Was I genuinely happy to see her?

She stretched both arms over her head as if she'd woken from a refreshing night's sleep. "No need to worry about me. I'm the one who asked Nate to rescue you two from that guest. Her energy was outright hostile. Besides, I trust Nate completely. He can't help being a natural charmer. That's who he is, and I celebrate that."

Since when had Sarah become so . . . likable? Before I could consider an answer, I heard my name being called from nearby.

"Over here." A waving hand caught my eye. The pretty twins I'd checked in yesterday were stretched out on two lounge chairs. One had on a casual blue sundress while the other wore high-waisted black shorts and a hot-pink tank top with a splash of glitter along the neckline.

I approached the pair. "Elle and Lila, right?"

They exchanged a look of surprise before nodding. "You've got a good memory," one of them said. They were the mirror image of each other. I wasn't sure who was who.

As if reading my mind, the sister in the sequined separates grinned. "I'm Elle."

Sister number two, Lila, put an arm around her twin. "As in Eleganza Extravaganza."

"*RuPaul's Drag Race* fans," I noted in appreciation. There could be a whole book dedicated to the genius catchphrases in my favorite show.

"That's right. We're both fans, but Elle gags over anything sparkly."

Elle put her hand behind her ear to show off a dangling crystal earring. "Swarovski crystals are this girl's best friend." She grinned at her sister. "After you, of course."

I was glad to see Bob's death hadn't dampened everyone's spirits. "So you two are holding up okay?"

Elle snuck one more look at Lila. Her smile briefly faltered. "Mm-hmm."

I glanced from one to the other. "You don't need to pretend for our benefit. It's okay to be upset by what's happened. The death of a guest paired with a big police presence doesn't exactly gel with a girls' weekend vibe."

Elle let out a big breath. "It's been a shock."

Lila nodded. "Life's tough sometimes. But we'll get through."

It was nice to see the pair had resolved their differences. They'd seemed a little out of sorts during check-in. "You mentioned food when you arrived. I wrote down a few of my favorite restaurants in town and left the list at reception. If there's anything we can do to help, don't hesitate to ask," I told them.

"Know a good divorce lawyer?" Lila asked. Elle stiffened at the question.

My eyes widened. She had me there.

Kat sidled up next to me. "Got mine on speed dial."

Lila squeezed Elle's hand, flashing Kat a grin. "Good to know."

Kat eyed the pair quizzically. "Listen, I've been legally single now for all of nine months. And after muddling through the pain of marriage to a two-timing slimedog, I can tell you divorce can be liberating. I feel like a phoenix rising from the ashes."

"This is Kat, by the way," I said. "My business partner and best friend. She ditched the dud and revamped her life."

Elle swallowed. "Appreciate the support. We come from a very traditional family where divorce is considered shameful. It took a while for me to come to terms with the truth: that I couldn't stay married to someone like him."

Lila frowned. "A controlling and manipulative a—"

"Stop." Elle's eyes filled with tears. "I know that now. Is there anything wrong with seeking out some closure?"

Kat's expression softened. "Ultimately, it's your life. You get to decide. But hey, look at me now. I was where you are not that long ago. For me, all it took was one road trip, two nights, and three bottles of wine."

Lila looked impressed. "And you managed to come up with all of this?"

"It's not quite that simple. This was my grandparents' house," I explained. "When my grandmother passed, my mom and aunt put it up for sale, but it's a massive house with an extensive property and needed a lot of work, so it stayed on the market for over a year with no bites. Then Kat and I were on our annual girls' trip, and we realized we were both burnt-out in our careers and ready for a change. Combined with the fact that my brother had been scouring the area for the perfect location to open a bar—*then* it all came together."

"That's a great story." Lila turned and looked into her twin's eyes. "See? This is proof that life doesn't end with divorce."

Kat reached forward and squeezed Elle's arm. "Take it from me—a different perspective can help you see the truth. Sometimes the best dreams are born from nightmares."

Elle nodded. "You're right. I'm taking back control."

"We've all had a gruesome reminder that life is short," Lila said. "We need to seize every moment we have and squash anyone who gets in our way."

I cringed. After witnessing a caved-in skull this morning, I found her words hit way too close to home.

Our conversation was cut short by a young mother and son bursting through the lobby exit. The boy, giggling with energy, bounced a small red rubber ball against the nearby wall. It rebounded off a lounge chair and the back of Kat's head before dropping into a nearby planter.

"Ethan!" the mortified mom snapped. She caught the ball and turned to Kat. "I'm so sorry."

Kat smiled at the woman and then down at the cowering boy. "I've got two younger brothers and a strong noggin. Nothing to worry about here."

The woman confiscated the ball and gripped the young boy's hand before looking at Kat gratefully. "Thanks." They shuffled toward the pool, the frazzled mom leaning over and scolding her son as they went. She put two towels on a nearby seat, hooked her bag on the chair, and dropped the ball inside. She waggled her finger at him and warned him not to move while she went to grab them a snack.

With wide eyes, he promised, and she turned her back and strode toward the bar. He stayed put for all of about two seconds before hopping out of the chair and digging his ball out of his mom's bag.

"Speaking of worries," I said, turning my attention back to Lila and Elle. "The police will be done here soon, and things can get back to normal."

Elle's eyebrows perked up. "Any suggestions for afternoon activities other than the pool? There's only so much sun I can handle in a day."

Kat ducked. "Heads up." A red flash zinged past my head. We all watched as the young boy continued his bouncy-ball attack, hitting both guests and furniture with uncontrolled vigor. His mom, on her way back with a large order of fries in hand, saw him and began a hot

85

pursuit. She'd almost reached him when her foot caught on something nearby. *Noooo!* It was a Stella McCartney purse strap sticking out of Lila's lounge chair. I held my breath as the mom toppled over. Somehow she managed to save the fries and stop herself from going headfirst into the pool, but just barely. She turned and mumbled an apology to the purse before setting down the food and returning to her mission of taming the beast—or rather, the boy.

Sarah approached our huddle, holding her hands together over her heart. "Don't you love the energy of children? Such free spirits."

Kat huffed. "I prefer my spirits in a martini glass."

I stifled a grin and held out my hand toward Sarah. "Elle, Lila, this is my sister-in-law, Sarah. She is our resident yoga instructor."

Sarah held out her hands, palms up. "Together, we can improve your body flow and breathing techniques."

"That might be nice," Elle said. Lila looked less excited.

"We're also working on getting a bicycle tour set up," Kat offered.

"And if neither option appeals to you," I said, "Stick a hashtag *notreadytoadult* sign on your door and share a bottle of wine."

Lila looked at her sister. "Whatever you want to do is fine by me."

Elle grinned. "You're such a liar." She turned to the rest of us. "No judgment if we choose the latter?"

"Hold that thought." I excused myself and walked back to reception, where I grabbed a bottle of chilled rosé from the small wine fridge along with two wine tumblers. I returned and handed over the goods. *Rosé All Day* was scrolled across the side of the glasses in white cursive script.

"Does this reassure you?" I asked.

Lila clapped her hands together. "We've found our people, sis."

Elle nodded. "You're like a wine whisperer."

The women thanked us, gathered up their gear, and strolled across the lounge area toward their room, arm in arm.

Sarah, Kat, and I made our way back inside. Sarah wandered over to the sofa and picked up a magazine.

Kat and I reconvened at the floor-to-ceiling window near the front entrance that overlooked the street. "Nice work, partner." She and I high-fived. At least one problem was solved. What next?

I looked outside and watched my mom schmoozing with the reporter. It gave me an idea.

"Jess," Kat said. "What's up? You look schemey."

"I think it's time we step up and help the police. As long as we don't know what happened to Bob, chances are the press and the police are going to be hanging around. And that's not good for business. Think about it, Kat. Between the Momfia and us, we have a lot of brainpower."

"I love the enthusiasm, but cops don't like interfering civilians, even well-meaning ones."

"Kat, c'mon. You're a Murderino. Do I really need to list the number of times civilians helped solve crimes and bring about justice?"

"True. But it's usually cold cases."

Sarah peered over her magazine. "Hold up. What the heck is a Murderino?"

"A Murderino is someone obsessed with true crime," Kat explained. "It was born from the *My Favorite Murder* podcast. It's smart and sexy, just like us."

Kat and I high-fived again.

"Riiight," Sarah said, clueing in. "I listened to that once. Too gruesome for me. You two are kinda like the hosts."

Kat grinned. "Karen Kilgariff and Georgia Hardstark? That's so sweet, Sarah. They're my heroes."

I put my hand up. "I want to be Karen."

Kat clapped. "That means I'm Georgia."

Sarah's eyes shifted between us. "Uh . . ."

Oh, right. Sarah's comparison wasn't meant as a compliment. So what? Besides, she was playing right into my plan, whether she meant to or not.

I elbowed Kat. "Seriously. We've got style and smarts."

Kat groaned. "And we are both hilarious."

Our eyes locked. "Okay, I'm in," Kat said, throwing her hands up. "But I'm no patsy. I'm fully aware you're manipulating me, you sly fox."

I feigned a pout. "*Moi?*"

Duke got up and stretched, then strolled over to Kat, where he rubbed his head on her leg, demanding to be petted. She obliged before looking back up at me. "We'd better not end up in handcuffs again."

Sarah's mouth dropped open, a look of horror on her face.

My hands flew up in a defensive stance. "I thought that *Keep Out* sign was part of the Halloween décor. Besides, this is completely different. A man has lost his life at our B and B, and the reputation of our business is at stake."

Kat and Duke crossed the room and peered out the window. "We do know this town and its secrets, don't we?"

With Kat on board, I was feeling good. I also had to admit Sarah had been a big part of convincing her to hop on. "I may have the best sister-in-law in the world," I said, giving Sarah a ginormous smile.

Sarah looked up. She didn't return my smile. "Oh no. I'm not down with this." She threw the magazine back on the table and stood up. "I'm going to go set up some yoga mats."

"Just don't mention anything to Nate, then," I called over as she made a hasty leap toward the door. She reached over her head as she scurried away, giving me a thumbs-up.

I looked back at Kat. "Where do we begin?"

Chapter Ten

B efore we could start on our investigation, Kat and I needed a list. I lived for lists. Was there any better satisfaction than crossing off a page of to-dos by the end of the day? A big no from me. I kept a stash of pink notebooks in the storage room along with a selection of colorful pens. When inspired, purple ink was my jam.

Before I could gather my supplies, however, a couple came into the reception area looking for suggestions on where to have a private picnic.

"Does that mean you're free to go?" Kat asked them.

The couple laughed. "The detective said people are allowed to leave as long as they check in with him before they check out," the woman said.

"Uh-oh," I said. "Should we prepare ourselves? Are people feeling apprehensive about their stay here?" No one had booked for only one night. Would people run for the hills, leaving us empty on our second day of business?

"Not us," the man said. "We're not worried, and it didn't seem like anyone else was either. The police said to stay alert but told us there was no reason to think anyone else was in danger. Besides, we're here now. Nothing is going to scare us off."

The woman patted her husband's arm. "My husband means it took a lot of planning for us to organize the trip. We wouldn't mind a little more alone time, though. The mood in the lounge is fun, but we're ready for something more intimate. Is there anywhere nearby you can suggest? Maybe something outside, yet private?"

"We've spent lots of time in our room, but we want to shake it up a little," the man said with a not-so-subtle wink at his wife. She blushed in return.

Kat pulled out a map of the area. She circled our location, then drew a line across the street, followed by another circle not far away, near the water. "Just across the road you'll see a pathway that snakes through some bushes. It leads to a small alcove with a great beach. There's no sign, but it's not hard to spot. It's only separated from the main beach area of Fletcher Lake by a scattering of trees and bushes."

"Why isn't it marked?" asked the woman.

"It gets pretty overcrowded in the valley during high season. We townies like to keep this one just for ourselves."

"Ah, a secret beach. I like it," the man said, putting his arm around his wife's waist. He pulled her close as she grinned up at him and leaned her head on his shoulder.

"You'll love it," Kat said. "The unofficial name of it is Evergreen Beach. There's only one pine tree, which is rumored to be over a hundred years old." She leaned in closer to them. "The dense canopy underneath is just tall enough for a romantic tête-à-tête, if you get my meaning."

The woman flushed, and she and her husband both giggled. "Thanks for the tip," the man said. "It's our first weekend away from the kids. Fresh air and romance is exactly why we're here."

"Then you've come to the right place," Kat concluded. "One sec; let me get you one of our signature baskets."

She scurried out to the closet, returning a minute later with a woven wicker picnic basket. "This is the quintessential kit. It has everything you need: blanket, glasses, and—" She paused and reached into the small bar fridge behind the reception counter. She grabbed a bottle of wine and put it inside the basket. "Voilà! A chilled bottle of rosé. On the house, if you promise to spread the word."

The couple thanked her and left, whispering to each other all the way out the door.

I elbowed my friend gently. "Nice touch."

Kat shot me a satisfied grin and pulled out an espresso cup from under the counter. She headed for the espresso machine, looking very pleased with herself. I left her to it while I made my way back to the supply closet.

En route, I peeked out the back exit. For all the complaints about our B and B turning into a prison, it seemed that people were willing to put up with the police presence as long as they were tended to and comfortable. All signs of strain and stress were gone. A few guests on white loungers next to the pool were scrolling through their phones while others took turns doing cannonballs into the water. Nate was handing out pitchers of complimentary drinks, too, which probably helped.

With my brother on top of the outdoor area, I could focus on my new task. I turned around and marched down the hallway until I reached the closet. I stepped inside, switched the light on, and shut the door. Where had I put those notebooks? Everything was organized, but the place was packed with housekeeping and other supplies from floor to ceiling.

I thought back to my run-in with Lars and to the bloody shirt he'd had in his possession. Why did he feel the need to hide it? Lars was lots of things, but violent had never made the list, except for one particular Thanksgiving . . .

Lars had been put in charge of the cooking. The turkey burnt, and an argument ensued. Bob said Lars was useless. Lars snapped and punched him in the face.

A chill went through me at the memory. I tried to rub away a fresh crop of goosebumps. Was it possible Lars had snapped again? No, I couldn't see it. Not without a good reason, at least. And that had been a single punch. Murder was a whole different can of kapow, right?

I peered around the closet, biting my lip, shifting stuff on the shelves. Was there any chance the soiled shirt was still here?

The door swung open and I let out a little yelp, whipping my head up with a sudden jerk and slamming it into a shelf. Mom stood at the open door. I glared at her while rubbing my head, trying to push past an unsettling feeling of déjà vu.

"Jessica, why do I keep finding you in the closet?" Mom said. "I shouldn't need to tell you that running a bed-and-breakfast is going to require you to face people, not avoid them like the plague."

I stifled the urge to roll my eyes. "Mom . . ."

She pushed her way in and began peeking behind the stacks of supplies. "At least tell me you're not hiding a guy in here again."

"See anyone?" I squashed myself up against a shelf as she squeezed past me. "I might be in a dry spell, but I haven't resorted to dating the Invisible Man quite yet."

She ignored the comment and reached down behind the stack of pink notebooks I'd been looking for. With her thumb and index finger, she pulled out the bloody T-shirt. "What's this, Jessica?"

"Ew, Mom! Drop it," I said, whacking her wrist, knocking the garment onto the floor. Most people would think twice before putting their hands on a soiled shirt, reminiscent of any one of a dozen scenes from *Law & Order: SVU*. But after thirty years of working with teenagers, nothing fazed my mother. She examined my face, waiting for an explanation.

"You don't want to contaminate evidence," I said.

"Evidence?" Mom's eyes were sharp and alert. "What are you saying, Jessica? Evidence pertaining to what, exactly?"

I steeled myself and met her gaze. "Lars was holding that T-shirt when I found him here this morning. How did you even see it behind the notebooks?"

"I'm your mother." The most overused and unsatisfying answer ever. A better one would have been to finally admit she was part bloodhound. No wonder that was the nickname given to her by her students. At least the one people were willing to share with me. "So why is Lars using your supply closet to stash his dirty laundry?"

I swallowed. "He's worried it might implicate him . . ." I couldn't finish the sentence.

Her eyes widened. "In his stepfather's murder?"

I shrugged. "Something like that."

She leaned over and checked to make sure nothing else was hidden behind the stacked boxes. "Innocent people don't hide evidence."

"Scared people do all sorts of outrageous things, Mom. Didn't one of your students try to jump out the window when he was summoned to your office?"

She finished her search, then stood back to examine me. "That was on the first floor, Jessica. And the student got stuck halfway, making the whole situation that much worse for himself. The rest of the school year, people referred to him as Winnie the Pooh instead of Wayne." She paused. "My point is you're not doing Lars any favors. We need to hand this shirt over to James right away."

"I'm not disagreeing, Mom." My voice came out as a whine. I cleared my throat and stood taller. "If I knew where Detective Holloway was right now, I wouldn't hesitate."

Mom nodded. "Glad to hear it."

I relaxed a little. "Good. Although there may be no need. He may have already concluded that Bob slipped, hit his head, and fell into the water. And in that case, we don't need to even have this conversation or bring up inconsequential items."

"Including blood-soaked clothing?"

"Exactly."

Mom opened the closet door. "Luckily we won't have to face that decision, since he's in the lobby looking for you."

"Is he ready to watch the video footage?"

"I would imagine so. After all, it wasn't a ghost that killed Bob Strapp."

I froze. "What do you mean?"

"Time for you to find out."

Always the rip-the-Band-Aid-off type of mom. She pulled me out of the closet and marched me back toward the lobby, where Detective Holloway was waiting. For some unspoken reason that filled me with dread.

His elbow was propped up on the front counter and he was chatting casually to Kat, as if just stopping by for a friendly hello or dropping off the daily soup special from Eddie's Place. But as Mom and I approached, the detective and Kat stopped their conversation and he stood up to his full height. It was hard not to notice his broad shoulders and ripped arms as he moved. His impenetrable gaze caught my roving eye, and I felt my cheeks burn and quickly shifted my focus to Kat, who gave me a *caught you* smirk.

"Here she is," Mom stated. "As promised." She pushed me forward, like a bounty hunter handing over a fugitive. "And Jessica, don't forget to give him that bloody T-shirt Lars stuffed in the closet earlier."

I cringed at her description before attempting a casual friendly smile. Maybe Detective Holloway would think Mom was employing the British use of the word *bloody*, which might give me the chance to explain it on my own terms in my own way.

When I mustered up the courage to meet his gaze, I had my answer. *Nope. Not a chance.* One look at him and I knew that would definitely not be the case. Clenched jaw. Probing eyes. Was it too late to run back to the closet and hide?

When no one else said anything, Mom didn't hesitate. "Go on, Jessica. Show him."

"Thanks, Mom," I said in a way that told her I was anything but thankful before turning my attention back to Detective Holloway. "Lars didn't give it to me. And I didn't know it was still in the closet. He had it with him earlier when I found him. He must've forgotten to give it to you."

"*Forgotten?*" Mom snapped. I glared at her. She crossed her arms but said no more.

A pang of guilt shot through me. Was I throwing Lars under the bus, outing him like this? No doubt. Then again, given Mom's persistence, did I have a choice?

"Can you show me the T-shirt?" Detective Holloway said. "Where is it now?"

His friendly demeanor had cooled. Not that it mattered. I had more important things to worry about. "It's still in the closet. I'll show you."

"It was stashed behind some cleaning supplies," Mom added helpfully. "I grabbed it, not realizing what it was, so my fingerprints will be on it. I hope that won't complicate matters."

Detective Holloway told her not to worry. When I stole a glance back at Kat, who'd remained silent, she looked about as impressed with me as everyone else in the room. Only Duke came to my defense, standing at my feet, looking up with unwavering support. I bent down and gave him a pat. A proverb floated through my mind: *Be the person your dog thinks you are.* Words to live by? Easier said than done. I took a breath and marched to the closet, Detective Holloway following close behind.

Chapter Eleven

The soiled T-shirt lay balled up on the floor between a full box of bottle openers and a case of stemless wineglasses marked with the slogan *#savewaterdrinkwine*.

Detective Holloway donned a pair of gloves and bagged the T-shirt. When he turned around, his expression had turned grim. "Can you spare a few more minutes?"

A sense of unease set in. "Okay. Do you want me to set up the video feed?"

"It's on my list."

His list? Uh-oh. If he was anything like me, a list came into play only when there were more than three items. What else could there be?

He must have sensed my apprehension, because he added, "Don't worry. There's just a few more things I'd like to go over with you. I promise it won't take long."

"Yeah, of course," I heard myself reply. His assurance did little to settle my nerves, but what else could I say?

"Okay, good." He held up the evidence bag. "Mind walking me around the building? I need to drop this off first."

"Sure." My mind began to spin as I followed him out. If Lars had killed Bob, he didn't deserve my help. My loyalty could withstand some weathering, but it had limits. Then again, I couldn't picture Lars as a murderer. He was an idiot, yes, but he wasn't cruel or hateful. And the victim was Bob. The only family he had left. What possible motive would Lars have had to kill his own stepdad?

We walked in silence back to the lobby. He paused at the door. "Be right back." I watched him hustle out the front door toward his car. When he reached it, he opened the trunk and dropped the T-shirt inside.

Movement behind me shifted my attention to the reception desk. Penny had arrived and was on duty. I could see by her red-rimmed eyes that she'd been brought up to date. The couple who'd borrowed a picnic basket earlier had also returned. Apparently there was no corkscrew in the basket; Penny apologized and made her way back to the supply closet to grab one. Duke was snoring in his bed. *Goofball.* Mom and Kat were seated on the sofa, eyes locked, talking in low tones. They didn't even notice me. What were they talking about?

Before I had a chance to ask them, Detective Holloway stuck his head in the door. "Mind if we go the long way around?"

"No problem."

He held the door open, and I stepped outside to join him.

He patted his shirt pocket. "Shoot. I forgot something in the car. Let me just grab it."

"Sure, okay." I followed him back to his car. He unlocked the door and reached inside to grab a small notebook that lay on the passenger seat.

"Sorry about that." He locked up the car and tucked the notebook into his pocket.

I frowned. "What exactly are we doing now?"

"Don't worry, this isn't an interrogation. I'd like you to accompany me back to the area near where Mr. Strapp died. Kat said you'd be the one to notice anything out of place."

Phew. Couldn't argue that. My eye for detail had gone into over-drive during the final days before opening. We were charging premium prices for a stay at the Pearl. It wasn't just about the individual rooms. It was an atmosphere, an attitude. So it had to be perfect, right down to the labels of the essential oils on display. To be Instagram worthy, details mattered.

Before we made our way out back, I decided now was the time to ask a few questions of my own. With no one else around, it was the perfect opportunity. "Mom said Bob didn't just slip on the rocks. Do you know what happened?"

He looked at me. "We're starting to get an idea. Sounds like your mom's filled you in. Guess I have Helen McKay to thank for that."

I stifled a grin. I couldn't read his face to decide if he was an ally or an enemy. His expression was straight up impassive.

"Are you saying Mom was right? He was murdered?" I searched Detective Holloway's face for confirmation.

He hesitated before answering. "All I can say is that his death warrants an investigation."

I kept my eyes on him. "But people don't regularly drown in two feet of water. Or was it blunt-force trauma? Obviously, I noticed he had a head injury."

He pressed his lips together in a tight smile. Was he going to answer my question? Before I could find out, the squeaky door of an unmarked van parked just beyond our property swung open. A man leapt out the back. He careened toward us, equipped with a large-lensed camera with a boom mike attached. I froze. The cameraman's face was hidden behind his lens, but the three red letters on his ball cap told me everything I needed to know.

STT.

Could things get any worse?

His voice bellowed as he moved in. "Sheriff Holloway, can you tell us what's going on?"

The detective stood up straighter. He took a step forward in a protective stance and assessed the man, unfazed. "It's *Detective* Holloway, and when we have something to share, we'll make an announcement."

The cameraman shifted his attention—and his camera—toward me without missing a beat. "Who are you? The wife? The mistress?"

I stared into the camera as if mesmerized by the shiny glass lens. It wasn't that I'd never daydreamed of such a moment, but in my imagination, I'd been on a red carpet in a vintage Chanel dress, not on asphalt wearing uninspired yoga basics (not even my Lulu gear).

Duke must've been woken by the squeaky door of the van and sensed my alarm. In no time, he'd pushed his way out of the lobby doors and was at my side in seconds. This time his approach wasn't friendly. There was no mistaking the tone of his barks: f-bombs all the way. The cameraman got the hint and retreated, one hand up in fearful defeat. *Good boy!*

Once there was a respectable distance between the cameraman and me, I told Duke to shush. A throat cleared behind us. I smelled tea tree shampoo and didn't need to turn around to recognize the commanding voice. Mom had joined the party. "This is the woman who will give you an exclusive if you give her a little breathing space. Play by her terms, you win."

Finally, the face behind the camera popped up. A middle-aged man with ruddy cheeks and a receding chin eyed us.

"You a lawyer?" he demanded.

"Valerie Byrne. And this is Jessica, owner of the Pearl Bed-and-Breakfast. I was just speaking with some of your friends out front."

He said nothing but watched her intently, as if trying to decipher if she was lying.

Mom walked up to him, now with an expression colder than Siberia at Christmas, her spiked heels just inches away from crushing the tips of his toes. Without dropping her head, she surveyed him from above. "I'll tell you what I've told them. Respect our boundaries and we'll respect your deadlines."

The man's chin receded farther into the folds of his neck as he surveyed my mom, who now stood almost directly above him.

An almost imperceptible nod brought a smug smile from Mom. Her hand shot out in front of her to shake on the deal, nearly jabbing him with her perfectly polished nails, and she awaited his response.

He flinched before extending his hand almost against his will, as if pressured by the overflowing confidence exuded by Mom. He wouldn't be the first. She reached forward and took it in hers, giving it a hearty shake.

"Good on you, Rick," she said. "It is Rick, isn't it?"

His mouth flopped open. "Yes, ma'am."

"Excellent. Your friends mentioned you'd be up here first, camera in hand. I like ambition, Rick. You and I will get along just fine. Now run along, and I'll see you when I'm ready."

"Yes, ma'am," Rick said again, well aware he'd been schooled. His camera was now at his side.

Without another word, he took a few steps backward before turning tail and scooting back to the safety of his crew as fast as his stubby legs could take him.

"Thanks, Mom," I said. Her effect on the cameraman hadn't surprised me. I'd seen it before. It never failed to impress me, though. And serve as a reminder to stay on her good side.

"You're welcome," she said. "I caught a few episodes of *Keeping Up With the Kardashians*. I was conjuring up my inner Kris Jenner."

I grinned at her. "You nailed it. Now can you take Duke back inside? Detective Holloway and I need to talk."

"I suppose," she said, with a hint of reluctance. "But don't take too long. We need to come up with a plan to deal with these vultures. Once word spreads, there'll be more. I'd like to know how we're going to handle it."

"I promise," I called out as she and Duke went back inside.

"Guess your mom's got herself a job," Detective Holloway commented, once she was out of earshot. "A win-win for everyone."

I grinned at him. "Except them."

He paused as we rounded the corner. He was peering up at the security camera. "You said this is in working order, right?"

The equipment had seen better days. It was at least a decade old and was haphazardly mounted with a few screws and a lot of pull ties. "I think so. As you can see, the cameras weren't professionally installed. There's one here, one at the bar, one at reception, and one on the second story overlooking the common area. My aunt set them up yesterday."

He stood directly under the camera and stretched both hands out. "We might get a break. It's aimed more toward the parking lots, but it's a fisheye lens, so if we're lucky, it might catch part of the gazebo."

I looked ahead. "It's possible, but no way it has the pond in view."

"That might not matter."

I thought about it. "You're right. If Bob was supposed to meet someone, it would've been at the gazebo, not the mucky pond below. So we might not see a crime, but we might see the lead-up and the killer in wait."

The corners of his mouth turned up. "If innkeeper doesn't work out, you should come find me. You'd make a decent detective."

I nodded my thanks and felt my insides warm. My grandmother would've loved this man. Subtle and smart, like Columbo, her favorite TV sleuth. "I'll ask Kat to cue up the video feed. She and Aunt Marnie set it up on the office laptop."

He thanked me, and we marched ahead until we reached the same low fence we had the day before. This time I made sure to land on my feet instead of my face. With that hurdle managed, I relaxed a little and strode side by side with him past the gazebo and approached the pond. He lifted the surrounding yellow police tape and invited me to pass under. I ducked down and scooted underneath.

He scanned the water and the shoreline before turning back to me. "Can you look around and tell me if anything looks different since Mr. Strapp's death?"

I did as he asked, but beyond the trampled grass, likely the result of EMS personnel, nothing stood out. As if reading my mind, Detective Holloway approached my side, and we stood together at the edge of the water, just feet from where Bob's body had been found.

"Small details are what I'm looking for. Something only you would notice."

I surveyed the landscape again. Looked like the same old pond as before. "Can you be more specific?"

"I'm trying to figure out if there was a struggle."

"Oh." I thought back to the gash on the back of Bob's head and surveyed the water. There were an awful lot of smashy items around, specifically oodles of rocks that covered the bottom of the pond. Could one of them be responsible for causing a fatal blow? Or was I off base? Detective Holloway still hadn't divulged the cause of death.

Another question popped up, and with it a glimmer of optimism. "Is it possible Bob had a heart attack and collapsed?" I tried to make my voice less hopeful than I felt.

"Your sister-in-law told me she found him facedown. If he'd collapsed and hit his head as he fell, he would've been faceup. This was no accident."

A chill went through me. "I thought you weren't ready to make that call."

"Publicly, I'm not."

"So why are you telling me?"

"I don't want our primary suspect to manipulate you into thinking he's a victim too."

My face flushed. *Ouch.* "I wouldn't protect a killer."

He held my gaze long enough that he didn't even need to mention the bloody T-shirt. "It's not easy to find out someone we care about is capable of murder."

A burst of frustration hit me. Why was he so sure Lars had done this? Bob was Lars's stepfather. "I'm not some lovesick teenager. If Lars is guilty, I'd tell you to lock him up and throw away the key. But I know Lars, and he's not capable of killing anyone, let alone the only family member he had left."

"Emotion isn't always rational. Bob and Lars were seen arguing last night. And I'm not ready to convict; I just want to figure out what happened."

Why did everything he said sound so reasonable? That Lars had been in a fight with Bob wasn't news. Lars hadn't hit himself.

Duke appeared next to me, as if on cue, and sat at my feet. Since I'd adopted him from the local shelter, he'd become a second shadow, never allowing me out of his sight for too long. Especially when I was stressed or upset. My heart swelled as he looked into my eyes. Kat might be my ride or die, but Duke would be sitting in the sidecar.

"What do you think, Duke? Sniff anything suspicious?"

He wagged his tail, happy to be included. I kicked off my sandals and began to shuffle around the shallow water barefoot. Duke waded a few steps ahead, then looked up at me, as if asking *What are we doing?* "No idea, Duke." I'd been particular when prepping the B and B, but I'd stopped short of organizing rocks in the pond.

I was about to give up when Duke's tail began to wag and he let out a double bark. Eyebrows raised, I looked at Detective Holloway, then waded over to where Duke was focused on a shallow area near the water's edge a few feet from where I'd been standing. Upon reaching him, I bent down to examine the water more closely.

My breath caught. One rock didn't belong. It was baseball sized, bigger than the others surrounding it, and contained flecks of gold and silver. I recognized it as one of a dozen rocks I'd moved next to the gazebo. Guess I *hadn't* stopped short of organizing rocks. I straightened up and craned my neck to see the other ones in the grouping I'd formed. They were still arranged in a line along the side of the gazebo. During the morning yoga sessions, the reflection of the sun off the rocks gave a beautiful glittery effect, a perfect pairing for the yogis' sun salutations. A sinking feeling hit my gut. I didn't need a detective to tell me this could be a clue.

Chapter Twelve

I waved Detective Holloway over. "Look at this."

Duke wagged his tail as the hunky lawman approached. "What are we looking at?"

I pointed out the rock and explained its significance. "This rock is not like the others. No way this could get here without someone dropping it here on purpose."

He reached into the water with a gloved hand and retrieved the rock in question. "Good find." He held it up to examine it, then swore under his breath.

I frowned. "What's wrong? If an attacker used that as a weapon, isn't it a good thing we found it? Evidence?"

"Anything that gives us a clearer picture of what happened is helpful. It's just unfortunate it was fully submerged in water."

My frown deepened. "Why?"

He shook excess water off the rock, then took a closer look. "Water prevents us from lifting fingerprints or DNA."

Shoot. That's never mentioned on TV. "Could that be a clue in itself?"

He stretched back up to his full height and surveyed the area. "Hidden in plain sight."

"Exactly." No one but me—or Duke, who'd been with me when I'd moved them—would raise an eyebrow at its location. I swallowed. "That must mean the killer is a guest here."

He gripped the rock in his hand but shifted his focus to me. "How do you figure that?"

"Anyone else would've removed it from the property. Only someone staying here would consider taking the risk of leaving it nearby."

He raised his eyebrows. "Huh. You could be onto something."

A shiver ran down my back. With only ten guest suites at the B and B, it wasn't a comforting theory.

"You okay?" He closed the gap between us. "If this is too much, we can stop."

"It's a lot." I met his gaze. "But I'll manage."

"Is there any chance Mr. Strapp came here for a late-night yoga class? Yoga in the moonlight or something?"

I shook my head. "No way. First session isn't until tonight."

"Yet she was here last night?"

"Of course." Why was he asking me this? "It was opening night. Nate was working, we had entertainment set up, and Sarah stuck around to see the show."

"You saw her, then, last night?"

I drew back. *Wait. How did this become about Sarah?* "Why are you asking?"

"Curious," he said. "Usually people who get up at five in the morning aren't known for late nights at the bar."

I stiffened. "Last night was special. It's not like she was drunk."

His eyes were fixed on mine. "So you did see her?"

My mind raced back to last night. "Yes, just before the show."

"What time was that?"

"Close to eight o'clock," I said.

"You're sure about the time?"

I nodded. "She came by to apologize for an earlier argument."

His face remained stoic. "Does Sarah often argue with people?"

I gave him an exaggerated smile. "Just with me."

"Okay." He didn't smile back.

Note to self: Stick to the facts. "She's a yoga teacher, remember? It's all about namaste for her."

"So you'd be surprised to learn she was seen arguing with Mr. Strapp yesterday?"

I frowned. Why would Sarah have had a run-in with Bob? *D'oh! No-brainer.* The man was a lech and had no filter.

"Listen," I said, my voice firm. "If Sarah told Bob off, you can bet it was a reaction to some gross comment he made to her, if not worse." I shuddered.

I sounded confident, but I thought it weird Sarah hadn't mentioned anything to me. Then again, maybe she'd talked to Nate. What if Bob had gone too far, cornered her when she was alone? Would she have felt trapped and reacted by hitting him harder than she meant to? When I was younger, he'd certainly made me feel uncomfortable, although he'd never put his hands on me. But predatory behavior tended to escalate. Was it possible he'd gone after Sarah and she'd defended herself? It wasn't out of the realm of possibility that she had been alone in the gazebo, setting up or practicing her poses.

What if he'd come in and hit on her or tried to make a move? She was stronger than her size suggested. She might not have been mastering the big West Coast waves since she'd moved here with Nate, but she'd maintained the typical surfer bod: a rock-hard physique with six-pack abs, strong shoulders, and a neck to match. Bob was much bigger, but he couldn't compete with her mastered movements.

I abandoned my musings when I noticed Detective Holloway still watching me. If we'd been on a picnic or at a candlelight dinner, I wouldn't have minded the attention. But here and now I got the impression he had more questions, none of them pertaining to wine preference or movie picks. I crossed my arms and glowered at him. Sarah might not be my soul sister, but I still felt protective of her and didn't want to answer anything that might get her into trouble.

I took a few steps away from the shoreline and called Duke back. "Are we done here, Detective?"

He scratched the back of his neck. "Yeah, almost. Any more thoughts on Lars? Your brother doesn't seem too fond of him. Want to tell me why?"

My face flushed. Was that why I was really here, so he could pepper me with questions? "Lars and I broke up years ago. What do you expect me to say?"

"I'm not really sure. Anything that comes to mind, I guess."

"You might not like the sentiment."

The side of his mouth lifted. I flinched. Did he find this cute? Frustration and anger bubbled up in me.

"Why are you asking me about all this again anyway? I've already told you everything I know."

"Lars canceled his show last night, has a banged-up face, and hid a bloody T-shirt in a closet." He paused. "I'm asking you because he's lying to me, and I'm hoping you won't do the same. He trusts you, and I need you to trust me."

I dropped my hands to my sides. "Look, I want the truth as much as you do. A man is dead, and my business is at stake."

"Cooperate, then. Tell me what you know. If Lars is innocent, there's nothing to hide."

He was right. "Lars isn't a bad guy. I'll admit he's a little self-involved, but it doesn't go any deeper than that. There's no darkness lurking beneath the surface."

"Not even in his relationship with Bob?"

I shrugged. "Like I said, we haven't been close in years. I'll admit I was never a fan of Bob's. He was a creep. But he stepped up after Lars's mom died. My guess is Lars felt an obligation to include him in his success."

"But they had issues?"

Did a wiped-out college fund count? Probably, but it was ancient history and not mine to share. "Doesn't every family have issues?"

Detective Holloway left it at that, and we strode over to the gazebo. Duke lingered, taking time to sniff all the scents left behind by the earlier commotion. He surveyed the area where Bob's body had been found.

A ping from my pocket alerted me to a text. I pulled out my phone and saw it was a message from Kat. The security camera footage was cued up from last night. A flutter in my stomach told me to be prepared. What would we see? More importantly, *who* would we see?

I held up my phone. "It's Kat. The video is ready to play."

We picked up our pace. Duke's eager barks told me he thought this was a game. Maybe he was right. But if we were all pawns in this game, who was the gamemaster? Guess it was time to find out.

Chapter Thirteen

When we passed back through the gate by the bar, the low whir of the blender told me margaritas and daiquiris were in demand. The scent of citrus hit my nose. Sarah stood with her back to us, slicing up a big pile of limes with a sharp paring knife. Strong grip. Capable hands.

"Hey," a loud voice called. The greeting pulled me out of my thoughts. Nate popped out from under a nearby umbrella, an empty serving tray in his hand, a big smile on his face. The sight of him made me jump, and his smile faded a little as he glanced from me to Sarah. Could he read my mind?

"'Sup?" I said, forcing a grin. Sarah turned at the sound of my voice and waved at me, still gripping the knife in her hand. *Don't look at it*. A beam of light reflected off the steel blade and hit me in the eye. I flinched. Served me right, suspecting my sister-in-law of murder. Maybe this was fate's way of reminding me to check myself.

Sarah turned back to her task and the large pile of limes she had yet to prepare. Nate approached us, a stern look now settled across his features.

"What's going on?" he asked me, only briefly glancing at the detective by my side.

"Just going over a few things. Hoping to turn up some clues."

"Good," he said. But the shadow that crossed his face told me he didn't really mean it.

I took a step closer and gripped his arm. "Everything okay?"

Nate eyed me briefly. "Yeah." He glanced at his wife. "Better now." What exactly did he mean by that? Were things better now because Sarah had calmed down, or were things better now because Bob Strapp was dead?

A titter of laughter pulled our attention toward the pool. In the shallow end, a small gathering of women had circled around a cute brunette in an aqua bikini. She shushed them before stretching out her arm, phone in hand. "Everyone say, 'Girls' weekend!'" The group did as they were told, speaking in unison, striking various poses as she captured shot after shot.

Nate bent down and gathered a few tumblers placed precariously at the edge of the pool. Good thing we'd decided to invest in premium acrylic barware. Broken glass and pools weren't a good combo. Nate called over to the selfie group, "Don't forget to tag us on social."

The brunette craned her neck to smile at him. "Of course: at *pearlbnb*, hashtag *designinspo*, hashtag *girlsweekend*, hashtag *bestplaceever*."

He held his free hand up. "Excuse me. I'll keep my mouth shut. Clearly, I'm dealing with pros. I might hit you up for a few tips later on."

She giggled. "Happy to oblige, as long as you keep the drinks coming. Hashtag *thiscallsforwine*."

He gave her a thumbs-up and stood up to his full height. When he turned back to us, I saw that his broody look had vanished. Maybe I'd imagined it. "Have I told you how glad I am you agreed to partner with Kat and me?" I said.

He arranged the dozen or so dirty tumblers on his tray, then glanced up at me. "At some point I'm sure I'll miss the city, but running my own bar has always been the end goal. Even if I'm working seven days a week at the beginning. So right back at ya, sis."

Detective Holloway surveyed the scene. "You've done a good job settling things down, Nate."

"That's my job," Nate said. "Once your guys left, it wasn't all that hard. Especially since George Havers offered to play an acoustic set to help out. Between the bar and the music, the good vibes are back."

"You're a lifesaver, bro," I said.

He tipped his head toward me. "I do my best."

My attention shifted in the direction of Lars's room. The shades were drawn. Nate followed my gaze. "I'm no miracle worker. No sign of your boy. Between his stepdad's passing and his rival's superior showing, my guess is it'll stay that way until he slinks back to California."

"Any particular reason you're not a fan?" Detective Holloway said.

Nate tensed and looked from the detective to me. I gave him a warning look. He glanced back at Lars's room before answering. "Let's just say he's always played too fast for me."

Detective Holloway seemed to linger on Nate's words before turning back to me. "Let's get moving. I'm anxious to see what we can learn from that video footage."

I nodded. "Sure."

Nate's grip slipped momentarily, and the tray teetered. Quick reflexes steadied it again, and he glanced up at me. "There's footage?"

I frowned. "Auntie M installed security cameras yesterday. Didn't I tell you?"

"No," he said. "You didn't."

"It'll lower our insurance by twenty-five percent."

Sarah waved Nate over. A couple was at the bar, waiting to be served. Sarah could sling beer, but anything more complicated she left for Nate. He held one finger up. "I gotta move. Duty calls. I guess Marnie's Deadhead days taught her a few things after all. I'll see you later."

The detective turned to me. "Deadhead?"

"My aunt followed the Grateful Dead around for years. When she couldn't afford a ticket, she sometimes charmed a security guard to let her in. Apparently, she picked up a few tips along the way." I shot him an embarrassed smile. "It explains a lot."

"Gotcha," he said.

We watched Nate hustle back to the bar. He leaned in and gave Sarah a quick kiss before grabbing two large bottles of liquor. He twirled them in his hands like a gunslinger in the Old West and pointed them toward the waiting couple. The pair laughed as he leaned in and said something we couldn't hear.

Nate doted on Sarah in a way he never had any of his previous girlfriends. My stomach did a flip. How far would he go to protect his new wife?

Detective Holloway and I turned and made our way back inside to the reception area. Kat stood at the desk, posture rigid and lips pinched, listening to a guest's rant about customer service as Penny cowered behind her. The thirsty blonde hair, short pink dress, and reek of sickeningly sweet perfume told me who the nitpicker was before she even turned around. Had the complaints come from anyone else, I would've been more concerned. But in this case? I couldn't care less.

I held up a finger to Detective Holloway, signaling I needed a second, then cleared my throat loud enough to drown out the speaker and said, "Britt's in a snit. Isn't that what people used to say?"

Kat's mouth dropped open, then curled into a grin. I stood taller and raised my chin. Britt whirled around, her unnaturally full cheeks red hot.

"What did you say?" Her words were raspy and sharp.

I raised my eyebrows in a display of mock innocence. "Isn't this our thing now? Exchanging witty banter using high school nicknames? I'm Jess the Mess; you're Britt the Snit."

Her nostrils flared as the flush from her cheeks deepened. "We don't have a *thing*, Jess. We were never friends."

Duke sauntered in from the pool area and sat at my feet. A low growl told me he wasn't a fan either. I reached down and rubbed one of his ears, then looked back to Britt. "Guess I forgot."

The curl in her upper lip told me I'd succeeded in getting to her. Satisfied, I shifted my focus to Kat. "What's going on?"

Kat scratched her forehead, trying to cover her grin as she focused on the computer screen in front of her. "Britt wants information about another guest. I've explained to her that I can't give out any personal information, but she feels like an exception should be made in her case."

I tut-tutted. "Don't you think it's time to lay off Lars, Britt? It seems he has his hands full right now with more important things than a hometown groupie."

Britt's chin jutted forward as her eyes narrowed into slits. "I'm looking for Paula, not Lars, if you must know. She's not answering my texts or my calls."

I shrugged. "And that matters because?"

"I'm worried, okay?" Britt snapped. "She hasn't been back to Fletcher Lake since her parents' divorce."

Paula's dad had been the owner of the hardware shop in town. It went out of business after he lost a bunch of money. He and Paula's mom broke up, and he took off to California, leaving Paula and her mom to move in with her grandmother in Rochester. I could see how that might make a trip back tough.

If Britt was truly concerned, I'd be touched. But her sour mug wasn't giving me sympathy vibes. Then again, maybe her face had settled into a cemented expression of dissatisfaction. Like laugh lines, only different. A perma-sneer?

"Kat," I said in a softer tone. "Can you call Paula's room, see if she's there?"

Britt huffed. "Don't you think I've already checked? No answer."

"We're not in the business of policing private affairs."

Britt gritted her teeth. "George is a married man."

And there it was. The real reason she was looking for Paula. Paula had abandoned her for someone new. "Britt, stop." The sharp tone in my voice made her flinch, but I continued. "How is this any of your business? Paula is a grown woman. Never mind the fact that I'm not even sure if George is staying here."

"He is," Kat whispered in my ear. "Aunt Marnie told me she checked him in last night under an alias."

Britt glanced from me to Kat and back again. "Find my friend, or I'll call the cops and report her missing."

Detective Holloway stepped forward, hand in the air. "Hold up. Can you make an exception and confirm if he's a guest? We have our hands full, so if we can resolve this quickly, I'd appreciate it."

Britt folded her arms over her chest and gave me a smug look.

"Fine," I said through gritted teeth. "He's here."

"Thanks, Jess," the detective said. "Seeing as I'm at hand, why don't I take a stroll over to George's room and find out if Paula's with him? From what Nate said, George has been entertaining guests, but I'll pop over and check. Good?"

Britt gave him a curt nod. "Thank you. I just hope he's not giving Paula a private performance."

I wrinkled my nose. *Ew.*

Detective Holloway ignored her crude remark. "If Paula's there, I'll make sure she's okay and let her know you're looking for her. Then we can all move on with our day."

"That'll work," Britt said.

I blinked a few times before speaking. "And if there's no answer?"

Britt flung her hand in the air. "Then you'll have to use your pretty pink master key to make sure my friend is all right. I demand it."

Before I could argue, Detective Holloway spoke again. "Let's take this one step at a time." He turned toward Britt. "Wait here."

Britt shot him a nasty look but didn't argue. She marched over to the sofa and slumped back in the seat, turning her attention out the window.

Kat tapped on the computer until she found the room number. "Suite seven."

I nodded and told Duke to go sit behind the desk. Detective Holloway and I headed out in silence.

While I hated to concede a point, I had to admit it did seem strange that Paula would ignore Britt. It would be like Duke deciding one day he'd no longer listen to my commands. Then again, George's star was rising. Hair or no hair, the man was hot. "Thanks for acting as ref back there, Jame—" My face reddened and I cleared my throat, mortified. "Sorry, Detective Holloway."

He looked at me. "James is fine unless I'm conducting an official interview."

I frowned. "I thought you preferred formality."

His eyebrows bunched together as he cocked his head to the side and looked at me quizzically.

I cleared my throat. "You told Lars . . ."

"Ah, that. You're not the only one with an old rivalry here."

I took a closer look at him. His deep-brown eyes and taut jawline reminded me of Australian hottie Jacob Elordi. No way I could forget that mug. "Where do you know Lars from?"

He coughed and rubbed an eyebrow with the back of his hand, shooting me an embarrassed grin. "State championship, senior year."

A jolt went through me. "What did you say?"

He gave me a strange look. "You remember that game?"

Everyone remembered that game. Lars had found out the week before that Bob had lost his college fund in bad investments. He usually played running back on the school team but asked to switch to the defensive line during halftime. With our team down by a huge margin, the coach agreed to give him a chance. Lars channeled his unbottled rage and lingering grief over his mom into pummeling the other team with dirty tricks and vicious tackles. He got thrown out for unnecessary roughness, but by then the game had turned around. Fletcher High won, and by all accounts, Lars was a key factor.

Things had begun to make a lot more sense. Lars had been a brute that day. He'd played with savage aggression. Could this be why James had homed in on him right away?

I began walking again, slowing my pace to give myself a chance to explain. "Lars wasn't himself that day. It was the anniversary of his mom's death, and he'd just found out he wouldn't be going to college."

"Really?" James said. "Wasn't aware of that."

I took a deep breath. "Were you injured during the game?"

I'd known a few of the players from the other team had sustained more than your average football bumps and bruises, although I couldn't remember the details.

"Doesn't matter. He'd had a bad day. I get that." Then he shrugged. "Hard not to wonder if it happened again."

I swallowed. "Right." A sinking feeling in my stomach told me Lars was in bigger trouble than I'd realized.

We continued along the corridor in silence until we reached George's room. When we got there, James pressed his ear against the door. He pulled back and gave me a friendly nod, then knocked three times. There was no answer. He tried again, this time adding, "Police. Open up."

That got the attention of the occupants. There was a loud thump before the shuffling sound of footsteps approaching. The click of the lock sounded, and the door swung open.

George Havers, shirtless and out of breath, stood in front of us, using a towel to shield his lower half. He didn't look pleased to see us. "Yeah? What is it?"

"Detective James Holloway. We spoke earlier today."

"Sure," George said, looking from James to me. "I already gave you my statement. What else do you need?"

"There's some concern about the welfare of another guest of the B and B, and I've been informed she may be here with you."

"Who's asking?" he said gruffly.

I piped up. "It's the guest's cousin."

Before George could respond, another voice spoke up. This one was higher pitched and angry. "Are you kidding me?" George stepped back and allowed a blotchy-faced Paula to yank the door open so hard I cringed in anticipation of it flying off its hinges. Paula's hair was a sea of tangles, the tips of her ears peeking out on either side. Between that and her green eyes and impressive scowl, she was a dead ringer for the angry cat I'd seen repeatedly in recent memes. Interesting. I'd always thought of her as more of a mouse.

"Hi, Paula." I said. "Britt's worried about you."

The scowl deepened as her eyes latched on to mine. "As if! She just doesn't like that I'm ignoring her."

Paula was right. "I'll let her know you're fine."

119

"Do that," she said, ready to slam the door shut.

George grabbed it before she could. "Is that really why you're here? You thought I mighta hurt her?"

"Britt seemed genuinely concerned," James said unapologetically. "It's my responsibility to follow up."

Paula ignored him and glared at me. I cleared my throat. "Britt said you'd been looking forward to the visit. She assumed you'd be out and about a little more."

"Like it was my idea to come here." Her voice oozed resentment. "Who do you think makes the decisions, Jess? Britt's not just my cousin; she's my boss. She has no right to send the cops chasing after me because I took a day off from being her servant. Seriously? I thought you'd see through her concerned-cousin act."

I bit back a retort Paula probably didn't deserve. After all, she was right. "Like I said, we'll pass along the message."

"Thanks," Paula said in a sarcastic tone. "Can you go now?"

James nodded. "I think we're done here."

"Hold up," George said, a sheepish grin creeping onto his face. "Can we borrow your handcuffs?"

James's jaw twitched. "No."

"Then we best be saying goodbye." George snaked his hands around Paula's waist and sidled up close behind her. "We're only here for another day, and we have plans."

"We do?" Paula asked with a husky voice.

"Come back here and see."

Paula turned to face him and slid her hands around his neck.

He swept her up and carried her toward the bed, craning his neck at us as the door began to close. "We good?"

James and I nodded adamantly, letting the door click shut. We stood there for a moment in silence. Had it gotten hot out here? I shifted in my flip-flops, my mouth now too dry to speak.

"Right." James spun on his heel and gave me an official nod. "I guess that takes care of that."

I nodded. "Absolutely. Do you want to go make a video—uh, watch the video, I mean?"

"Yeah, let's do it. The video." His hand ran through his hair as he huffed out a breath. "Watch the security video."

We marched away in silence. If anyone noticed us, they'd likely guess either we'd been scorched by the sun or that we secretly belonged in the tomato family and were in some sort of human disguise.

Chapter Fourteen

As we approached the reception area, James reached past me and held the door open. My nose wrinkled as I breathed in the smell of stale candy floss. *Britt. Rats.* I'd hoped Kat might've chased her away, but instead, my raven-haired partner had disappeared.

A hot-pink sticky note scrawled in messy black ink stuck to the top of the reception desk explained she'd gone to help a guest set up a hammock on their balcony. *Ha, unlikely story.* My bet was she'd picked up the phone and had a one-sided conversation in a desperate ploy to get out of Dodge.

Could I blame her? Not for a second. Self-preservation was a worthy trait in a best friend. Duke was nowhere in sight either. He must have made the wise decision to join Kat in her escape. Only Penny remained in the lobby. She greeted us with a rigid smile as she carried an espresso over to Britt. The queen bee lounged comfortably on the cushy sofa, feet up, snark on.

"Let's hope you've got it right this time, Jenny."

Penny's smile faltered as she set down the drink. "It's Penny. And I sweetened the espresso with maple syrup, since you didn't like the regular sugar, the raw sugar, or the agave syrup."

"I suppose it'll have to do, then." Britt took a sip from the white demitasse cup. She dismissed Penny with a wave of her hand, then peered up at us expectantly. Penny brushed past me, mumbling a plethora of obscenities under her breath, which I pretended not to hear.

Open next to Britt was the travel section of *Hudson Valley Magazine*. Fletcher Lake had been showcased in its summer edition.

"So?" Britt said in place of a greeting. "Did you find my cousin?"

"So," I repeated back in my most conciliatory tone. "Paula is fine. You don't need to worry."

"*Fine?*" she snapped. "Where is she? I wanted you to fetch her, not find her."

James stepped in before I had a chance to bite back. "We let her know you were concerned. She will catch up with you later. Right now, she doesn't want to be disturbed."

Britt let out a royal huff and swung her feet onto the floor. The last dribbles of the espresso splashed out of its cup, soaking into her logoed Coach pumps in epic karmic fashion.

"That thankless tramp! After begging me to bring her to this dive, she bails on me?"

"Paula told us it was you who brought her here," I said, with a game show grin. "For work," I added, using air quotations. "Or was that her trying to cover for a failed mission to finally hook your claws into Lars, after giving it your all in high school?"

Britt locked eyes with me, her fists balling up at her side. For a second, I thought she was going to attack. "Wrong and wrong, Jess the Mess. Like Paula said, my trip here is strictly business. But as always, you have no idea what you're talking about."

James sighed. "Enough." He placed his hands gently on my shoulders, eased me back, then inserted himself squarely between us.

"Britt, I think it would be best for you to cool off somewhere else. Maybe go for a swim or take a walk into town."

I fought the urge to stick my tongue out at my nemesis, settling instead for a Britt-worthy smirk.

Jaw clenched, Britt shifted her focus to him. "I see. She got you too, huh? Just another victim." Her head whipped back toward me, lip curled, teeth bared. "How do you do it, Jess?"

I batted my eyelashes at her. "Do what?"

A low growl arose from her throat. "I think I'm gonna puke."

She gave me one last withering glare, then stalked off without another word. When she was out of earshot, James turned to me. "I'd let Kat be in charge of Ms. Sanders for the rest of her stay."

I stifled a laugh. "No arguments here. Britt brings out the worst in me."

"It seems to go both ways."

Penny approached and picked up the empty espresso cup. "Jess?"

I turned and smiled at her. "What's up, Penny?"

"I forgot to mention your mom asked me to let you know she had to leave but wanted you to call her ASAP."

"Got it," I said. "Thanks for letting me know. I'm going to hole up in my office for the next little while, if you need me."

"K, boss." The receptionist turned to James. "I have a message for you too."

He raised his eyebrows. "Oh?"

She shuffled her feet and cleared her throat. "Lars Armstrong called three times asking if you were around. I guess he doesn't have your number. Anyway, he wants to leave his room. Says if you're not there soon, he's going to sue the police for, like, something? I can't remember the rest of the message. But he's mad."

"Right," James said. "I get the gist. Thanks, Penny."

Looking relieved, she nodded and scooted back behind the safety of the reception desk.

I checked my watch. "If you need to be somewhere, I can wait. I need to call my aunt anyway. I want to let her know what happened before she shows up to work."

"Got the whole family working here, huh?"

I laughed. "My aunt sorta came with the place."

"That's a new one. I've heard of B and Bs inheriting ghosts. Never aunts."

"We may have some of those too." I grinned. "I'm full of surprises."

"Apparently." The corners of his mouth lifted. "I'll put that on the back burner of questions I may need to revisit. In the meantime, I guess I better go talk to our suffering superstar."

"Lars isn't that bad. Underneath the flash, he's a decent guy."

My concern must've shown. "I'll give him a fair shake, okay? That much I can promise you." He tapped the doorframe and gave me a two-finger salute.

When he was gone, a feeling of unease set in. I'd never really stopped to seriously consider the possibility Lars could have killed Bob. Was I wrong to be so certain? My thoughts drifted back to the bloody T-shirt in the closet. Why was Lars trying to hide something if he hadn't done anything wrong? And what about the piece of fabric stuck in the fence?

It wouldn't be long before I'd see the video. There was no point in wasting time contemplating what I didn't know. I marched to my office before any more distractions could get in the way. Butt in chair, phone out. Time to focus on the task at hand. I tried calling my aunt at her home.

The phone rang. I let it go for a dozen or so rings before giving up. Next up: Kat. I pulled my phone out and started typing.

Me: *How do I start the video replay on my laptop?*

Kat: *There's an icon on your desktop. It's all cued up, ready to play. But don't start it yet.*

Me: *Why?*

Kat: *I'm a Murderino. Watch it without me and you're next.*

Me: *Not funny!*

Kat: *Not joking!*

Me: *Hurry up then. James will be here soon and he wants to see it.*

After a brief pause another message popped up.

Kat: *James, huh? You move quick.*

Me: *??*

Kat: *Last time I saw you, it was still Detective Holloway.*

I snickered but didn't reply. Three more dots appeared.

Kat: *Give me 5. I'm helping Nate and Sarah at the bar. Wine is flowing faster than the Hudson.*

Me: *Good to hear.*

I slipped my phone back into my pocket. Someone cleared their throat behind me. I swiveled in my chair, then flinched. A now-familiar face was watching me. Nicky. I straightened up. Was this guy sneaky on purpose? Five bucks said yes. He reminded me of a Roomba, always on the move with the sole intention of collecting dirt. I glared at him. "Don't you ever knock?"

He, in turn, gave me an icy once-over. "I thought you saw me."

I stiffened. Did he mean now or the morning of the murder? This was a game to him. I returned his glacial expression. "What can I do for you?"

Without breaking eye contact, he sidled farther into the room, closing the gap between us. Had the room shrunk? I wasn't used to having people I didn't know or like in my micro-sized office. I scrambled back in my chair, pushing it back until it hit the desk. He leaned in and hovered over me, blocking my view of the door. My heart sped up.

Wait a minute. No way I'll let him intimidate me. I shot up to face him.

He was at least half a foot taller than me. When I'd first seen him, I'd thought he was closer to my height. But I hadn't accounted for the exaggerated slouch, now gone. His looming figure blocked the exit, and I swallowed hard.

Don't let him get to you.

I tilted my head up to meet his gaze, rolling my shoulders back to let him know he didn't scare me. At least not that I was willing to admit. "What do you want, Nicky?"

"A bottle of rosé." He spoke in a whisper, leaning closer to my ear. "For George."

I took a step back, cringing as his hot breath hit my neck. Anger seethed inside me. "Give me some space."

He drew back but kept his eyes on me. "Sure thing, Jessica."

"Thank you." I crossed my arms. "Now let me get this straight. You want a bottle of rosé for George?"

"Yes, ma'am."

"But you work for Lars."

"Not anymore. We parted ways."

I frowned. "Since when?"

His mouth slid into a smirk. "Curious girl, aren't you?"

"Nope. I'm a grown woman, Nicky. But the timing of your career change strikes me as odd."

"I know a sinking ship when I see one. Best to get off before it pulls me under."

I narrowed my eyes. "Are you talking about Lars?"

He shook his head. "No, I'm talking about wine. I'm just here asking for rosé, remember?"

I pushed past him and stormed down the hallway into the lobby. I didn't need to look behind me to know he was on my tail. "Sit down." I pointed at the lobby sofa.

Penny was standing at the reception desk, advising a honeymooning couple about activities in the area. I squeezed by as she spoke. "There are bike rentals at the café down the street. You could power up with a cup of java, then head out. Trails are all over the place. I could highlight some of my favorites, if you like. Or you could window shop. It's only a ten-minute walk into town. We've got a cheese shop, a candy shop, a brew pub with a patio—"

"That's the one," the man said. "Hon?" The woman nodded. Penny pulled out a map and a highlighter from under the counter.

Sitting nearby, Nicky waited, his eyes fixed on me. The hair on the back of my neck stood up as I bent down and grabbed out a bottle of wine from the mini-fridge we kept behind the desk.

Bottle in hand, I approached Nicky and handed him the wine. Kat walked into the lobby with Duke trailing behind. Tail wagging, my perfect pooch rushed to my side. I bent down and gave him a pat, his pretty eyes calming my nerves. Kat gave Nicky a scathing look. "Thirsty?"

"Depends what's on the menu," he said, licking his lips.

Kat's eyes widened, and she looked at me. "What did this kid just say to me?"

I pointed at him. "Not a kid."

"Good. I don't like to punch children." She turned to Nicky. "Speak to me like that again and I'll smack you."

He grinned at her. "I knew you were an untamed mare. Come find me anytime."

She pointed to the door. "Get out!"

"Yes, wild filly." He took the wine and shuffled out the door, leaving us gaping openmouthed after him.

Kat tilted her head. "I'm at a loss for words."

"You could start with *ew*."

"That'll work," she said. "Ewwww. Now, can we get back to the amateur detective bits so I can block that image out of my mind?"

"Yes, please," I said, nodding adamantly. "The man-child seems to get off being weird. Time to move on."

I pulled out a treat from my pocket and gave it to Duke. He swallowed it whole, then returned to his bed next to the reception desk, where he plunked down and closed his eyes.

Kat and I went back to the office. The small room looked inviting and cozy again, now that Nicky wasn't in it. The artificial palm tree in the corner and the old wood desk provided just enough room for two.

Kat gestured around. "How are we going to fit a third person in here?"

"Good question." The room had been designed with only Kat and me in mind: a place to discuss brand strategy, number crunch, and do some online marketing, not to do a group analysis of our video feeds or talk suspects, especially with the police.

"You two can sit down," I said. "I'll squeeze in behind."

"Is this a ploy to get cushy with Detective Dish?"

"That's *so* not funny."

"Would you prefer Detective Dreamboat? Captain Hotstuff? Constable Nice A—"

I held my hand up. "Stop it, you fiend. I'm trying to sort out a murder here. Mind out of the gutter."

She pouted. "You're no fun when you're playing the earnest meddler."

I shifted my attention to the computer. "I'm trying to make sure we still have a business to meddle with. Can you focus, please?"

She harrumphed. "Fine. Cue it up then, partner."

"Thank you." I said, opening the laptop. My breath caught as the screen lit up and a series of photos of Bob Strapp filled the screen. I frowned. Someone had searched Google images for him. But who?

"What is it?" Kat asked, craning her neck to see.

I opened the laptop wider so she could get a better look. She leaned in and squinted. "Why are you looking up Bob Strapp?"

"Not me."

"Then who?" she asked.

"Curious guest?"

We offered use of the office to our guests as a perk, so we left the door unlocked. If I'd been staying somewhere and someone had been murdered, I could see myself looking the victim up too. There were several other windows still open: the bakery's hours, an old photo of Main Street, the official *Sing This!* website, and local breweries in the area.

"Guess I better make sure we have a strong password set up for our stuff," I said. "I'm wondering if offering this service was a mistake."

"Maybe." Kat reached forward and double-clicked an icon on the desktop. Her fingers got to work, and a minute later, a grainy video feed filled the screen.

There were four separate videos, each taking up a quarter of the display: reception and the lobby, the pool/bar area, the upper hallway, and the back of the house. The last one had its camera pointing toward the gazebo and the pond where Bob's body had been found.

I glanced back at her. "Can you bring up last night's feed?"

She nodded. "Now, or should I wait for James?"

I shrugged. "We could watch a preview."

Kat didn't respond, instead setting the parameters for the time in question: the point in the night when George had gotten up onstage. I stretched backward and pushed the door of the office closed. Our heads huddled together, Kat and I each stole a glance over our shoulders to make sure the door had latched. She reached forward and pressed enter on the laptop.

Chapter Fifteen

The time stamp in the bottom corner of the screen read *20:10*, just after eight PM. There were two cameras, so the screen was split into halves. One shot overlooked the bar and pool area where I'd been in the process of announcing to the crowd that Lars wouldn't be playing.

"Yikes, look at those frowns. Good thing George Havers showed up last night." Kat paused the video and pointed to the unhappy faces caught on camera.

I shivered. "You won't hear an argument from me."

"If George hadn't saved the day, I would've sought Lars out and killed him for letting you down."

I cringed at her lack of tact. "You mean us. He let *us* down."

She shook her head. "Nope. I only agreed to his show in the first place because you wanted to do it. It takes a lot to lose my approval. He did that on prom night, and I never trusted him again. So his flaking out a second time on another big night didn't faze me."

Heavy promos featuring Lars had been circulated on our social media for over a month. His upcoming appearance had snagged mentions on several gossip feeds and national entertainment sites, never mind that it had been the talk of Fletcher Lake. I'd been so proud.

Now the burn of humiliation roared inside me. "Am I that much of an idiot?" I reached forward and was about to press enter again when Kat grabbed my hand.

"No." She shook her head. "I'm sorry; I'm being a jerk. Maybe I'm a little bitter after all."

"Good. I don't want to be the only one."

She sighed. "When Lars reached out to you, offering to come and play, I was wary. But when he didn't cancel and showed up yesterday with his big smile and bigger talk, I came around. I'm mad at myself for letting him weasel his way back into your life. No, *our* lives."

I picked at my fingernails. "Yeah, me too. But I'm not into him anymore. You and Nate seem to think I've got feelings for him still. Honestly, I don't."

"Then why do you keep defending him? Think about it. He was hiding a bloody T-shirt in the closet. And Bob was not a good guy. After the crap he pulled with Lars's college fund, it was clear the man had no boundaries. We both know that most murders are personal. Lars is the most likely candidate."

"I'll admit he makes bad choices, and he's selfish, even self-absorbed. But deep down, he's a decent person." My voice rose along with my temper. "I wish you'd stop trying to convince me otherwise. I don't want to date him again, okay? Can't you believe me and leave it there?"

"Fine."

The room was quiet for a minute. It wasn't like Kat and me to be at odds like this.

I rubbed my temples. "Look, I'm sorry."

She sighed. "Me too."

"Can I start the video now?"

"Go for it."

I pressed play and braced myself for what was ahead.

The screen showing the backs of the rooms, the parking lot, and the gazebo was quiet, which made sense, since everyone had been watching the show. The other screen showed me informing the crowd of the complimentary drink hour. It wasn't the hit I'd hoped. I turned to Kat. "You're right about George. We were so lucky he showed up."

"Lucky doesn't even begin to describe it."

Her words lingered in my mind. "Then how about weird?"

Kat paused the video again and looked at me. "I was joking."

"I wasn't. Think about it. Lars has done some less-than-stand-up moves, but it's not like him to cancel a gig. If you'd seen him yesterday, you would've agreed he was psyched about the show."

Kat's hand hovered above the play button, but she turned her gaze on me. "Have you asked him why he crapped out on us?"

"I haven't had the chance," I said. "But obviously, something went down."

"I totally understand where you're coming from, Jess. But look at the facts. A black eye and a dead guy are two strikes against him. Let's hope, for his sake, he wasn't alone at the time of Bob's death."

She shifted her attention back to the computer and pressed enter. The video continued. George Havers, my knight in shining leather, appeared in front of the stage.

"Is it me, or did George come out of nowhere?" Kat asked.

"Like a real-life superhero," I said.

"Lucky for us, George is as popular as Lars, if not more."

George's career was on fire. Plus anyone who watched *Sing This!* would know both men well. They had been the final two, and it had been a tight race for the win.

Even without sound, the reaction to George's appearance was clear: wide eyes and open mouths followed by big cheers and applause. Lars was popular, but if the crowd last night was any indicator, George Havers was proving himself to be the next big thing. Lars had nothing on him.

Kat's eyes were fixed on the screen. "Rumor has it there was no love lost between George and Lars. I don't know if that was a story created to pique interest in the show or if it was legit."

I leaned back. "If they weren't friends, why would George come here to watch Lars play?" I'd listened to enough true crime podcasts to know that a coincidence could mean murder. "And why would he come to his rescue when Lars was—"

"Cracking under pressure? Falling apart?"

I shot her a dirty look. "I was going to say having a bad night. There's enough real-life tragedy. Let's not add melodrama to the mix."

"Fair enough," she agreed. "Now shush. Let's get back to the tape and watch what happens."

The crowd began to bounce and move, their arms raised and their hands clapping as George grabbed his guitar from next to the stage and began to play.

Why did he have his guitar there? Had he planned to cut in on Lars's set?

I couldn't answer the questions that suddenly cropped up, so for now, I packed them up and tucked them away. The visibly excited crowd hooted and hollered even before the music began.

At the end of George's first song, he took notice of Paula. Kat rubbed her palms together as she watched the playback. "This is the part I was waiting for. The whole thing reminded me of that old Bruce Springsteen video with Courteney Cox, where he picks her out of the crowd." She broke off with an excited "And I'm here for it."

There was no doubt George had noticed Paula right off the bat. *Lucky girl.* What caught my attention, though, was the one left behind—namely, Britt the Snit, who was clearly unimpressed, given the scowl on her face. Had there ever been a time a guy had chosen Paula over her? A whoosh of petty glee coursed through me, and I cupped a hand over my mouth to stop a giggle.

"What's so funny?" Kat asked.

"The expression on Britt's face. It's priceless."

Kat scoffed. "Guess she wasn't in on it."

"In on what?" I asked.

"Choosing a woman from the audience to single out. I read somewhere he does it at every show. A little cliché if you ask me, but I guess it works to get the crowd going."

"And it's fun to watch," I said, trying to hide my disappointment that the initial meet-cute between him and Paula had been staged.

As if sensing my dismay, she added, "It's not a complete sham. According to the article I read, he likes to make that connection organically. Chances are the spark between him and Paula is genuine."

"It would be hard to fake that intensity," I said rallying my romantic spirit. "Besides, Paula doesn't even breathe without concrete permission from Britt. And Britt's expression in the video tells me she didn't know George was going to pick Paula. Besides, Paula and George are still going strong. No way that sort of bond could be manufactured on a regular basis. They're electric."

"Good point." Kat grinned. "Oh, look. Britt's storming off after Paula leaves her in the dust. What a baby."

"Wait a sec," I said, sitting up straighter.

"What?" Kat said.

"Here, look." I tapped the screen with my nail. "Britt storms off, but not in the direction of their room. She walks past the bar and heads out the back exit."

Kat bolted upright. "Not far from where Bob was killed."

In a panic, I closed the laptop. "What does this mean?"

She studied my face. "The Queen of Mean may have upped her game. Crap. What should we do?"

Before I could answer, there was a knock on the door.

Kat gripped my arm. "It's her! She's come to get us."

"Stop it." I swatted her away and swung my arm out to open the door. Standing there was James with a questioning look on his face.

"Hi." He craned his neck to look past me. "Decided to have a viewing party without me?"

My cheeks flushed. "We wanted to cue it up so it was all ready to go."

"Sure," he said. "May I?"

"C'mon in."

He shuffled inside. I leaned behind him to shut the door and couldn't help but smile as I saw the small emblem on his pants: Lululemon. *Huh.* No crumpled old suits or stinky cigars for this modern-day Columbo.

James and Kat exchanged greetings, and I offered him my seat.

He shook his head. "I prefer to stand, thanks." I sat back down and opened the laptop. Kat took control, setting the time stamp to restart at the beginning. Without another word, she pressed enter.

James hunched down and watched the scene unfold between George, Paula, and Britt. He leaned in as Britt exited. "Stop," he instructed. "Can you remind me what's back there other than the gazebo and the pond?"

"It's the public entrance for the bar, so it leads to the sidewalk. But if you head in the other direction, toward the back, we have a small firepit set up with chairs surrounding it," Kat said. "We had a few guests who weren't interested in the show that used it last night. Twin sisters. You'll see them moving in and out of the frame as they come in to refill their drinks."

James rubbed his jawline and gave an almost imperceptible nod.

"Considering how crammed it was near the stage, Britt may have decided to exit that way to avoid all the people," said Kat.

James accepted the explanation, keeping his eyes on the screen. Kat continued the video. James pulled out a small notebook from his shirt pocket and began asking us to identify people in the crowd. There weren't too many he didn't know, since he'd already become familiar with the guests and some of the staff of the B and B and the bar, to say nothing of my entire family.

A few of the local shop owners from Main Street were there, as well as the old music teacher from Fletcher High. James took down names and occupations, asking if there were any people who had a particular connection with Lars.

Nicky made a brief appearance on camera, bringing a drink to the stage and taping a piece of paper to the stage in front of the microphone. I'd seen that done before at small shows. It was a set list of songs to be played.

"Why do the weird ones always like me?" Kat complained.

"What's weird," I said, "is that Nicky started the day with Lars and ended up with George."

James quirked an eyebrow. "Did he tell you why he made the switch?"

I shook my head as he made a note in his book. Then he said, "I think we've identified everyone, so if you don't mind, I'll take the computer with me to review the rest on my own."

Kat and I both groaned.

"Sorry." James gave us each a sheepish grin.

Drat. We should've kept our chat shorter if we wanted to snoop. Kat put her hand on top of the laptop and was about to close it when a face peered out from a shadow on the screen.

My hand shot out to stop her. "Wait!" I paused the video, then leaned in and squinted at the screen. "Is that Travis Sanders?"

Kat mimicked my movements. "Where?"

I pointed to a corner of the frozen shot. "Oh yeah, that's him. No mistaking the hair on that chinny chin chin."

The guitarist's shiny dark mop had receded but remained as long and unkempt as it had been in high school. His signature black goatee, which had always reminded me of a burnt marshmallow, still clung to his chin.

James rubbed his jaw, as if made uncomfortable by the sight of the unruly facial hair. "Who's Travis?"

"He's Britt's brother and Lars's old bandmate. Rumor has it that he and Lars didn't part on the best of terms."

James wrote something down. "Interesting."

"Lars wanted to be a star," I said. "Travis wanted to make good music. In the end, their vision didn't match, and Lars moved on."

Kat pointed to the floor. "Leaving Travis in the proverbial dust."

James continued to write. "Was Bob Strapp involved with Lars's career at that point?"

I shook my head. "Not officially, I don't think."

"But . . ." Kat let the word linger before she continued. "Bob was always about the bottom line. He used to do investment banking before switching lanes and becoming Lars's manager."

"Can you show me how to zoom in?" James asked Kat. "And maybe slow down the playback?"

"Sure." Kat pushed a few keys and got the effect he requested. "That good?" Travis's face got bigger on the screen. She typed a few more keystrokes, and the zoomed-in video played at half speed.

Travis was standing near the back of the crowd, away from the lights and action. He disappeared from view after George's second song.

"Where did he go?" James asked.

Travis popped up again in the video from the other camera, just after nine o'clock. Shown only from the back, he was still recognizable by his unruly hair. He hugged the wall and disappeared again as he moved along the back of the B and B. The time stamp said *21:10*.

"What's he up to?" I said, as much to myself as the other two.

"Okay," James said. "I think I can take it from here."

Irritation flooded through me. I turned to look at Kat, who was giving James the stink eye. I did the same.

Throwing his hands up, he cleared his throat. "Sorry, you two. This is a police investigation. I only asked for your help since you both seem to know everyone around here and can show me how to use the playback on your computer. But we're done here. I need to take the laptop with me and view the video at the station."

I tsked. "But it was just getting good."

"Look!" Kat said, pointing to the screen.

She hadn't yet paused the video. In the corner of the screen, from the lobby camera view, we saw Lars stumble out of his suite backward as two hands shoved him out from inside.

My breath caught. "Uh-oh."

James leaned forward. "How do I stop this?"

Neither Kat nor I offered tech support. James began to press buttons at random on the keyboard as the camera continued to play. Bob stormed out of the room after Lars. His face was twisted with rage, and he appeared to be yelling. Lars raised his hands in front of his face in a defensive position, but the pair were far enough apart for us to read Bob's lips. They formed two words, over and over: "Get out."

James threw his hands up and abandoned the keyboard to focus back on the feed. The three of us watched in silence as Bob smacked Lars across the face with an open palm. Lars recoiled from the blow, one hand up to soothe the sting. Bob followed the smack with a finger in Lars's face, scolding him like a child. Lars lashed out with his free arm, creating enough space to stand up to his full height. His chest heaving with emotion, he towered over Bob. His fist flew up, making contact with Bob's jaw. The older man stumbled backward before returning to the offensive, taking aim at Lars with everything he had. One swift blow to the head caused Lars to wince with pain. Lars returned the hit with a powerful shove, knocking Bob off his feet. Bob scrambled up, keeping his distance this time. He spewed out a bunch of words before spinning on his heel and exiting out the front. Lars was left standing alone. Blood dripped down his face and onto his T-shirt before he wiped his brow with a shaky hand.

For a minute, I thought that was it. A slow breath eased out of me. This tape could prove Lars's innocence. The bloody shirt, the gash on his brow. It made sense now.

Lars turned toward the room door.

That's it. Go inside, Lars.

But at the last minute, he appeared to change his mind. Looking around as if to make sure he hadn't been seen, Lars trudged off after Bob. A minute later, both men appeared in the exterior camera. Bob was ahead, Lars a few minutes behind. I closed my eyes and sank back in my chair.

"Kat, shut this down," James said in a quiet voice.

"I'll try."

"Make it stop," he said more urgently.

"Aye, aye, Cap'n," she said. "You know we can watch this later, though, right?"

"I'm going to pretend I didn't hear that."

"Right." The video played on until the two men walked out of view. A moment later, two more figures could be seen in the upstairs camera: George Havers and Paula Davis. His arm was draped around her, and they were both smiling broadly. Paula paused at one door, likely asking George if it was his room. George shook his head, pointing down the corridor. Paula, as if sensing someone watching, looked up and gave a start as she took in the security camera watching their every move. She frowned and whispered to George before giving a smile and a wave to the camera. George pushed her hand down, and she leaned into him and kissed him hard on the lips. They drifted down the hallway to his room two doors down, where he reached into his pocket and pulled out his key card. They practically fell into the room together as the door shut behind them.

Kat and I both jumped at a sudden movement near the book nook, and Nicky came into view, hovering between two shelves, watching the couple as they disappeared into their room. He looked around before going gliding across the hallway and entering his room.

Then out of nowhere, Aunt Marnie showed up on the screen.

I sat up straighter. "What's Auntie M doing there?" A bad feeling told me I didn't really want to know.

I felt James's eyes on me. I turned to look at him. There was an almost playful lift to the corner of his mouth. "Doesn't she work at the B and B?"

"Of course. What am I thinking?" *That there is no reason for her to be up there? That I can tell by her ducked head and stiff movements that something is off?*

Aunt Marnie walked toward the camera and looked right into it, as if catching us looking at her. I turtled back. James leaned in closer to the computer, his smile now gone. Aunt Marnie's arm stretched forward until it looked like it was going to reach through the camera and grab us. My heart started pounding. *What's she doing?* Before I had a chance to figure it out, all the screens filled with static.

Kat closed the laptop noiselessly as silence filled the room.

Chapter Sixteen

I cleared my throat. "Didn't see that coming." My attempt at a casual tone failed, and my voice was tight and strained. Why had Auntie M felt the need to shut off the cameras just before the murder?

There had to be a reasonable explanation. Several possibilities existed. Had she recently read *1984* by George Orwell? Was she concerned about saving energy? Did she want to practice her signature moonwalk in secret for the upcoming Fletcher Lake talent show? All of the above were plausible. Then again, if it had been a philosophical objection, she wouldn't have installed the cameras in the first place. And I'd seen her do the moonwalk. She had perfect form and never turned down the chance to perform it for anyone willing to watch. Like ever.

Kat gave a slow shrug. "We could watch it again?" She turned to me, eyes wide. "Any idea what she was up to?"

My shoulders stiffened. "Auntie M is always doing odd things that most of us don't understand."

Kat's eyes flicked from me to James. "True. She's a wackadoodle."

James's face was unreadable. "Jess, did your aunt know Bob Strapp?"

A brilliant question, and with it, the tension began to ease from my shoulders. "No way! They were around the same age but worlds apart. My aunt spent her youth following the Grateful Dead on tour."

"She made corduroy purses and drove around in VW vans," Kat added. "Bob gave me more narc vibes than Deadhead—no offense."

Relief swept through me. Kat was right. "To this day, she keeps a homemade hippie pouch with a bouquet of basics just in case a van of like-minded hippies show up out of the blue and want to go on a road trip."

James cocked his head to the side. "Auntie M has a getaway bag?"

I felt my eyes bug out. "What? No!"

Kat rescued me. "Just a few toiletries."

I held my finger up. "But no soap."

"Should I ask why?" James said.

Kat shook her head. "I wouldn't."

It was too late. Anxiety had always made me ramble, and now I was on a tear. "You haven't heard that joke?"

James rubbed his jawline. "No. Do tell."

"How do you hide money from a hippie?" I didn't wait for him to respond. "Put it under the soap."

He frowned. "Your aunt doesn't bathe?"

Kat gave me a *cut it out* gesture with a flick of her thumb across her neck.

I could feel beads of sweat gather at my hairline. "Hard to say. Mostly she smells like incense."

"Right." James glanced from Kat to me with a look that said *don't quit your day job*, then added, "Do you think I can have the room now? I'd like to rewatch the footage on my own."

"Absolutely," I said, but my tone, even to me, sounded almost aggressive, like a football coach at halftime.

"We'll leave you to it." Kat grabbed my elbow with a pinch and pulled me up. "C'mon."

"One more thing," James said. "I might stick around. Is it okay if I help myself to another coffee?"

"Of course," Kat said. "We'll try and keep out of your way."

She shoved me out the door and shut it behind her. We walked in silence until we reached the reception area. She pointed to the sofa. "Sit down."

I did as I was told, flopping onto the comfy seat. "Ugh" was all I got out. Duke hopped out of his bed and ambled over. He sat on my feet and rested his head on my leg. No matter what, *he* still loved me.

Kat dropped down next to me and let her head fall back against the cushion. She patted my leg. "Don't worry. There's so many other things to be freaking out about; let that one go."

I had no words. She was right.

We watched a young couple at the reception desk. The man had a baby strapped to his front, and the woman was wearing a backpack with a small rubber giraffe on one side and a water bottle on the other.

They were examining a brochure with Penny. She glanced up, then flipped the pamphlet over and tapped it with a pen. "Here's a map of the area," she explained to the couple. "All our favorite spots to visit are highlighted."

"We're hoping to find an easy hike within walking distance," said the woman. "Any suggestions?"

"You betcha." Penny said. "There's an easy loop here." She circled a spot on the map with her pen. "You can access it on the path across the road. Take your first left to access the walking trail; otherwise, you'll get to a dead end, a small clearing by the water. It only takes about forty-five minutes to do the whole loop." She paused for a moment, then added, "Fair warning, though; the nearby alcove may contain a couple enjoying a romantic hideaway."

"Sounds like us a year ago," the woman said, smiling at her husband.

"Yeah, and look what happened," he said, planting a kiss on the top of the baby's head, which was barely visible in its snug cocoon. He gave his wife a wink. "We'll stick to the path, thanks."

Penny went into more detailed directions as my mind began to drift back to Aunt Marnie. Was there any way she could've known her actions might protect a killer? And what was James thinking? Did he place her in the suspect pool? The thought terrified me.

I gave my head a shake. Enough moping. Time to figure this out before things got out of hand. "So what did we learn from the security footage?"

Kat focused on the ceiling. "Lars got in a fight with Bob before he was killed."

"Which we already knew." I pulled my hair back into a ponytail, securing it with an elastic band I kept on my wrist. "But we picked up a few nuggets we didn't know before."

"True." Kat sat up straighter and looked at me. "Like why was Travis there?"

"Exactly. Didn't you say his and Lars's relationship ended on bad terms?"

She held up her hands. "That's what I heard, but don't quote me."

I thought back to the footage. "I could see Travis showing up if he'd known George would be playing, but there was no way he could've known Lars was going to cancel. Or could he?"

"Good question. And why did Travis head out back?"

"Right." I stood up and started pacing. "Where was he going?"

"If your aunt hadn't turned off the cameras, we might've been able to answer that question."

I couldn't argue that. "Guess I should start by questioning her, then."

Kat scoured the hallway to make sure no one was around to overhear us. Penny was still chatting with the young family at reception, and the exits were all clear. "James will be asking too. Better warn her the fuzz will be coming around."

My aunt's time on the road with the Grateful Dead had made her wary of the police. There'd been a rivalry between the Deadheads and the police that usually resulted in at least a few arrests. While my aunt swore she'd never partaken in any illegal substances, she blamed an undercover cop for snagging her favorite Frisbee and had held it against the whole force ever since.

Up until now, it had been a joke. This time it wasn't so funny. I stopped pacing and dropped back onto the sofa. "She's scheduled to work later, but I better go warn her, just in case."

Kat stood up. "I'd come, but I've got that appointment at the bank to go over our terms."

We'd recently applied for a secure line of credit, since we'd pooled our money to renovate and had little left over for day-to-day operations. Mom had seen the paperwork in my room and called her friend, Judy Sheehan, the VP of Fletcher Bank, asking if she'd be able to lower the interest rate. Judy had agreed to take a look at our file in spite of the fact that we'd been told the rate was finite and nonnegotiable.

I stopped pacing and tapped my watch. "Never make the Mom-fia wait."

"Right," Kat said. "I'll have my phone off for a bit. You all right?"

"Fine. I'm going to head over to see my aunt right after I sit down and write a list of my to-dos."

"Meditation with a ballpoint pen."

"You said it, sister."

Kat agreed to call me right after the meeting to let me know how it went. I needed to talk to Aunt Marnie and Lars. And my mom, who'd been suspiciously unintrusive. Radio silence with her was not a good sign.

I approached the reception desk, where Penny was straightening up the front display of wineglasses and coffee mugs adorned with our logo.

"How's everything going, Penny?"

"It's been busy," she said. "Guests are making requests, and the phone has been ringing off the hook."

"Is the reservation page down on our website?" I asked.

"It's not people looking to book rooms. It's reporters asking questions. Your mom told me to take messages for now and say 'No comment' to anyone who pushed for details about what happened."

"Right," I said. "Before my mom left, did she give you an update on the scene outside?"

Penny shrugged. "Only that she'd taken care of it."

"What does that mean?" I asked, more to myself than to Penny.

"It might have to do with Lars," Penny said. "She had me deliver a note to him. It was folded up, so I couldn't read it."

"You saw Lars?"

"Briefly. I brought him the note. He wanted to know where you were. I told him I didn't know."

With a double tap on the desk, I smiled at her. "Thanks, Penny."

I grabbed a paper and pen from the counter. The *Cool Vibes Only* logo scrolled across the top of the page taunted me. I scribbled over the words and wrote *Anxiety Rules!* above it, then headed for the bar.

Chapter Seventeen

It was time to write a list to prioritize my jumbled thoughts. Could I squeeze in a visit with Lars before calling my mom and going to my aunt's? And what about work? That had to remain a priority, yet it was piling up too. Social media engagement was the key to our success, and I had promised myself to stay on top of it. I couldn't fall behind on only the second day of operations.

Yet as I began to rank tasks in my head, nothing topped finding Bob's killer. A man had lost his life. Whether I liked him or not, that still came before anything else. And when people I cared about were emerging as suspects, all those important business things felt much less urgent. Realizing this made it crystal clear what I needed to do.

Nate looked up from behind the bar as I approached. Sarah was in the middle of leading a yoga session by the pool, giving me the chance to speak to him without her there.

Nate had the chalkboard down and was in the process of updating the bar specials. "Hey, you, what's up?"

"We need to talk."

He put down the chalk and wiped his hands on the bar towel draped over his shoulder. "Should I be worried?"

"Why were you being weird when you found out cameras were installed?"

His face flushed. "Why are you asking?"

"So I can sleep tonight without having nightmares about seeing your wife's face behind bars."

He eyes went wide. "Did you inhale too much of Auntie M's incense again?" He put air quotation marks around the word *incense*.

My expression flattened. "Just answer me. Apparently, Sarah was seen having some kind of argument with Bob."

He blew out a loud breath. "Because the guy was checking out her butt and she told him off. What's your problem?"

No surprise there. "And the cameras? Why did you wig out about them?"

"Not for the outrageous reason you're thinking. Sarah is a lover, not a killer." He looked at me with a *Know what I mean?* look. But I didn't get it. He dropped his head back. "I was a little tense last night, okay? So, on break, we snuck into the woods and . . ." He rolled his hand in a gesture suggesting I finish the thought myself.

"Oh! Oh . . . yup, okay. I get you." I wrinkled my nose.

"We good now?"

"What time did you . . . take a stroll?"

"Nine thirty or so."

A server dropped a tray nearby. Nate grabbed an order chit from the machine behind the bar and poured two glasses of wine. He put them on the tray, and the server left.

I waited until she was out of earshot before asking my next question. "Did you see anyone near the gazebo or the pond?"

Nate smiled sheepishly. "No, but we only had eyes for each other. If you need to know the exact time, check the video feed."

I huffed out a breath of frustration. "Not possible, thanks to Auntie M."

He frowned. "What do you mean?"

"She shut the cameras off."

"Why?"

"Good question. I need to find her and ask."

He lifted an eyebrow. "Does that mean Sarah and I are off the hook? Or would you like a sample of our DNA too?"

"I'm just trying to sort this mess out, okay? If it makes you feel better, Auntie M will be facing much tougher questions. Did you happen to see her after the show last night?"

He leaned in close. "Have you lost your mind?"

"Indulge me."

"Fine. Let me think . . . Last call ended with the show. George hooked up with someone and disappeared, but most people lingered until about eleven. We shut things down, and the crowd slowly made their way out. By then the office was closed, but I don't remember seeing Marnie milling about with everyone else. I think loud music gives her headaches these days. Why does it matter?"

"Shutting off the cameras dashed any chance of capturing what happened to Bob on video."

"That's odd. Then again, that's Marnie." He clapped my back.

I blew out a long low sigh and felt my shoulders slump.

Nate stood up taller. "Jess, our aunt is about universal love and understanding. Surely you can't be worried she got mixed up in Bob's death. No matter how much she hated him." He reached under the bar and brought up a box of chalk. Under today's specials, he wrote *Strawberry Gin and Tonic*.

It took me a minute to process the implication of what he'd said. "Marnie knew Bob?"

He glanced up, then did a double take. No doubt he recognized my pallor as panic. He held his hands up, palms forward. "Settle. They went to school together. It can't be a surprise that the guy was a jerk back then too. Guys like that don't just up and become weasels overnight."

"Okay, but how do you know she didn't like him?"

"I saw them arguing earlier in the parking lot."

My heart began to beat hard. Auntie M, unlike my mom, wasn't the confrontational sort. "Her too? When?"

His head bobbed from side to side as he thought about it. "Sometime during the show. I'd run out of tiny drink umbrellas and went to the supply cupboard to find the spare box. The reception desk was unstaffed, which I found odd until I heard raised voices and looked outside. Bob and Marnie were at each other's throats. I approached them to see if she was okay, and she shoved a brown paper bag at me. She asked me to throw it out, explaining she'd lost her appetite, then stormed off. Bob made an excuse and skedaddled, leaving me standing there with a bag of carrot sticks and a cucumber sandwich. Come to think of it, I haven't seen her since." He scratched his head. "With everything going on, I'd forgotten about that."

This didn't make sense. What would Marnie and Bob be arguing about? I pulled out my mobile, then put it away. The questions I needed to ask her weren't the kind to be asked over the phone. "I need to go find her."

Nate put both hands on my shoulders. "Jess, relax. Bob Strapp was a very unlikable character. He had no friends in town and was a bad dude. Lars's mom got suckered in by his cheap charm, and Lars followed suit. If I had to put money down, my guess is that he pissed off the wrong person and got knocked out too close to the water. Drowning probably was a by-product of a bad night. This may sound harsh, but karma has a way of catching up with people."

Could Nate be right? Before I had a chance to mull it over, I heard someone call my name. The voice behind me was familiar and the musky scent that went with it unmistakable.

I turned to see Lars watching me. "Hey."

He lifted a hand. "Hey yourself."

Nate gave him a salute. "Y'all right, man?"

Lars shrugged. "I don't know anymore. I'm supposed to be waiting in my room for James to come back, but I can't sit still. Thought maybe a whiskey could help me chill out."

Nate put the chalk away and brushed his hands off on the bar towel on his shoulder. "Sure thing."

Lars made his way to the bar and hopped onto a stool. "Thanks, man."

Nate surveyed the pool area. "Would it be better if it were brought to you in your room? Not sure how well it would go over if the police found you drinking here."

"Good point. Jess, would you mind making the delivery? It would be just my luck to have Detective Holloway show up and me not be there."

I nodded. "Yeah, no problem. I'll bring it right over."

Lars stood up and drew closer to me. "Thanks, babe." I took a step back and patted his arm before he turned on his heel and slunk away.

Nate made up the drink in about three seconds flat, then set it down on the bar, eyeing me. "Jess, it'll be okay. The cops will figure this out, and we can get back on track. I feel bad about what happened; no one deserves that fate."

My brother was starting to sound like Sarah. But I didn't disagree.

A couple approached the bar, and Nate breezed over to take their order. I picked up the drink and set off in the direction of Lars's room.

When I got there, Lars opened the door before I even knocked. He grabbed the drink and shot it back.

I glanced around before entering. "Are you okay?" It was a silly question, but I had to start somewhere.

He wiped the back of his hand across his mouth and set the empty glass down on top of the mini-fridge nearby. "I'm in trouble, babe."

"You said that before." I squeezed past him and sat down on the edge of the woven rattan lounge chair next to the bed. "Tell me what's going on."

He looked up at the ceiling. "I screwed up."

My hands gripped the edge of the chair. "I'm listening."

He rubbed the back of his neck and looked at me. "Bob came by my room last night, and we got into an argument. Now he's dead. I think Holloway's going to try to pin his murder on me."

I swallowed. "Why do you say that?"

Lars's jaw tightened. "That's what happens, babe. These cops get an idea in their head and run with it, no matter what."

"Tunnel vision."

He frowned. "Say what?"

"Tunnel vision. That's what you're describing." I'd heard the term used on *My Favorite Murder*. Investigators targeted one individual, filtering evidence to accord with their singular belief, regardless of all the facts. It was a phenomenon that had led to several wrongful convictions. I wasn't convinced James was guilty of tunnel vision in this case, but I could see why Lars felt that way. Should I bother pointing out to Lars that if James suspected him, it was likely because the evidence repeatedly pointed to him?

"Call it what you want," he said with a shrug. "But that guy has it in for me."

I stood up and looked out the window. The pool was in full view. The Pearl was my dream come true. Guests were smiling and laughing, enjoying the amenities we'd worked so hard to perfect. And it could be gone in a flash. Unsolved murders didn't sit well with prospective vacationers.

"Kat says James is a decent guy, a good guy," I heard myself saying. I stepped back and watched Lars's reflection in the glass. "An old football rivalry won't change that."

"Kat? As in your bestie who hates me as much as Holloway?" His tone was bitter. It was a big departure from his usual die-hard optimism. I felt a roiling in my gut. Time to save this sinking ship before it was too late.

"Listen." I turned to face him. "It's James's job to figure out what happened. Of course he needs you to explain why there's blood on your clothes. That's a reasonable request. He needs to cross you off the suspect list, right?"

Lars ran a hand through his hair. "Not so sure that's *James's* intention. And since we're on the subject of intent, when did you two become so close?"

Was he for real right now? "Cut it out, Lars. Your plate's already full." In a softer tone, I added, "Now tell me what he said."

He cursed under his breath and sank down on the bed, dropping the macho-man persona. "He only asked a few questions before getting a call. He said he had to go but he'd be back soon and told me to stay put. Like, is he even allowed to say that?"

I frowned. What would take precedence over interviewing a suspect? "What was that all about?"

He threw up his hands. "I was too glad to see the back of him to ask any questions. Now listen, babe, I may not have much time. There's something—"

My phone began to play the Darth Vader theme. *Mom. Shoot.* "I better run. Mom's been waiting for me to call her back. I can't put her off any longer."

I walked back toward the door. I opened it, but before I could leave, Lars reached out and grabbed my hand. "If I tell you a secret, will you promise to keep it?"

A cold sensation trickled down my spine. "Lars—" I began.

Before I could say any more, a figure appeared in the doorway. It was James. I wriggled my hand free and dropped it to my side, silencing my ringer.

James didn't seem to notice, his eyes focused on Lars. He cleared his throat. "Lars, you need to come down to the station with me."

"Why?"

"I need to ask you questions in a more formal setting. You may want to bring a lawyer."

Lars looked at me with wide eyes. "Jess?"

I swallowed. "Call your lawyer."

Lars patted the pocket of his jeans. "My phone. I left it at the bar."

I turned to James. "Can Lars have a minute to grab his phone?"

"Go ahead. I'll follow you," James said to Lars.

Lars didn't hesitate. He sprinted out the door like he was back on the football field at the state championship.

James took a step back. With a wave of his hand, he invited me to join him on the walkway. I left Lars's room, shutting the door behind me. "What's going on?"

We fell into step with each other, heading toward the bar. "We got an anonymous tip that's propelled the case forward. I can't say any more."

"Are you going to arrest Lars?" I asked, trying to sound casual.

James looked straight ahead and didn't blink. "He's not in handcuffs yet."

I leaped ahead and stood in front of him, demanding he look at me. "*Yet?*"

He didn't shy away from my gaze. His intense brown eyes looked straight into mine. "Physical evidence, motive, and opportunity. That's what I require to move forward on a suspect."

I said nothing. There was nothing to say. He pointed past me. "Can I go now?"

I moved out of his lane. He was done with my questions. But I wasn't ready to be dismissed. I pressed on with my inquiries as he picked up the pace. "What was the call you got earlier about? The blood on Lars's T-shirt? Because Lars already said he and Bob had a fight and we witnessed it on the video."

The corner of his mouth lifted. His head tilted to one side, catching my eye. "Convenient, isn't it?"

"Not for Lars." I threw my arms up. "I assume by now you know that no one liked Bob. He had no friends here."

"There's a lot of jerks in the world, Jess. Most of them don't end up murdered."

The thought of Lars being charged with murder made my stomach churn. Underneath his brittle veneer was a vulnerable guy who hadn't had an easy life. With no one else in his corner, I had to be there. "You're wrong about Lars."

James gave me the side-eye. "Are you sure it's not the other way around?"

"Have you even considered that someone from Bob's past could have done this? The man hadn't been back to Fletcher Lake for years. Don't they say revenge is best served cold?"

"That's a long time to wait." He turned to face me. "Listen, Jess, I'm not trying to be flippant, and I'm not done investigating, promise. But my boss wants movement on this case, as I'm sure you and all your guests do."

I shook my head. "Not if it means sacrificing an innocent man."

"What is it with him? Most people aren't so determined to help their ex, especially after a rocky ending."

I frowned. How did he know how things had ended with Lars and me?

As if reading my mind, he said, "I watched the video, remember? Ditched on prom night? That's rough."

My face flushed. *Ugh. Thanks again, Britt.* "He had a radio thing."

"You don't need to make excuses." He held my gaze again. "You deserved better."

The color deepened in my cheeks. I couldn't argue with that. "Thanks."

"You're welcome."

What were we talking about? Lars, right. I'd almost forgotten. I cleared my throat. "Anyway, despite the rocky end, the relationship had its ups too. Lars was the first person I met after my dad died who eased the loneliness I felt. He'd just lost his mom, and we bonded. I won't deny our romance was an epic failure, but we were friends first. And I know he's a good person deep down. So I can't stand by and let him take the fall."

Two young women strolled past, each with a daiquiri in hand. They both ogled the detective, whispering to each other as they passed us. James ignored them; his eyes remained on me.

"Like I told you, Jess, I'm not done investigating. But for now, I need to follow protocol and do my job. That includes formal interviews with persons of interest."

"But like you said, you watched the video," I pointed out. "It shows more than one person in the area when Bob was killed. There were at least two other people in the vicinity."

"Including you aunt," he said gently.

A sense of indignation rose up in me. "Is that a joke?"

"I wish it was." His phone pinged. He pulled it out and looked at the screen before shifting his eyes back to mine. "Your aunt prevented what might've been an open-and-shut case." He held up a finger and took a few steps away to respond to an incoming message.

I rubbed my hand over my face. He was right. What had Auntie M been thinking? Right now, it didn't matter. More important was a list of potential suspects who were not in my circle of trust.

When James was done, I was ready. "What about Travis Sanders? Or Britt? Is it a coincidence they both headed back to the area where Bob was killed? Maybe they had a reason to want Bob dead. Maybe there's some dark family secret that Bob was exploiting. Have you thought of that?"

He held up his hands. "Okay, slow down. The brother-sister combo has crossed my mind, okay? Listen, I appreciate you taking the time to give me your insights, but right now I need to follow the evidence, wherever it leads me."

And that, as they say, was that—the end of our conversation. We were almost at the bar when Lars popped back into view, phone in hand. He looked from James to me and back again. He reached out and grabbed my hand, drawing me closer to him and away from the detective. "Are you upsetting Jessie?" he demanded. "Leave her alone, man. She's got nothing to do with this."

James kept his eyes on me. "Try telling her that."

Lars tried pulling me closer still. This time I held my ground and shot him a *cut it out* look. The Neanderthal headbutting was interrupted as the music became louder and a familiar tune began to play over the speaker system: *It's Raining Men* by Geri Halliwell. I whipped my head round to the bar and saw Nate with a smug grin on his face. He gave me a double thumbs-up. I shot daggers at him with my eyes.

Luckily, neither James nor Lars seemed to notice. They were too busy staring each other down. "Have you talked to Nicky yet?" I heard Lars say over the music. "He got into it with Bob last night too. Quit on the spot."

James scoffed. "Convenient to accuse the one holding all your dirty little secrets, isn't it?"

"Can I have a minute alone with Jessie?"

"You've got thirty seconds. I'll head out to the parking lot. But if I have to come back to get you, I'll use the cuffs."

"You got it, man," Lars said with a sneer.

James turned and headed toward the exit. "The clock's ticking," he called over his shoulder.

As soon as he was out of sight, Lars turned to me. The tough-guy act deflated along with the puffed-out chest and rolled-back shoulders, making him shrink about two sizes. He looked at me with wide, frightened eyes. "You've got to help me."

The earnestness of his plea caught me off guard. "How?"

"There are things I've done I'm not proud of. You need to find out where Travis Sanders and George Havers were when Bob was killed. They have motives too. Big motives."

I didn't like the sound of this. "I saw the video. George was with Paula, but Travis may not have an alibi. Why don't you just tell James what you know?"

He shook his head. "I can't. I don't trust him. You see how celebrities' mug shots somehow get leaked to the media. I bet a million bucks that clown would do the same thing to me. Can you look into it, Jess? Please."

"And if I find something?"

Lars's phone beeped. He glanced down at it and cursed as he read the message. I leaned closer to see what it said. The message was from a blocked number: *Ten seconds and counting.*

He groaned. "That's gotta be Detective Dud. Babe, do you have my back?" His eyes met mine. He was scared.

I let out a long sigh before answering. "I'll do what I can, okay? Better not keep him waiting."

He reached out and squeezed my hand. "Thank you."

I gave him the most reassuring smile I could muster and lightly pushed him toward the exit. "Go." He obeyed, and we started to walk.

We'd almost reached the door when he suddenly whirled around and planted a kiss firmly on my lips. "I never should've let you go."

I staggered backward, speechless. He glided past the pool and flung the side door open. He walked through without another look back.

What just happened?

Chapter Eighteen

Focus, girl, focus! Gotta find out about Travis Sanders and George Havers. It's not about the kiss. Lips locked when emotions run high. Nuff said.

I wiped my mouth with the back of my hand and ignored my thumping heart. Time to concentrate on what really mattered. Instead of hanging around the bar where Nate would ask too many questions, I kept my eyes down and made my way back to the refuge of reception.

When I reached the safety zone, I let out my breath. How long had I been holding it? Penny was on the phone. She gave me a friendly wave, then turned her attention back to her computer screen. I plunked myself down onto the sofa. How was I going to find out if George or Travis was involved in Bob's murder?

Duke got up from his station and greeted me with a double bark and a wagging tail. I reached down and gave him an affectionate pat. "Any ideas, pal?"

Duke barked and licked my knee. I scratched his ears as I began to formulate a plan.

Based on the video, we could assume George had been busy at the time of the murder. The same couldn't be said about Travis. So where do I go from here?

Kat sailed into the room. The bounce in her step told me she was feeling good. She shimmied up to me, making it hard not to grin back.

"Bank meeting went well?"

Duke barked again, and his tail started wagging. Apparently, I wasn't the only one sensing Kat's good mood.

She snapped her fingers to the beat of some imaginary pulsing music. "Super. And after such an awful morning, the vibes have picked up around here, too. People are actually enjoying themselves again. I hadn't taken Sarah for a DJ, but I've got to admit, she's good."

I blinked. "DJ? What do you mean?"

"She moved the speakers that were behind the bar to center stage, and she's taking requests. You were out there. Didn't you notice? Your brother wanted Geri Halliwell to kick it off, of all people. What's that about?"

"Don't ask."

I'd been so focused on the conversation with Lars I hadn't paid attention to what was happening around the pool—with the exception of Nate's song choice. Wasn't that where I should be? Focusing on guests, making sure the vibes were right?

Kat moved in closer to me. "You okay?"

"Yeah, fine," I grumbled.

She took a step back and covered her mouth in mock horror. "Uh-oh."

I rolled my eyes. "What?"

"You only use that word when things are anything but fine." She sat down. "Want to fill me in?"

With the weight of Lars's request, I was ready to collapse. Instead, I spilled my guts—leaving out the kiss, of course.

The grave expression on Kat's face told me she wasn't pleased.

"Are you as stumped as I am?"

"You need to be careful, Jess. I don't like this."

I shrugged. "Me neither."

She reached her hand out and tried to tuck my hair behind my ear. I swatted her away like a pesky fly. "What are you doing?"

She tried again. "I'm trying to show you a bit of tenderness, but you're making it very difficult." I flinched, and we entered a hand flap smackdown until eventually she gave up. "Okay, look. You need to consider the possibility that Lars is manipulating you."

I pulled both my legs up into a crisscross applesauce pose and met her head on. "In what way?"

"By sending you on a fruitless mission. A wild-goose chase."

"Why would he do that?"

"To muddy the facts. We watched Lars and Bob get into a fight just before Bob was murdered. That's a fact. If Lars can get you to dig up dirt on people Bob didn't like, it could act as a distraction."

My eyes narrowed. "You think Lars is using me to weaken the case against himself."

She gave me a one-shoulder shrug. The weasel shrug. "James might see right through this sort of tactic. But you . . ."

My phone pinged. Another text. Most likely my mom again. I ignored it and finished Kat's sentence instead. "Will get him off by creating reasonable doubt, even if he's guilty. Is that what you're trying to say?"

Kat nodded. "Pretty much."

"I see."

Penny cleared her throat loudly from across the room. We looked at her expectantly. She looked from me to Kat. "Everything okay?"

We both nodded. "Peachy," Kat said in a sour tone.

"Riiiight." With that, Penny reached under the counter and grabbed a box of overstock to refill our small shelf of shop goodies, wisely deciding to leave us alone to stew.

We watched her in silence. I let Kat's words sink in. Part of me wanted to storm off in an outrage, demand an apology, and refuse to speak to her for the rest of the day. But I couldn't. She might be right.

It hadn't occurred to me that Lars might be using me. Maybe it should have. I didn't see him as a killer, but I could see him messing with the investigation to hide truths he didn't want uncovered. He'd already admitted to me that he was holding back on telling James everything he knew, even though he was the prime suspect. I had to concede that Kat was right to question his motives in asking me for help. Was this all a game to Lars?

I folded my arms across my chest and sighed. "Okay, I'll admit it's possible."

Kat's expression softened. "I'm sorry, Jess. I've been thinking about this all day, and I couldn't let it go. However, I have an idea that could satisfy both of us."

"What is it?"

"You and I are going to double down our efforts, dig deeper, then tell James everything we find out, regardless of what we uncover. I know I said okay before, but this time I'm in a hundred percent."

"You mean it?"

"Yes. I know you care about Lars and I understand why. You're my best friend, and I want to help you do what you need to do. But you have to promise to agree to my terms."

"Okay. I'll share everything we learn with the police. Promise." I held my hand over my chest.

She tapped her chin. "Good. I think we should start with an online search of everything to do with George Havers. If we look deep enough, chances are we'll find something. Lars and George have been rivals since the first episode of *Sing This!* Let's find out the dirty details. Somewhere along the way, one or both of them must've done something to fuel the fire. Who's to say there won't be a motive in what we find? Big money and big egos can turn things ugly."

I thought back to the video. "George went off with Paula after his show. He has an alibi."

"Yes," Kat said. "But who's to say he didn't leave his room afterwards?"

"Good point."

Kat tapped my knee. "How about this? Let me handle the online stuff. I had to do some deep dives for background checks at the investment firm when I was interning. I've got a few ideas of where and how to search."

I nodded. "Perfect. I'll go see Travis. It's been a while, but we used to be pretty tight. It wouldn't be off the radar for me to stop by and say hello to him and Ashlyn."

Kat scrunched up her nose. "Just don't go all J. B. Fletcher and get yourself in trouble."

"Yes, boss."

Before she could respond, the front door flew open and the twins Elle and Lila traipsed inside. Their cheeks were rosy and they were smiling from ear to ear.

Penny threw her arms out. "Hey, you two. How was your adventure abroad?"

Elle patted her damp forehead with the back of her hand. "Awesome."

"We had a great day out," Lila agreed. "Your itinerary was spot-on."

I looked from one to the other. "Someone fill me in."

Elle spoke first. "Lila and I decided it was a little too early to uncork the wine, so we left it on ice and headed over to the bakery. We rented bicycles there and hit a few hot spots."

Lila strode over to the self-serve Nespresso machine and popped a caramel macchiato capsule into the machine. "There's a lot to see in your little town."

"The bookstore? The candy shop? It's all so charming," Elle gushed.

Lila rubbed her belly. "Don't forget the poutinerie."

"We managed to get there just in time for their afternoon special," Elle said. "Extra cheese with every order. Good thing we burned some calories riding around."

Lila waited for her drink to finish brewing and breathed in the sweet scent. "A quick caffeine fix and I'll be ready for a shower."

"You go ahead. I'll meet you upstairs," Elle said.

Lila took a sip and smacked her lips. "Delish. You want one?"

Elle looked out the back door toward the bar, scanning the crowd. "I'm going to grab something at the bar."

Lila followed Elle's line of sight. Her spine stiffened. She threw back the shot of espresso as if it were whiskey at a gold rush saloon. "Seriously?"

"Just a spritzer," Elle said. She didn't wait for a response, making a beeline for the bar. "See you soon," she called over her shoulder.

Lila let out an exasperated breath, then turned on her heel and stomped out after her sister.

"Did I miss something?" Kat said.

"I think we both did." More trouble was brewing. Good thing Nate was used to dealing with drama. As every experienced bartender knew, emotions could run high after a few drinks. The question was what—or who—had triggered this sudden change of mood in the twins.

Penny approached the sofa cautiously. "You two okay now?"

Kat slung her arm around my neck and pulled me close. "Never better."

Penny nodded. "Good."

I noticed she was fidgeting with her hands, unusual for our normally chill receptionist. "Penny, what's up? Are you okay?"

She dropped her hands to her sides. "I don't want to throw anyone under the bus, but I was supposed to be at my boyfriend's house an hour ago. I'm not sure who's supposed to be on the afternoon shift, but no one's shown up."

"That's odd." We had only three receptionists on staff, and one didn't start until next week. That left Auntie M. She wasn't normally more than fifteen minutes late for work. An hour was pushing it, even for her. "Let me pull up the schedule. I have it on my phone."

An app on my phone called #Lifesaver kept all of my files organized, and it definitely lived up to its name. "Here we go. Let's see." One quick glance and I could feel a big headache coming on.

Kat looked at the expression on my face. "What is it? Who's tardy for the party?"

"It's Aunt Marnie." I shook my head. "She should've been here ages ago."

Kat turned to Penny. "Normally I'd tell you to head out, but today . . ."

"I get it. We'll postpone dinner. I'm not really in the mood to eat anyway."

"Thanks, Penny."

Kat hunkered down at reception while Penny called her boyfriend to break the news. I tried calling Marnie's house. No answer.

"Where could she be?" I wondered out loud. "She's normally only fifteen minutes late. If she was held up somewhere, she would've called."

"Maybe James asked her to come to the police station for an interview. Ask why she shut down the video?" Kat suggested.

"Maybe, but I got the impression he'd be focusing on Lars for a while." I peeled myself off the sofa. "Do you mind if I drive over and make sure she's okay? I was going to stop by Travis's, but that'll have to wait."

She shooed me away. "Go for it. I'll start my online search on George while I hold down the fort."

I gave a short whistle. Duke stood up and stretched. I grabbed my keys and wallet from under the reception desk, and a pack of matches fell to the floor. We kept them there for the firepit out back, which reminded me: tonight was our first proper firepit social.

I snapped my fingers. "I have to remember to pick up the ingredients for s'mores while I'm out."

Kat licked her lips. "Get extra marshmallows and chocolate bars."

"Noted." Duke and I headed out, determined to get a few answers and a lot of treats.

Our signature vehicle for the B and B was a pink-and-white vintage Volkswagen van. I'd bought it at a discount out west after it had been used in a TV pilot that hadn't been picked up for production. As such, the van was in pristine condition. It worked well for driving guests around and served as a backdrop for our social media pics.

Duke, tongue hanging out, rode shotgun in the front seat as we made our way through town. I placed my phone in its dashboard cradle and rolled up my window. "Hey, Siri, call Momster."

Half a ring later, my mom picked up. "Jessica?"

"Hi, Mom."

"Finally."

"Sorry it took me so long to get back to you. What's going on?"

"A lot." She cleared her throat. "We need to go over a few things."

169

Whenever my mom used vague terms, I knew she'd signed me up for something I had no interest in doing. Like a Zumba class. Or a first date.

"Mom, you know I'm up to my eyeballs in work, right? I don't have time to go for a coffee with Bernadette's nephew Harry again. And besides, he smells like meatballs."

"He's a lovely young man. Bernadette says he's a wonderful cook too. Maybe he'd just finished whipping up a spaghetti Bolognese. Had you thought about that?"

"I'm a vegetarian, Mom. It's kind of a dealbreaker for me. Besides, even if that were true, did he forget to bathe after baking the balls?"

"Now you're starting to sound like Yvonne."

"Who's Yvonne?"

"Yvonne Gordon from the bank. She was so picky about who'd she'd go out with she ended up childless and alone."

"Better than having mini meatballs."

"Anyway, Yvonne told me today that Bob Strapp had been barred from every financial institution in Fletcher Lake."

I sat up straighter. *Hold the Bolognese.* "What? How's that possible? Wasn't he a financial adviser?"

Mom cleared her throat. "Not for long, according to Yvonne."

"What exactly did she tell you?"

A squirrel ran across the road in front of the van. Duke put his paws up on the dashboard and began to bark. "Shh, Duke, sit." Duke dropped down and curled up in the seat. "Sorry, Mom."

"It's okay. Duke just wants to be heard. Like Yvonne, really. She took care of her niece when her sister was sick, remember? Anyway, she came to see me at school a few years back and signed her niece up for a semester. I looked out for the young lady and made sure she fit in okay with her peers. Good kid, really."

"Mom—"

"My point is Yvonne trusts me, hon."

Now we were getting somewhere. "Super. Now dish the dirt."

"Fine. She mentioned Bob's stint at Sanders Investments. She wouldn't go into details but implied he'd burned enough bridges to be run out of town."

"That's a juicy tidbit, Mom. Thanks."

So Bob had worked for the investment firm owned by Britt and Travis's dad before he became Lars's manager. I'd assumed he'd quit his job to join Lars. Maybe I'd had it wrong.

"Speaking of juicy, you need to start thinking about what to say to the camera crew hanging around outside the B and B. I told them you'd call to set up an exclusive interview with them."

I cringed. "You're kidding."

"I'm not. You put me in charge, remember? The truck parked outside the B and B after they received an anonymous tip that Lars Armstrong had died. I let them know it was not Lars but his stepfather."

I gritted my teeth. "And?"

"And they refused to stop asking questions until I came up with something to make them back off. That's when I thought of you doing an exclusive."

I sighed. "Fine."

"Good. And if your nerves get the best of you, let Lars do the talking."

"*Lars?*"

Mom cleared her throat. "Didn't I mention he needs to be there too?"

"Mom!"

There was a pause. "I wanted them to leave you alone. They drive a hard bargain, Jessica. Besides, it's better he give some sort of statement before rumors about him start swirling around. It could kill his career."

Since when had my mom become so concerned with Lars's career? Had the spirit of Kris Jenner taken over my mother? "I don't know about that."

"Listen, I've dealt with the fallout of gossip my whole professional career. It may have only been at the high school level, but the basics are the same. It's better to be in control of the narrative, trust me."

She was probably right. "When and where?"

"Today, at some point. I said you'd call before four o'clock and set something up."

I glanced down at my watch. "That's in less than two hours."

"Don't forget to look your best. The spotlight is on the B and B. You didn't ask for the publicity, but you've got it. May as well use it to your advantage."

"I'll do my best. Now I've gotta go."

"Okay, hon. Talk to you soon."

"Bye, Mom."

I hung up. How was I going to explain this to Lars—and James? I just hoped they saw the logic in my mom's argument. James would have conditions. Lars would want time to do his hair. I shoved the phone back in its holder. I'd make sure to call and let the guys know once I was done with my current mission. Whoever said multitasking was a gift had never had a mom like mine.

Chapter Nineteen

Aunt Marnie's modern tiny house was a bright wood prefab structure just under four hundred square feet. It adhered to all the building code requirements and had every modern convenience yet was an homage to her tree-hugging, hippie ways. It was simple but pretty, with wildflowers growing in place of grass on her front lawn and lavender shutters adorning the windows. The wind chime hanging above the door tinkled as the familiar scents of Auntie M—patchouli and sandalwood—drifted through the open window.

"Auntie M?" I called through the window. No response. Duke helped out with a few loud barks, triggering a shuffling sound. A minute later, there was a loud click and the lock turned. Duke's nose wiggled, then, tail wagging madly, he pushed hard against the simple wood door. It swung open and he rushed inside, likely smelling the scent of a nearby cat. Last time I'd counted, Auntie M had three.

"Stay out of my cookie jar, Sir Duke!" her voice called out. He hopped up on the nearby sofa as Auntie M emerged from behind the door.

"Jess?" she said, her voice cracking. She cleared her throat, rubbing her neck and looking at me with uncertainty. "What are you doing here?"

Her easy breezy demeanor had vanished, and dark circles framed her eyes. I reached out and put a hand on her arm. "I was worried about you when you didn't show up for work today."

"I'm sorry," she said. "I must've slept in. Am I late?"

My eyes narrowed. "It's almost two thirty."

She began flitting around the open room. "Whoa! It's later than I realized. Let me get my purse. I'll come now." She looked around in search of her handmade bag.

I put my hands up to stop her. "It's okay, Aunt Marnie. We've got it covered."

She slowed down, allowing me to get a better look at her face. Her eyes were puffy and bloodshot, with fresh tears threatening to fall. "I'm sorry I let you down."

My mouth went dry. Frequent lateness had never spawned tears before. "Auntie M, what's going on?"

My tone was sterner than I'd intended. She sank down in the nearby orange papasan chair.

"I was getting ready for work this morning, listening to the radio, when the announcer came on and said there'd been an unconfirmed report of a death at the B and B. I tried to call, but there was no answer, so I rang the police station. Helen answered. She filled me in."

Helen must've gotten a call to come in early to hold down the fort. With a major incident like a murder, chances were that the small police force wanted all hands on deck. I leaned over Marnie's chair. "What exactly did she tell you?"

"That there'd been a death at the B and B. She reassured me it wasn't any of you, but I begged her for more information." She swallowed hard before continuing. "She told me Bob Strapp had died."

"Okay." I waited for more.

"I almost came in, but the more I thought about it, the more I figured the fewer people, the better. The police wouldn't want a mob of spectators milling about."

Logic had never come naturally to Marnie. She was lying. "Did you know Bob?"

Instead of answering, she got up and ambled across the room, where she picked up a glass figurine shaped like a fish. "Have I shown you my new prized possession?" She held it up for me to see, the sunshine glinting off the fish's tail. "It represents Pisces. It's hand blown. I ordered it off Etsy."

I pinched my lips together. "Can you answer my question?"

She held the fish up to the light, turning it in her hand. "Mr. Strapp was a guest at the B and B. I saw him around. Don't you love how the different angles change the path of the reflection?"

"You knew Bob as more than just a guest, didn't you?"

She clutched her fish to her chest and looked at me with wide eyes. "What do you mean?"

I folded my arms across my chest. "You were seen arguing with him yesterday in the parking lot."

Red splotches appeared on her face. She licked her lips. "He . . . ," she started, then blurted out, "He had double-parked. When I asked him to move, he got a bit testy."

Our eyes met, and she looked away. Not a good sign. "Auntie M, are you sure there wasn't more to it?"

She shook her head but didn't meet my gaze. A whistle from the kettle gave her a start. "I'm making tea. Would you like some? I mixed up a chamomile-lemongrass blend. It's delicious."

"Okay." My stomach was in knots. Aunt Marnie could be a space case, but she'd never been evasive, not even when broaching awkward topics, like the time I'd had to bail her out after she was arrested at an environmental protest out west. Truth and honesty had always gone hand in hand with Auntie M. Until today.

I watched her scoop out a heap of loose tea from a tin and divide it into two separate infusers. She placed one in each mug and poured steaming water from the kettle, replacing the lingering smell of incense with the sweet fresh scent of the infusion. I breathed it in, hoping the calming properties of the chamomile would work their charms on my jumpy aunt. I sat down at her small round oak kitchen table, waiting for the tea to steep.

She grabbed a nearby glass jar and offered me an oatmeal carob chip cookie. Although it wasn't a perfect pairing with the citrusy taste of the tea, I grabbed two and stuffed one in my mouth.

"Kat and I watched the security camera footage from last night," I said through a mouthful of sweetness.

The jar slipped from Auntie M's fingers and crashed to the floor. She gave a choked cry, and for a minute she didn't move, her face turning red. "Oops."

I hopped up and grabbed a broom out from behind the sofa. "Don't worry, I got it." It didn't take long to sweep up the mess.

"Thanks, Jess." She watched me dump the glass shards and cookie bits into the garbage can. "This has all been so upsetting. You know, this isn't the first time a guest has died while staying at the house. It happened when my mom was first taking in boarders. Never talked much about it, but I know it haunted her."

Goosebumps prickled my skin. "Figuratively or literally?"

She looked out the window. "Never really said."

I shook off the creepy feeling rising up my spine. *No. I refuse to add ghostbusting to my list of to-dos.* I put the broom away, then reached over and squeezed her arm. "Come sit down and drink your tea."

She did as I instructed, breathing in the heady scent before taking a sip.

I pressed on. "As I was saying, Kat and I went over the video." I decided not to mention James had been with us. Auntie M was spooked enough. "We were surprised to see you near the back camera. Any particular reason you decided to turn it off?"

She blew on the tea and sat back in her chair. Her tense features softened. "Love was in the air."

Love?

I rubbed my index finger across my forehead to hide the worry lines. "Do tell."

"A spark had ignited." She spread her palms out across the table. "I was Cupid's wingman."

Had she not heard me right? "I'm asking about the video, Auntie M."

"Exactly."

"What does love have to do with the security camera?"

Her grin spread. "George Havers was entertaining a lady friend. His assistant, Nicky, came into reception and asked if I could help provide the lovebirds a little privacy."

Wait, what? I already knew from watching the security video that George and Paula had hooked up last night. Juicy, sure, but it was hardly a matter of national security. "Isn't that what closed doors are for?"

"For us noncelebrities, yes. But if reporters got hold of Mr. Havers in a romantic tryst, it might complicate his life and put him in the spotlight for all the wrong reasons. Back in my day, musicians had more freedom to invite eager fans for a more intimate set, if you know what I mean." Her cheeks turned pink, and I fought the urge to cringe. "Anyway, you know how vicious gossip magazines can be nowadays. Downright awful, if you ask me."

I wanted to ask why she then insisted on reading them every week, but I bit my tongue. It could easily slip into a case of oversharing, and now wasn't the time. Instead, I pulled my phone out and typed *George Havers* into Google. There were all sorts of headlines that came up in tabloid feeds: George Havers gets his third straight hit, George Havers wears leather pajamas to bed, George Havers was the real winner of *Sing This!*, George Havers channels Elvis while songwriting, and . . . *Bingo!* George Havers's marriage is in trouble. *Pay dirt!* According to various sources, George was in the middle of a separation.

After sifting through the headlines, I was beginning to understand why the country crooner might be wary of unfamiliar cameras, especially any that might capture proof of him stepping out on his wife. I'd heard that one of the main sources for both print and online gossip sites was hotel and restaurant staff. No one at the Pearl would compromise a guest's privacy for a few bucks—at least I didn't think so—but George wouldn't know that. Could I blame him, then, for his request?

I thought back to George's show. There had been a moment when he'd wagged his finger onstage, bringing Nicky forward. At the time, it hadn't struck me as odd. I'd assumed he was asking the time or making a drink request. Guess I'd been wrong. "Auntie M, what time did Nicky come by?"

"Oh, I couldn't say for sure. But it would've been a few minutes before you saw me on camera."

My mind raced. "When you disabled the camera, did you see anyone else around?" Maybe the killer had been watching and had seen her action as an opportunity.

Auntie M frowned. "I don't know—I wasn't paying attention. Why are you so interested?"

"Switching the camera off may have prevented Bob's murder from being recorded."

Color drained from her face, and her lips began to quiver. "Oh dear."

I reached across and squeezed her hands. "It's not your fault. You couldn't have predicted that someone would take advantage of you going out of your way to help a guest."

Could the timing have been a coincidence? Unlikely. I racked my brain for who might have been in the vicinity or known about the plan. George, Paula, and Nicky, for sure. Was this a clue, or did it make things even more complicated?

I drank some more tea and checked the time. As much as I wanted to stay and make sure my aunt was okay, I had to get moving. "Listen, Auntie M, you did nothing wrong, so don't worry about it. The police will sort everything out, okay?"

She bristled at the mention of the police. "You think so?"

I stood up. "You had no way of knowing what was about to happen." I reached down and gave her a hug. "Sorry to rush off, but I gotta run."

She pushed back her chair. "I'll follow you back. Can I stay a little later and make up the time I missed?"

There was a lot to do, and she looked exhausted. "Are you sure you're up for it?"

"Yes, of course. I'd prefer not to miss my shift."

"Okay," I said. "Do you want to come with me and Duke? I don't mind driving you home after."

"No, I'll take my motorcycle. The fresh air will do me good."

My aunt's so-called motorcycle was actually an electric scooter that putt-putted around town at a maximum speed of twenty miles per hour—another source of constant conflict with my mom. It was sky blue with a bouquet of artificial daisies attached to the front of it. "Sounds good." I gave her a peck on the cheek. "See you there."

I opened the front door. Duke hopped off the couch, tail wagging and tongue out. "C'mon, let's go." Duke bolted out the front. I slid the side door of the van open, and he hopped into the front seat. Then, with a wave to my aunt, we headed out.

The trip back left me torn. While I couldn't imagine Auntie M as a murderer and her explanation about the camera made sense, she'd lied to me about her altercation with Bob Strapp. Her story that she'd argued with Bob over a parking spot made no sense. To her, the dividing white lines in a parking lot were mere suggestions that I'd rarely seen her abide by, and she drove a scooter. The argument had to be more personal, something she didn't want to share. But what? Auntie M was a let-it-all-hang-out kind of person who never tried to hide her flaws, her past, or her mistakes. Even if Nate was right and they'd gone to school together, that had been a long time ago. What could be worth arguing over decades later?

Then there was man-child Nicky. He was quickly becoming my number-one suspect. Means, check. Opportunity, check. What about motive? I'd have to look into that one. Obviously, there had been no love lost between him and Bob, but murder might be a stretch. How could I find out more with Lars tied up at the police station?

Wait. Kat had caught Nicky's eye. Maybe he'd be willing to open up a little if she was the one asking the questions. She'd been known to wrap more than one man around her little finger. Could she coax Nicky into a confession? If anyone could do it, it would be Kat. Solving the murder, exonerating people I cared about, and getting back to our *Cool Vibes* motto were the priorities. I just had to convince my best friend to chat up the sneaky creep.

Chapter Twenty

Before I returned to the B and B, I stopped by the local grocer to pick up the s'mores supplies and some bottled water. Duke waited outside the store in the shade while I ran in. I grabbed a cart and made a beeline for the baking aisle, stocking up on marshmallows, chocolate, and graham crackers. Satisfied I had an ample supply, I grabbed a few cases of water and made my way toward the cashier.

Just ahead of me was a familiar face. Armed with a large bag of lemons in each hand, Nate turned at the sound of my voice. "Well, well, well."

"Hey, sis. Fancy meeting you here."

"What are you up to? I swear I saw you with a huge pile of lemons earlier today."

His eyes widened. "It's been cocktail hour, every hour. Great for tips, but I hadn't anticipated how busy I'd be." He peered into my cart and grinned at the sight of the goodies. "Lunch?"

I fought the urge to whack him with a chocolate bar. "We're doing s'mores tomorrow night. Kat and I thought it would make for a perfect Sunday evening activity. Low-key but fun."

"Sweet. Can you sneak one to me when you do it? Sarah's not a big fan of marshmallows."

I rolled my eyes. "What's wrong with marshmallows?"

"She thinks I'm a sugar junkie and is adamantly against gelatin."

"Then it's a good thing she'll be busy with her evening yoga session." I reached my hand over to a nearby chip display and grabbed a large bag of Doritos to my cart for the drive back. "Other than sugar issues, things okay on your front?"

"Don't fret. Most of the guests are super chill. It's a good vibe. Sarah's even won over your archenemy. She and Britt have bonded over a shared love of Justin Bieber."

I groaned. "They're Beliebers?"

Nate dropped his head in mock shame. "In Sarah's defense, she used to live down the street from his cousin or something. He's Canadian too, you know."

I gave him a disparaging smile. "Not all Canadians know each other."

"Maybe that's just what they tell us." He shot me an impish grin. "Either way, Sarah saved everyone else from Britt's incessant moping. Without a fan club of her own, she's lost."

"I have to admit, Paula's whirlwind romance with George Havers seems a little intense, don't you think? They've been inseparable since his show."

"I've already come to think of them as Peorge. You know, like Ben Affleck and Jennifer Lopez are known as Bennifer." He shrugged. "Who knows. Maybe with Peorge it was love at first sight."

We reached the checkout. There was one customer ahead of us, but he was almost finished. Nate stacked the water on the conveyor belt and pulled his wallet out from his back pocket. Old-school. I preferred tapping my Apple Watch. I dropped the lemons, s'mores ingredients, and Doritos on top of the water, then glancing around to make sure no one else was in earshot, I lowered my voice. "According to *SST,* George is going through a divorce and has been married several times."

"Focus on the positive, Jess. Connections are forming. This is a good thing." He turned to the cashier. "Hi, Zoe."

The young woman with pink hair and a lip ring grinned up at him. "Hi, Nate." She scanned the groceries.

He passed her his bank card. "When are we going to see you at the Cool Vibes Café?"

"Soon, I hope." She turned to me. "Me and my friends love the aesthetic you and Kat Miller chose."

My eyes widened. *Move over, West Coast kids. Fletcher Lake had raised its game.* "Thanks. Glad you like it."

She narrowed her eyes. "You don't recognize me, do you?"

I looked from her to Nate. He quirked an eyebrow. "Look a little closer."

Zoe's cheeks flushed. "Everyone tells me I have my mom's eyes. Some people curse at having hooded eyes, but look at Blake Lively and Kate Hudson, right?"

I leaned in and looked closer. *Shut the front door. I know those eyes.* "Is Parker your mom?"

She nodded. "Yup. Mom said babysitting you two was like false advertising." She snorted. "She calls me the Energizer Bunny, says you two were way more chill. I just started working here."

Parker had been my and Nate's favorite babysitter. She and her boyfriend got married right after high school, and I cried when Mom said Parker couldn't look after us anymore. She announced her pregnancy three months later.

Holy guacamole! How was this girl that baby? I did the math in my head. It had been over twenty years. "Wow, do I ever feel old."

Nate patted my shoulder. "You are nearly thirty."

"Twenty-eight and a quarter, thank you very much." I turned to Zoe. "And please say hi to your mom. I just moved home from San Francisco, and I haven't seen her since I got back."

"She was going to come to your opening until she heard that guy was there." Her eyes widened. "Guess that won't be a problem anymore."

I frowned. "Who? What guy?"

Zoe's face flushed. "Sorry. Mom always says my mouth works faster than my brain. I know he's dead. I didn't mean any disrespect."

My mind raced to put two and two together. "Your mom didn't come because of Bob Strapp?"

Zoe slapped her forehead. "That was his name. Sorry, I forgot."

Another customer approached the checkout, and Nate pulled on my sleeve. "We'll let you go. C'mon by anytime. I think you're going to love our Pink Panda: vodka, pineapple, strawberries, and a splash of lime blended to perfection."

"Me and my friends will be there next Saturday. I literally can't wait. Hashtag *chillday*, hashtag *amazing*."

Nate laughed. "Bye, Zoe." He picked up the water. "Shall we?"

I grabbed the two bags of groceries. "We shall."

Zoe gave us both a hearty wave. "Bye, guys."

I waved back and followed Nate out. Duke barked an excited greeting as we came into view. Nate gave him a thorough ear rub before heading to the van. I pulled the keys from my front pocket and slid open the side door. Duke hopped in, and Nate placed the cases of water on the floor. I dropped the bags on the passenger seat, grabbing the lemons and passing them to him. "How is Parker's kid already drinking age?"

"Zoe just turned twenty-one. Besides, Parker was young when she had Zoe." He glanced back at the store. "Beware. Zoe's a yapper."

"Yeah, I got that. Any idea of what she meant by the Bob Strapp comment?"

Before he could answer, his phone dinged. He pulled it out from his back pocket. "It's Sarah. She's covering, but it's getting busy; she needs help. I gotta run. You heading back?"

I hesitated. "Yeah."

He raised an eyebrow. "Uh-oh. What's up?"

"I'm trying to figure out how to bribe Kat. I need her to charm Nicky so he starts spilling his guts Zoe-style. Not sure how it'll go over."

"Refresh my memory—who's Nicky again?"

"The creepy man-child who lurks in corners. He's got light-blue eyes, stringy hair, and a slouch that makes him look about two feet shorter than his actual height. He's Lars's or maybe now George's assistant?"

"Right, I know the guy. He was spouting off at the bar earlier about knowing who killed Bob."

"Seriously?"

Nate waved a hand dismissively. "He was trying to impress a couple of women who were way out of his league. His theory was the same as everyone else's: Lars for the win."

I swallowed. "Kat will find out one way or the other."

"You may be out of luck. I just saw him crossing the street toward the path to Evergreen Beach." He scratched his head. "Tell me again why you want Kat to chat him up? She's more Jennifer Lawrence than Jennifer Garner."

"What does that mean?"

"Everyone knows not to mess with JLaw. She's more attitude than charm. If you want to charm him, maybe try Sarah or Duke."

"I'm ignoring the fact that you skipped right over me to suggest a creature who tongue bathes. The point is that Nicky likes Kat. He practically drools every time she bothers to even sneer in his direction."

"Loves the chase. I get it."

"You know what I don't get? That he's at the beach. It seems like an awfully pleasant pastime for him. Although it could be the perfect place to trap him."

He leaned an arm against the van. "Jess, what are you up to?"

"One sec." I pulled my phone out and texted Kat.

Me: *Where u?*

Kat: *In town. In hot pursuit of a red rubber ball and a screwdriver.*

Me: *Ack! Is Auntie M pressuring people to do one of her random scavenger hunts?*

Kat: *Ugh, no. Boy lost ball—can't stand the crying. Plus there's a loose door handle. Couldn't find the toolkit.*

Me: *Abandon mission. Meet me at the pathway entrance to Evergreen Beach. Asap.*

Kat: *Why?*

Me: *No questions. I need your help.*

Kat: *omw*

Nate craned his neck, trying to see the screen. "Who are you texting? I can tell you're scheming."

"Sorry." I tucked my phone away. "I need to see what Nicky's up to. I asked Kat to meet me at the lake path across from the B and B."

He clucked his tongue, a habit he'd picked up from Mom. "Jess, there's a murderer running around. I don't think now's the time to play amateur sleuth."

I frowned at him. "If not now, when?"

"How about never?"

I brushed off his concern. "Give me half an hour. Kat and I will be together. Remember, I'm your big sister, so you need to listen to me."

"And I'm your younger yet wiser brother. Besides, we're only a year apart. And I say no."

We walked around the van, and I hopped into the driver's seat. "A year and a quarter, remember? Now step back before I run over your toes."

He retreated just enough for me to close the door. Using the manual window crank, I rolled down the window. "We good?"

"At least have your phone handy and make sure the location sharing is on."

"Fine." I went into Settings and shared my location with him. "There. Now you can see where I am. Can I go now?"

"Fine. But wait for Kat out front. Deal?"

"Yes, Mom."

I rolled up the window and started the engine. Snack time. I fished out the chips from a bag and stuffed a handful into my mouth. I flipped one over at Duke, who'd been roused by the crinkling sound. Then, waving at Nate, I put-putted out of the grocery store lot. As I crunched and munched my snack, I couldn't help but wonder if there was more to the town's aversion to Bob then I knew. Sure, he was a sleazeball, but to change or cancel plans to avoid him? That surprised me. Parker, my old babysitter and mother-of-a-grownup, was not one to create drama. I'd been away from Fletcher for too long. It was time for me to get caught up on all the down-and-dirty bits I'd missed.

Chapter
Twenty-One

Within three minutes Duke and I had inhaled nearly the entire bag of chips and pulled into the B and B's parking lot. I scanned the area while Duke relieved himself. The media trucks laid low, likely thanks to my mom's finagling. There was also no sign of Nicky or Kat. I locked the doors, dropped off Duke inside along with the groceries, and tucked my phone into my yoga pants. Then I skipped across the road and waited. I stood behind a tree across from the B and B and out of sight.

I didn't have to wait long. Kat was born with a lead foot. She barreled into the parking lot, hopped out of the car, and surveyed the tree line. I stepped out and waved my twig-like arms.

She gathered her mass of long hair and hustled toward me. With expert speed, she piled her locks on top of her head, then secured them with the emergency scrunchie she kept on her wrist. It didn't slow her down. "What's going on?"

"Shhh. I think Nicky's around. Nate spotted him heading toward Evergreen Beach maybe half an hour ago."

She eyed me warily. "Is this a riddle? Let me give it a go. Why'd the man-child cross the road?"

I squatted behind my tree and yanked her sleeve till she also ducked down low. "I'm going to ignore the thick sarcasm, because you hit it on the nose."

"Seriously, Jess. I rushed back because Nicky went to the beach?"

"The guy is up to something. I can feel it. I need you to be nice to him. It's the only way we'll get him to talk."

She frowned. "Are you serious right now?"

"I will bake you chocolate cupcakes."

"Last time you baked, the cake bent the spoon."

"Then I'll *buy* you a vanilla cake. And melt fudge ice cream to go on top."

"You know I can't resist that combination. Fine, let's move." She stood, turned on her heel, and hit the narrow path that led to the water.

The alcove was masked by a line of trees and bushes that separated it from Fletcher Lake's better-known main beach area.

Halfway down the path, Kat stopped. "Did you hear that?"

"What?"

"There was a rustling." We waited a minute. Nothing. She tiptoed forward, me close behind, then paused. "Stop breathing in my ear. I can't hear anything."

I dropped back a few paces. The scent of her coconut-vanilla shampoo was replaced with the musty lake smell. The soft forest floor began to mix with sand as the trees grew sparse.

The glint of sunshine on the water suddenly appeared through the trees. At that same moment, we heard a yell for help. It was deep and guttural. It was also familiar.

Kat took off toward the sound. I followed. Twigs snapped under our feet, and we pushed branches to the side, abandoning any effort to be quiet as they swung back to hit us.

A wide opening between the remaining trees emerged not far ahead. Kat got there first. She stopped so suddenly I plowed into her with the grace of an oversized puppy.

I drew back and wiped her sweat off my cheek with the back of my hand. "A little warning next time, please." When she didn't move, I tried to shuffle around her. She threw her arm out to stop me from going any farther, almost clotheslining me in the process.

"Hey, what the hell are you doing? You almost—"

"Jess, look!" She pointed.

I abandoned my complaint as I followed her line of sight.

A flash of déjà vu hit me. There was a figure standing over a motionless body. But this time, it wasn't Sarah hovering over Bob Strapp. It was Lars standing over Nicky, who was lying on the sand.

I clapped a hand over my mouth to stop from screaming. *Oh no! Not again!*

As if sensing our presence, Lars turned. His eyes were wild with something: Fear? Panic? I wasn't sure. He was dripping wet and shirtless, with only a pair of shorts covering his lower half.

"Jess! Kat! Help!"

Kat and I exchanged a brief look before racing over. When we reached Lars, he was shaking so badly I thought he might pass out. I gripped his forearm hard to steady him.

Kat dropped to her knees and examined Nicky. For the first time since he'd been in town, his hood was drawn back. There was a bald spot at the back of his head, not far from a gaping wound on his temple, where a trickle of blood could be seen. His eyes were open but unfocused.

Kat looked up at me and shook her head. She didn't need to say the words. Nicky was dead, and we all knew it.

I spun Lars around to face me. "What happened?"

He balled his hands into fists. "I don't know."

My stomach churned. *"I don't know"? Is that the best he has?* In that moment, I understood why my mom hated those words.

"Lars, just tell us what happened." My words were measured and quiet.

Lars roughly shook my hand off his arm and stepped back. "I have no idea. It looks like he hit his head and fell, or—"

Kat brought her face closer to the wound. "There's a gouge in his temple."

I bent down to take a closer look. How could this happen again?

"Lars," Kat said. "Have you called the police?"

He patted his sopping-wet pockets and pulled out his phone. "I was just about to."

Kat shot me a raised eyebrow. He caught the exchange and shook his head. "I didn't kill him! I swear, I didn't kill him. You've got to believe me!"

Kat pulled out her mobile and called 911.

As she spoke with the operator, Lars moved closer to me. Instinctively, I flinched.

He looked hurt. "You're scared of me?"

I shook my head but couldn't meet his gaze. I didn't know what I thought anymore.

"Babe, you've got to believe me. I wouldn't kill anyone. I think someone's trying to set me up."

I forced myself to look at him. "Tell me."

He edged closer and leaned in, ready to whisper in my ear.

Kat yanked him back with one hand, her phone held up in the other. "The cops are recording every sound. Keep your hands where I can see them."

Lars retreated, wrapping his arms around his six-pack.

There was no blood on him. No signs of a fight. No new scratches on his chiseled body. Then again, he was soaking wet. Besides, if he'd surprised the much smaller Nicky, there might not have been a struggle at all. And was it a coincidence or was it a convenience that Lars had just washed off any chance of DNA evidence?

I wanted to ask him who would do this. Who would kill Nicky and ruin Lars's life by pinning a murder—two murders—on him? But I didn't get a chance. A piercing scream cut through the air, chasing away any other thoughts.

Elle and Lila, the pretty twins staying at the B and B, appeared at the other end of the cove, frozen in place. They'd come through a makeshift parting of the bushes that led to the better-known stretch of public beach. One of them had on a still-wet black bikini and held an open bottle of rosé while the other wore a pink dress with a matching scarf. She was carrying a Pearl picnic basket at her side. It would've made for a perfect Instagram post if there hadn't been a dead body in the way. A dead body in plain sight.

Both women were visibly shaking. The twin in pink looked at her sister. "Elle, you okay?"

The bottle of wine slid from Elle's hand, the contents soaking into the sand. Lila dropped the picnic basket and reached for her sister. But Elle dashed forward before her sister made contact. Elle ran across the beach, Lila right behind her. When Elle reached the spot where Nicky lay, she dropped to her knees next to him.

Lila tried to pull Elle back, but her sister didn't budge. Her eyes were fixed on Nicky, and she muttered three words over and over, as if she were possessed.

"Not my husband. Not my husband. Not my husband."

Chapter
Twenty-Two

The muttering faded away as Elle laid her face on Nicky's still chest. Was she checking for a pulse or overcome with grief? Her floral cover-up began to soak up Nicky's blood. My heart sank for her.

Lila crouched next to her sister, putting a hand on her back. Lars drew closer. He bent down, his face tight as he fought back tears. "I'm sorry," I heard him say, his voice cracking with emotion. "Nicky's gone."

Lila's face remained stoic, but Elle raised her head and glared at Lars, her face crimson. "Go away."

Lars looked back at Kat and me. His face was blotchy, and his breathing bordered on hyperventilation. Panic was setting in. But he wasn't our problem right now.

Kat and I exchanged a look and moved closer to the sisters. Lila began to sway back and forth like she might faint. Kat swooped in and grabbed hold of her while I squatted next to her sister.

"Elle?" I said softly. "It's Jess from the B and B."

She sat back on her heels, covering her face with her hands. I reached down and stroked her hair as she rocked back and forth. She stopped moving, and I leaned in closer. "C'mon, let me help you up."

Elle allowed me to guide her up, as Kat tended to Lila. "That's it," I heard Kat say. "Slow and steady."

Elle kept her face mostly covered, shielding her eyes. I squeezed her shoulders and leaned in closer. "I'm so sorry, Elle."

Elle sat down hard on a nearby stump, a long sigh deflating her. I sat beside her. "Nicky was your husband?"

"His name's Nico. Only Lars and Bob called him Nicky. They loved to tease him, to get under his skin." She looked up and gave Lars a pointed glare. "Didn't you, Lars?"

Lars stared down at the sand.

Lila, who'd managed to regain a sense of calm, approached. She crouched down and grabbed her sister's hand, peering up into her eyes. "You okay?" This was the first time I'd had a chance to see Elle's face. Her complexion was clear, not blotchy. No tears either. Which made it weird when Lila reached up and caressed her sister's face with her thumb. It would've been a natural gesture had Elle's cheeks been wet. But they were dry as a desert.

I rose so that Lila could join Elle on the stump. Lila and Elle sat in silence, huddled close. I remained nearby, mostly out of a sense of obligation, although I couldn't deny my curiosity had been piqued. *If there are no tears, does it mean Elle's apparent heartbreak is an act?*

My thoughts were interrupted by Lars approaching us. Elle went stiff, her face turning a deep shade of red as her mouth contorted into a snarl.

"This is all your fault," she practically spat at him. My breath caught as she spoke. I didn't get the sense she was acting anymore.

Lars flinched at her words before shaking his head slowly and mumbling a denial under his breath. "No, no, no."

Elle's chest began to heave, and her breaths grew ragged. Then, without warning, she lunged at Lars. He grabbed her outstretched hands before she could claw at him. She pulled her fists away and clenched them in front of her chest. "You treated Nico like dirt, as if you're some kind of Greek god." She paused, wiping the back of her hand across her mouth. "Know what you are, Lars? A one-hit wonder, a nobody. You cheat and lie, and you never like to get your hands dirty. And now your pit bull and your errand boy are dead. What happened? Did you get tired of them? Or did they get tired of you?"

Lars's face turned stony as her vicious words battered his ego. Approaching sirens grew louder, silencing Elle. We all turned to watch the police rush through the narrow pathway and onto the beach. Behind a handful of uniformed officers came James, his eyes darting around, taking in the details of the scene and finally resting on Lars. His jawline tightened as he looked past Lars at the spot where Nicky's body lay.

He strode past us, pulling on gloves as he bent down to examine the body. Elle rushed over, Lila and me on her heels. He held a hand up to stop us from getting any closer. His gaze shifted from Elle's face to her blood-soaked dress. "Elle, is it?"

"Yes," she said.

"You knew the victim?"

"Nico," she said. "His name was Nico. He was my husband."

James took a harder look at her before responding. "This man was your husband?"

"That's right. He went by Nicky after Lars insisted on it, even though Nico hated the name. Lars took enjoyment out of hurting him. Guess this time he went too far."

So neither Elle nor Nicky had told the police they were married. Why not?

"I'm sorry for your loss." James gave her a curt nod. He switched his focus to a uniformed officer standing nearby and waved him over. "Officer Jensen, can you escort these women back to the bed-and-breakfast across the road and wait with them in their room until I get there?"

Lila looked behind her. I followed her gaze. The picnic basket and the now-empty bottle of wine still lay on the sand. "Should I leave that stuff here?" she asked me.

"I'll take care of it later," I assured her. "Don't worry."

She nodded. "Thanks."

The officer approached Lila and Elle. "Ladies?" He gestured in the direction of the pathway back to the B and B. "Please follow me."

With no other option, Elle and Lila linked arms and followed Officer Jensen in silence. Once they were out of sight, James ordered another officer to take photos. Two paramedics arrived on the scene. After the officers were done with Nicky, the medics placed him into a body bag, loaded him onto a gurney, then brought him back up the path toward the road.

Once they'd left, James strode over to the tree stump where Kat and Lars stood. I trailed behind him. We watched as the police strung up yellow tape around the perimeter of the crime scene. James had his face set to neutral. "Okay, who wants to fill me in?"

Kat and I looked at Lars, who clasped his hands behind his neck and looked up at the sky. "I guess that should be me," Lars said.

James pulled a notebook out. "Whenever you're ready."

Lars dropped his hands to his sides in a look of defeat. "An *STT* reporter I'm close to gave me a heads-up that Nicky had been sniffing around asking about money for insider information about Bob's murder. So when I saw Nicky sneaking out of the B and B, I decided to follow him. Once I saw him cross the road and take the path, I knew he was going to the beach. I waited a few minutes, then headed after him."

"And then?"

"Then nothing. I didn't see anyone. Figured maybe I'd been wrong and that he'd decided to go to the main beach area to check out girls or go for a walk. I went for a swim to clear my head. When I came out of the water, I spotted a shoe sticking out from behind some bushes. That's when I found him. I pulled him out into the open, thinking he must've tripped or something."

"Are you sure you didn't meet him here? Maybe you two got into an argument?"

Lars held his hands up defensively. "I didn't do this. I swear."

James ran his fingers through his hair. "I'm going to need to search you. Do you have a screwdriver or any sharp objects on you I should know about? Now's the time, Lars."

"I don't," Lars said, clenching his fists. "My clothes are piled over there." He pointed to a rock near the pathway, with running shoes neatly placed on top of some bright-colored clothing. "I swear, someone is setting me up."

James moved a step closer to him. "Hold out your hands, please."

Lars held them out, palms up.

"Now turn them over," James instructed.

Lars complied. Both sides were baby soft. He flipped them back and forth. "What are you looking for?"

"Early signs of bruising."

"Bruising where?" I interrupted.

James looked closer at Lars's hands. "On the knuckles. Sharp objects entering temples require some force."

My stomach turned at the description.

Lars continued to flip his hands back and forth. "You can check them every day for a week. I didn't touch the guy."

James quirked an eyebrow. "Right. You think this is an elaborate setup."

Lars took a step closer to James. "What if Nicky was supposed to meet someone and an argument broke out?"

"Anything's possible." James maintained eye contact with Lars as he spoke. "I just follow where the evidence leads."

Lars stared back. "Yeah? 'Cause it feels like your eyes are only on me. Maybe you should start to look around. You might find yourself a killer."

"It's beginning to feel like watching you is doing just that," James shot back.

My head volleyed back and forth, as if watching the finals at Wimbledon. But there could be no winners here.

Lars's voice quivered with rage. "Are you accusing me of something?"

I gave a little wave to try to break the tension. "Guys?"

Neither looked my way. Instead, James closed the gap between him and Lars, bringing him nose to nose with his number-one suspect. "Who else has a connection to both victims? Who else was in the area where both men were killed?"

"Stop it," Lars ordered.

James continued. "You see where I'm going, or do you need me to draw up a game plan like your stepdad used to do? Oh, wait. That would require two plans, wouldn't it? One with the illegal moves for your eyes only and one for everyone else."

Ding, ding, ding. Where's the bell to stop this match? I put a hand on each man's chest and eased them apart. "All right, nuff said, you two." This time I made sure my voice was loud enough to hear.

Lars's chest began to heave, and his lip curled as if he was ready to snarl his next words. Instead, they came out hoarse and low. "I'm tired of your sore-loser crap from the football field, Holloway. Get over it and move on."

"Move on? Like the player you took out with the low blow that tore his knee ligament and cost him a full scholarship? You didn't think twice to take someone down when you wanted to win, no matter the cost. What's the prize this time?"

"Your player just had an unlucky slip," Lars said.

"A leopard doesn't change his spots," James said. "That's you, Lars. Except you're more like a weasel. I won't let you win the game this time. Too much is at stake."

"You couldn't keep up back then. Doesn't seem any different now. That's why I've asked Jess to help out. While you ride out old resentments, she'll do your job."

James looked at me. A smug grin spread across Lars's face, and he added, "What did you say our unfriendly neighborhood cop had, Jess? Tunnel vision?"

My mouth dropped open, and my face went red. I eyed James as he searched my face for an explanation. What could I say? *Sorry, James, I didn't think Lars would mention it*? Why on earth had I assumed Lars would keep our conversations private? When would I learn that trusting Lars never paid off?

Hot shame ran through me as Lars stood taller. "Heard of that, bro? Or is your head stuck too far up your—"

"As it stands," Kat interrupted in a clipped tone as she stepped out from behind a thicket of trees. I'd been so caught up in the drama I hadn't even noticed her step away. "We have a new problem, folks. Maybe you two can pause the cavemen act and deal with the paparazzi filming this dramatic exchange."

We all turned to look in the vicinity from which Kat had emerged.

"Hey, buddy," Kat shouted. "You're busted. Come on out."

Sure enough, a fidgety figure in wrinkled khakis shuffled out, holding a small camera with an extended lens that blocked his face. James and Lars swore in sync, causing the photographer to lower the camera long enough for me to see his face. He waggled his fingers at us in a friendly little wave.

"Stop taking photos," James ordered.

The man moved closer and kept snapping shots.

"Bro, have you no boundaries?" Lars shouted. "A man died here. Publish those photos and you can kiss any more exclusives goodbye."

At that threat, the photographer obediently dropped the camera, allowing the neck strap to do its job, then held up both hands. "Don't fret, folks. A one-on-one with Lars can make these pics disappear. Some lady promised an exclusive, but I never heard back." He shrugged. "So I gave up and followed the action."

Double crap. I'd forgotten to call the number Mom had sent me to set up the interview she'd promised this guy.

Lars busted out a Hollywood smile and aimed it at the man. "Have I ever denied you, Rick? You know I'm a fan. Give me a sec here." Lars looked from Kat to me to James. "Can I go? Or do y'all want to see your lovely faces as tonight's headlines across the gossip sites?"

"Okay, get rid of that sleaze," James instructed. "But don't give him any details, and that includes the victim's name. I need to notify the next of kin."

"Wouldn't that be his wife?" Lars said.

James glared at him. "You want to stand here and argue?"

Lars shook his head. "Do I have to ask permission for a shower, Holloway, or do you want to bring me in again so the killer can keep killing?"

"Since your swim conveniently washed off any evidence, go ahead and shower." James thrust his finger in Lars's face. "But I'm not done with you. Make yourself available and don't take off again."

"Fine, I'll be at the B and B."

Lars stalked off across the sand, giving a wave to the cameraman, who'd begun filming again. Lars flicked his still-damp hair back and flexed his muscles as he moved, turning the photo op into a makeshift beach shoot.

Jeez.

A rustling from the tree line drew my attention away from the cringey sight. George and Paula emerged from the dense bushes. They were holding hands and looked disheveled and awkward. James approached them.

"Where did you two come from?" he demanded.

George cleared his throat. "We were out for a stroll."

"Here?"

George shrugged. "It came recommended."

Paula cleared her throat. "I hadn't been here since high school. The desk clerk—Marnie—said it hadn't changed."

"How long have you been in the vicinity?" James said.

"Not long. We were feeling a little cooped up in the guest room. What's happened?" George asked.

"Did you see or hear anything?" James said.

"We were a little distracted," George said, putting his arm around Paula.

"Miss Davis? How about you?"

Paula leaned back into George's chest. "Like George said, we were distracted."

George pulled her in closer with a protective arm. "You going to fill us in?"

"Go back to your rooms for now. If I have any more questions, I know where to find you."

"Until tomorrow," Paula said. "Then it's back to real life again."

"When do you leave?" James asked.

"Checkout time," George said. "We're taking advantage of every second we have." If I was going to solve two murders, it was time for me to do the same.

Chapter
Twenty-Three

After asking us a few more questions, James sent Kat and me on our way. We walked back in silence, single file along the well-trodden path. Who knew if there were any more paparazzi hiding out in the thick brush?

As the path emerged from the trees, freeing us of any possible eavesdroppers, I made a confession. "Every time I see Paula together with George, I have the urge to purge."

Kat threw her head back and laughed. I swatted her shoulder. "It's not funny. When did I become such a cynic?"

"Senior year, if I'm not mistaken." She grinned at me. "But don't worry. You're not the only one. They lay it on so thick, the rest of us are left gagging."

We crossed the road back to the B and B. Penny was still there. I felt bad for her; I'd hoped Auntie M would've been here by now to relieve her. But I gave her a wave and went back to my apartment to change. I wanted out of these clothes, because no matter how careful I was at the beach, sand always managed to sneak in. Kat came with me so we could discuss our options in private.

As soon as I opened the door, we came face-to-face with Aunt Marnie. She was putting on her shoes and her hair was wet. She smelled like lavender and strawberries, the very scents of *my* soap and *my* shampoo.

"Hey now," she greeted us.

"Auntie M!" Kat said. "There you are."

I quirked an eyebrow. "Why did you have a shower here?"

"Hot flashes." My aunt shook her head. "Worse than a sweat lodge. I hope you don't mind I used your place. I was dripping."

"Of course not." Should I bother asking why she hadn't showered at her own place? First things first. "Will you please consider getting a phone? Next time you're going to be late, I won't have to drive to your house to do a welfare check."

"Sorry about that," she said. "Time can get away from me."

"When did you arrive?" Kat persisted.

"Just over fifty-eight years ago," she said. "Or was it fifty-nine?"

As she began counting on her fingers, I went into my bedroom and changed quickly. When I got back, she was still counting. Kat and I left her to it and made our way back to the front desk, where Penny was organizing pamphlets from some new trendy businesses in town. "Penny, if you need to go, I can cover until Marnie's ready. She won't be long, I don't think." Although based on her math skills, I wasn't all that confident.

Penny checked her watch. "No worries. I rearranged my schedule. I'm in no rush now."

"You sure?"

"Mm-hmm." She grinned at me and went back to her pile. So many breweries, wineries, restaurants, and cafés were cropping up nearby, it was hard to keep up. The surge of tourists was made up of a younger hipper crowd, our target market. It was a risk to focus on such a specific demographic but selling out this season told us we'd made a good call.

Kat and I wandered back into the pool area. The scents of chlorine and sunscreen wafted through the air as guests took advantage of the dog days of summer. Duke, in particular, took the term to heart. Flopped in a shady spot on a yoga mat, my fluffy husky panted while presiding over a yoga session led by Sarah. I snapped my fingers twice, and he showed off a perfected downward dog stretch before sauntering over to me. I gave him a few treats, then watched him settle back down in the shade.

The pool was occupied by a family of four. The kids splashed around, filling the air with laughter and joy. A good sound.

"Want to grab a drink?" Kat asked. "I have some number crunching to do, but I feel like murder is a good reason to slack off."

"Definitely. Besides, I want to tell Nate what happened."

She looked over at the bar. "He's been keeping pretty quiet since Bob died."

Head down, Nate was hard at work, cutting lemons and piling the slices into a dangerously tottering heap. I spotted his phone sitting next to the cutting board and was willing to bet my prized pair of Louboutins that it was open to the location-sharing screen with my whereabouts lit up. Ever since my dad passed when we were kids, Nate had stepped into protective mode.

"Once I tell him what happened, he'll be sure to have plenty to say." *Starting with "I told you so."*

"Does he have any theories on who might've killed Bob?"

"Unlike almost everyone else around here, he hasn't really said. You know his *If I were a country, I'd be Switzerland* attitude."

"I've heard him voice a few opinions about Lars in the past. Not so neutral. Maybe he's just trying to protect Sarah."

I glanced at her in surprise. "What do you mean?"

"She was pretty shaken up after finding Bob's body," Kat said. "I wouldn't be surprised if she's asked him not to bring it up."

"I guess. But I'd like to know if he has any ideas, No one is more observant than him. He may have noticed something we haven't."

She frowned. "Like?"

"I don't know—a heated argument? A clandestine meeting?"

"Are those actual excerpts from *Dateline*, or are you paraphrasing?" she teased.

I huffed out an indignant breath and charged ahead of her. I didn't need to look behind me to know Kat was rolling her eyes.

Nate had the lemons prepped and put away by the time we reached the bar. He had a bottle of rosé in his hand, with two glasses sitting in front of him begging to be filled. We sat down on the nearest barstools. He looked from me to Kat, then back to me again. "Back away slowly. These glasses are already spoken for."

When we didn't laugh at his dumb joke, he groaned. No one was better at reading faces than Nate. The unsung talent of a professional bartender. "For the love of lemons. What now?"

I rubbed my forehead. "It's Nicky."

A server approached the bar. Nate poured the wine and slid the drinks forward. The server picked them up with a silent salute. I waited until she was out of earshot, then lowered my voice. "He's dead."

Nate's face drained of color. "When? Where? What happened?" His voice went up an octave with each question. A familial trait.

"Murder," Kat said bluntly. At least *she* kept her voice down.

"Lars found him at Evergreen Beach," I added. "He had some sort of head wound and had been left by the water."

Nate frowned. "Sounds like you're describing Bob Strapp's death."

"Yikes, I hadn't even thought of that," Kat said. "Coincidence?"

"No way. Whoever killed Bob must've killed Nicky too." Nate let out a heavy sigh. "When I saw Nicky earlier today, I knew something was up. He kept checking over his shoulder, as if worried someone was following him. I should've stepped in, asked if he was okay, but I didn't. I dismissed my intuition, assuming Bob's murder was just making him jumpy." He cursed under his breath.

"This isn't your fault, Nate," I said. "The guy was always sneaking around. You had no idea what would happen."

"Maybe not, but like you said, Nicky wasn't exactly the beach bum type." He brushed his hand through his hair. "Besides, he'd been shooting his mouth off about Bob's murder."

Hold the happy hour. "At the bar?"

"Oh yeah. He'd been my number-one customer since check-in. Bourbon on the rocks." He held up a forty-ounce bottle of Jack Daniel's. "I'm running low, and it's been only two days."

Kat clicked her tongue. "Loose lips sink ships."

I didn't like where this was going. "That would mean we're housing a killer." The idea had come up before. I'd hoped to forget it.

Nate shook his head. "Not necessarily. A lot of people have been milling around the bar. Locals too. I'd like to think it's my reputation as an amazing bartender, but it may have more to do with Bob Strapp's murder."

"Curiosity?"

"More like dancing on his grave. I've sold more champagne in the last day than I'd estimated for a month. People came to celebrate his demise."

My eyes widened. "I know people didn't like him but that seems a little extreme, no?"

"Not if he lost all your money."

"Do tell." As far as I knew, Bob Strapp had been disliked because he shot his mouth off a lot. A know-it-all who really knew nothing. But this wasn't the first time I'd begun to wonder if there was more to it.

"All I know is what Britt told Sarah."

"Which was?" I prompted.

"That Bob nearly cost her dad his business. But I have no idea whether that's true or if it's another case of Britt creating drama."

"Kat, have you heard anything about this?" I asked. As a local accountant, she would have the inside scoop. She had also worked at Britt's dad's company during college.

"Don't know for sure, but I'd be inclined to guess it's not true. Although . . ." She paused and bit her lip. "I did hear Bob caused problems *and* that Mr. Sanders almost lost his business. However, I'm not sure if the two are connected. Remember, I was only there during the summer months, so I wasn't privy to much."

"Some help you are," I teased. "The way I see it, anything Britt says should be taken with a mouthful of salt. Drama is like oxygen for her, a must-have for life."

"Hold on, I have another idea." Kat looked from me to Nate. "What if Nicky knew he was going to meet a murderer?"

"That doesn't make sense," I balked. "Why would he go and do that?"

Nate snapped his fingers. "He may have thought he could trust the person."

I couldn't see it. "But who? Nicky had a falling-out with Bob, no longer worked for Lars, and barely knew George."

Nate raised an eyebrow. "What about blackmail?"

"Nah. You overheard Nicky brag to guests that he knew who did it. If he planned to blackmail the killer, wouldn't he have kept his mouth shut?"

"Jess is right," Kat said. "No way he would've said anything if the killer was within earshot."

Nate smacked his hand down on the bar. "The killer might've been hiding in the shadows."

"Beating Nicky at his own game," Kat said.

Nate tapped his nose and pointed at her. "Ding ding ding."

"Are you suggesting someone lurked the lurker?" I had to admit this theory was plausible. "Who was around when Nicky was blabbing?"

Nate held up his hand, using his fingers to count. "Britt, Lars, George and Paula, Aunt Marnie . . ."

I racked my brain. "What about Travis? The twins?"

"Not sure about them." He scratched his forehead. "I could probably go back through my receipts to check."

Kat leaned over the bar and lowered her voice. "One of the twins was married to Nicky."

"You mean divorced from Nicky," Nate said. "The papers were delivered last week. She was just waiting for his signature."

My eyebrows shot up. "And you know this how?"

"Yesterday I had to act as ref. Nicky was sitting at the bar when one of the twins—Elle, I think—approached him. He clammed up, said it wasn't the time or place for a chat. Before Elle could respond, her twin stormed in and demanded Nicky leave. He said no, and things got ugly. She accused him of being a useless husband. He said Elle followed him, not the other way around. Then Elle teared up, said all she wanted was closure. That's when I stepped in. Elle left right away. Her sister told Nicky he'd better sign the divorce papers or he'd have to deal with her. Nicky returned to the bar and apologized. Said he didn't even know they were in town until last night."

Kat rubbed her hands together. "The plot thickens."

"Does that make Elle or her sister, Lila, the prime suspect?" I asked. "Because what Lila said sounds like a threat."

"You could be onto something," Kat agreed. "Bad husband and overprotective twin?"

A server dropped off two new orders at the bar, then went to seat a new table. Nate ducked down and retrieved two bottles of local IPA beer before popping off the caps. He looked from Kat to me. "Sorry, but I've got to go with Occam's razor." He grabbed an open bottle of rosé and filled three glasses, then double-checked the orders and grouped them together on a tray, ready for pickup.

I glanced at Kat. "What did he say?"

Kat shrugged, but a sticky-sweet voice behind me piped up. "Keep it simple, silly."

Britt. Just who I didn't need.

I turned in time to see her new bestie, Sarah, knock elbows with her, stifling a grin.

I glared at them, and Sarah flinched.

"Britt's kidding, Jess," Sarah said with a pout. "Gee whiz, what's up with you, sis?"

"Don't *sis* me, Sarah," I snapped. "I'm not in the mood."

"What I mean," Nate said slowly, shooting me a warning look, "is the simplest explanation is usually the right one. There's only one person I can think of with motive, means, and opportunity for both of these murders. And I'm guessing the police are thinking the same thing."

Lars. Nate had never liked him, but then again, neither had most everyone else. In a softer tone, my brother added, "He checks off all the boxes, Jess."

"Tsk, tsk. Nate the Great jumping to conclusions like that." Britt slid onto the barstool on the far side of Kat. She passed her empty wine glass to Nate and tapped it, indicating she needed a refill. "If you ask me, no one really cares who did the deed, or the deeds, as it now stands. Whether it was the hand of fate or the Ghost of Christmas Past, no one will even remember those two in a year. The whole town knows Bob was a class A jerk, and according to *STT*, the second vic was a wannabe guitarist whose wife had just filed for divorce. Hashtag loser." She turned to me. "Can I have an amen, sister?"

My mouth fell open, but I had no words. I wasn't sure what was more surprising: that *STT* had already reported the death of Nicky or that Britt was sort of on the same side as me, albeit in a cruel and heartless way.

A wicked grin crossed her face. "Admit it, Jess. The only reason you're sniffing around is to save yourself and Lars. If Bob and what's his face had died down the street and Lars had a neat and tidy alibi, you wouldn't give a sh—"

Kat slapped her hand down on the bar. "Shut up, Britt. Unless you have something useful to add, leave your two cents in the tip jar." She rolled back her shoulders, preparing for a showdown with Britt, whose face had twisted into an ugly sneer.

"Literally no one cares what you think, Katherine the Not-So-Great. Don't you have numbers to crunch somewhere?"

Kat sniffed. "You want to come at me? Give it your best shot. I literally couldn't care less."

It was Nate's turn to intervene. "Enough. Kat, stand down. And Britt? On the house." He filled her glass and pushed it toward her. "Please take this wine and go chill somewhere else with Sarah."

Kat and Britt glared at each other.

I leaned closer to Kat. "Ignore her."

"Gladly," Kat said, turning so her back faced Britt.

Sarah reached forward and picked up Britt's glass. "C'mon, Britt, I'll show you that hollow back pose you were asking me about." With one last withering look at Kat and me, Britt stalked away, following Sarah out the back gate.

A couple approached the end of the bar. Nate greeted them with a smile. He bounced toward them after a brief glance back at us. "You two need to stay away from her. Okay?"

Kat and I exchanged sheepish grins before mumbling our okays. Duking it out in our own bar wasn't exactly the next best step for our brand.

Nate turned his attention back to the couple at the bar. They ordered two frozen margaritas. He threw the ingredients into the blender and switched it on, then went back to chatting with them as the blender did its thing.

I propped my elbow on the bar and rested my chin on my hand. "Thanks for stepping in. Britt caught me off guard. For what it's worth, I thought you showed great restraint."

Kat clenched her fists. "I could kill that woman."

"Maybe not today. We've got enough bodies stacking up." I didn't blame her for feeling that way, though; I felt the same.

"Fair enough." She swiveled around on her stool and scanned the bar. The cool vibes had been reestablished. The place was hopping, and everyone looked happy. Even George and Paula had emerged from his room, both smiling broadly. Kat rubbed her face. "I think I need a little chill time. I'm going to hide in the office and scroll through funny animal videos on Reddit."

"Soul therapy? I like it. I'll join you after I butt in on Peorge."

She narrowed her eyes. "Paula and George? Why? We can't afford more trouble."

"I know. I'm just going to see if George wouldn't mind playing another set tonight."

"That would be a great way to maintain the chill mood. Although those two are nothing but hot, hot, hot." Kat wrinkled her nose as she watched the couple paw each other under the shade of an umbrella at the south end of the pool. Then, with a wave, she hopped off the stool and made her way back inside.

I sauntered over to where the couple were stretched out side by side, arriving just in time to see George reach out and give Paula's shoulder an affectionate squeeze.

Could their weekend fling last beyond the confines of our B and B? Hard for me to say. The closest thing I'd had to romance lately was a high five at the drive-in during a zombie apocalypse film.

I slipped off my flip-flops, which were still sandy from the beach, and ducked under the wide-brimmed umbrella. The two lovebirds seemed completely oblivious to my presence. I was about to clear my throat when I stepped on something sharp and let out a squeal of pain. Paula gave a start, and George flinched. *Way to make an entrance, Jess.*

"Hey, guys, sorry about that." I bent down and pulled a small pine needle from the bottom of my foot.

Paula rubbed the base of her neck. "Guess I'm not the only one on edge."

George sighed. "This is a great place, but duty calls. I've just been booked for a last-minute gig. I'm fixin' to leave before the sun hits the west side of Ashland."

I raised an eyebrow. "Uh . . ."

"Early," Paula said, shooting George an affectionate grin. "He means early."

"Right." I nodded. "I completely understand. I just wish we could figure out what happened here before you leave."

Paula reached out and squeezed George's hand. "That would be nice. But either way, I'll make sure to give this place a glowing review. You've done a good job, Jess. And," she added, her face flushing with joy, "it'll always hold a special place for us, won't it, G?"

"Like the roses from my mother's garden, darlin'."

"Thanks, guys, much appreciated." I squatted to be closer to their level. "I have one more favor to ask."

"Shoot," George said.

"Since this is the last night of your visit and you were so amazing last night, is there any chance you'd consider an encore performance? I'd like to see everyone leave here on a high note."

"Guess it's not exactly the opening weekend you were hoping for, is it?" Paula said.

Paula was so different when she wasn't filling the role of evil sidekick. It was possible I was beginning to like her. A calm self-assurance seemed to have blossomed, and I was here for it. "You can say that again."

She sighed. "It's kinda funny. Your nightmare weekend has been my dream come true."

George sat up and patted Paula's knee. "I'd be happy to do another show for you. It's no trouble at all."

I clasped my hands together gratefully. "Thank you."

We quickly established that his first set would start as the sun went down. With that done and dusted, I left the lovebirds to their canoodling and took my leave.

Time to move on to the next task on my list: a visit to another musician. Hopefully, that talk would go just as well as this one had. Travis Sanders had made an appearance in the security video, but I hadn't seen him since. He'd always been a quiet guy who liked heavy music and flannel shirts, like his idol Kurt Cobain. But as any good Murderino knew, sometimes the least assuming person had the most to hide.

Chapter
Twenty-Four

I knocked on the door of the modest wood cabin, then stood back to get a better look at the lilac and pink hydrangeas encircling the home. Like smart accessories on a simple outfit, the flowers prettied up the otherwise plain house while sending out vibes of welcoming and warmth. I marveled at the vibrancy of the colors and breathed in the sweet scent as heavy footsteps drew closer.

Travis's wife, Ashlyn, swung the door open. In spite of dark circles, her eyes were bright, and her face lit up when she saw me. Perpetually perky, Ashlyn had always reminded me of strawberry shortcake with a pecan crust, like my grandma used to make. With light-red curls, she was sweet and nutty, in direct contrast with Travis's quieter, broody nature. Hence the nickname Dread and Ginger, which the couple had acquired after she dragged him onto the dance floor during the spring dance of their junior year.

Ashlyn's hands were wrapped around a small bundle attached to her chest. Poking out of the top were two blue eyes under a dusting of wispy red curls, almost identical to Ashlyn's. My hands flew up and covered my mouth.

She swayed back and forth in the doorway. "Hi, Jess. This is a nice surprise!"

"You're telling me! Congratulations, Ashlyn!"

"Thank you. Good thing you didn't drop by thirty minutes ago. You might've thought we'd hatched a monster." She bent forward and touched her nose to the baby's head. A gurgle of laughter erupted, followed by a hiccup.

Ashlyn pulled her head back up and beamed at me. "She does that a lot."

"Such a cutie." I reached my finger out. A tiny hand gripped it. Little legs kicked from inside a light-pink sleeper. "What's her name?"

Ashlyn expertly freed my finger, then caressed the little hand with her own. "This is Janis."

I grinned. "No need to ask where she got her name. She's already stolen a piece of *my* heart."

Ashlyn and Travis had been inseparable since they first got together. When Travis was in the band with Lars, Ashlyn and I had been the dedicated girlfriends who showed up at every gig. We wore Sharpied T-shirts emblazoned with the band's logo, and we always cheered our hearts out, even—or perhaps especially—when the crowds were sparse. Ashlyn was kind and easygoing and all the good things that Travis's older sister, Britt, was not.

"C'mon in," Ashlyn said. "As long as you promise not to judge the mess."

"I swear to notice nothing other than your beautiful new daughter and your cheery bright smile."

Ashlyn backed up to make room for me in the narrow entranceway. I followed her and Janis into the small living room and took a seat on a well-worn blue velvet sofa. A squeak from underneath me made me jump, and I pulled out a small rubber giraffe.

Ashlyn's cheeks flushed as she held out her hand and took it from me. "Sorry."

The baby stuff competed with guitars and amplifiers, each piece fighting for dominance in the cramped room. Ashlyn stayed standing, gently rocking back and forth while rubbing the outside of the baby carrier attached to her middle.

A familiar scent wafted through the air, and I breathed it in. "Is that fresh-brewed hazelnut coffee I smell?"

"My guilty pleasure. After having none for nine and a half months, I allow myself two precious cups a day. Want one?"

"You know I do." How many nights had we slipped out of shows to find coffee to get us through the long, loud nights? Nothing hurt a boyfriend's feelings more than his girlfriend yawning during his set. "Aren't you worried it'll keep you up, though? I thought new moms were supposed to sleep as much as they can."

"Janis has decided she likes sleeping during the day."

"Like a vampire?" I teased.

Ashlyn giggled. "Exactly. It's pretty common for newborns."

She glided over to an island that separated the living space from the kitchen. A French press was waiting to be poured, a stack of white coffee mugs within easy reach. Ashlyn grabbed two and poured carefully, with fully extended arms to keep the baby away from the hot drink. "Janis will change her habits as she grows, but for now I rely on fresh brews to see me through. I savor every last sip."

"Good for you," I said. "Where's Travis?"

"He's over at the school but should be home soon."

Ashlyn didn't need to ask how I took my coffee; we were purists when it came to French press. She brought two steaming cups over to the sofa and passed one to me. "It's been tough for him. He's working extra hours these days. Poor guy's there from morning till night. Sometimes I wonder if we should put a bed in his office."

I'd heard through the grapevine that Travis had opened a music school in town. By all accounts, it was doing well, but running a small business was hard and a baby was expensive. "How does he manage?"

"The power of love." Ashlyn set down her coffee mug and pulled Janis free from her carrier. She put the wiggle-worm into a playpen, then picked her coffee back up. "Anyway, how about you? I've heard your new bed-and-breakfast is gorgeous. It will be my first destination when my mom comes to stay with us in a few weeks. Rumor has it Nate makes the best peach Bellini mocktails in the entire Hudson Valley."

"You won't be disappointed. Call me on your way over, and we'll have it ready for your arrival."

"I'll be daydreaming about it until then. Becoming a mom is the best thing I've ever done, but I didn't know this level of exhaustion even existed. But hey, you're probably feeling the same way. I've heard you and Kat have spent the last few months working your butts off to get ready for this weekend."

"It *has* been a little intense, but I still get seven hours of sleep most nights."

"Probably not in the last few days, I bet." She gave me a sympathetic look. "I'm sorry about what happened. It's so bizarre."

"That's for sure." My stomach churned. It was now or never. "I was a little surprised to see Travis there opening night."

She frowned. "Huh? No, he didn't make it. He was working late Friday night."

Weird. Why would he keep that from her? Before I could decide whether or not I should tell her, a loud black motorcycle roared into the driveway.

Janis began to gurgle and kick her miniature feet. I watched with delight. Ashlyn grinned. "She knows that sound."

I laughed. "A daddy's girl already, huh?"

"Through and through." Ashlyn beamed. "He's the best dad in the world too."

A minute later, the door swung open and Travis's tall, lanky figure appeared in the doorway. Before Ashlyn or I had the chance to greet him, he muttered a few obscenities under his breath and kicked away a small gathering of shoes at the doorway.

"Ash! I told you not to leave crap around the entrance all the time. How many times—"

He froze when he saw me. "Jess," he said. "This is a surprise."

I gave him a small wave. "Hey, Travis."

His eyes narrowed. "What are you doing here?"

Ashlyn shot me an apologetic smile. "Jess came by to meet the baby, hon." She gathered up her bundle of love and sashayed across the living room.

"Daddy's home," she cooed.

Travis's shoulders dropped and his face softened as he took his daughter into his arms, prompting another happy gurgle. A tiny hand reached out and grabbed his nose. He drew Janis up to his face and kissed her chubby tummy, then buried his face in her rolls of neck. When he looked up, all signs of trouble were gone, replaced by a goofy grin.

Ashlyn held out her hands and took the baby back, reaching forward to give Travis a kiss in the process. "You got to say hi to Daddy, sweetie. Now it's time for your nap." The baby began to fuss in protest. "Sorry, Jess, you'll have to excuse me." She took Janis down the hall, holding up the baby's arm to wave goodbye. I waved back. Ashlyn made it to the nursery just as Janis began to wail. *Tired? Hungry? Just plain mad? Can moms tell the difference?*

Travis dropped into a beat-up recliner and leaned back while pulling up the lever on the side. The footrest popped up and he sank back into the chair, clasping both hands behind his head. He pulled the elastic band out of his hair and shook his head, allowing a wad of thinning hair to settle over his shoulders. His thick brow furrowed and his dark eyes studied me, a cloud of suspicion drifting over his features. "Jess, it's good to see you and all, but tell me why you're really here."

I shifted in my seat. Travis had always been direct. "I'm sure you heard Bob Strapp was killed."

"I did." He didn't try to hide the upbeat tone of his voice.

I frowned. "Lars is in trouble. The police seem to think he killed Bob."

He snorted. "So you're looking for a scapegoat?"

"No. I just want to find the truth." My tone was firm. "I saw you were there that night and thought maybe you saw something that could help Lars."

"I know what happened," Travis said.

My mouth went dry. "You do?"

"Yeah. Lars finally stopped being a puppet and grew a pair."

Heat rose in my cheeks. Was this a joke to him? I glanced out the window as a rusty gray pickup truck raced down the quiet street. When I looked back, Travis was still watching me. I shook off the unnerving feeling it gave me. Time to get to the point. "Did you see Bob that night?"

He quirked an eyebrow. "Is that what my best pal said?"

When they'd been in the band together, Lars sung and Travis played guitar. Other members had drifted in and out, but those two had been inseparable from the day they'd met on the school bus, each carrying the same Def Leppard album.

Ashlyn reappeared. "Sorry to interrupt." She started to search the room, then picked up the rubber giraffe I'd sat on earlier. "Aha, there it is."

Travis reached into the back pocket of his jeans and pulled out a ratty old notebook. He tossed it onto the coffee table.

Ashlyn looked from the book to Travis. "Are you going to show Jess the new song you wrote for—"

Travis shot her a look. She stopped midsentence and bit her lip.

Odd. Why was a new song a secret?

The tension in the room had grown thicker. Before I was asked to leave or these two began to argue, I needed to find neutral ground. "I heard you opened a music school, Travis. My mom said kids around town fight for spots in the music camps during summer break."

Travis pointed to a framed photo on the wall. "Opened a year ago." The picture showed him and Ashlyn, prebaby, standing next to the town mayor, all smiling. Travis had an oversized pair of scissors in his hands. Behind him was a decorative red ribbon draped across the front of an obviously new shop with shiny guitars and trumpets displayed in the front window. The sign above read *The Music Academy.* "That was a good day."

"Do you still have time to play your own music?" I looked at his notebook. "You always wrote the best songs. Lars used to say he'd give his firstborn to have your talent."

Ashlyn plunked herself down on the couch and clapped her hands. "I remember that," she said with a laugh. "You used to tell him he'd better find another currency or you'd walk. It was so exciting how you two had your entire future planned out before the end of junior year."

"We were so young. Lars and I planned to live in Hollywood and eat caviar for breakfast. He wanted to have six kids, five dogs, and several gold records. No wonder we didn't work out."

"Priorities change." Travis's expression darkened at the mention of Lars. "For him, all that mattered in the end was the glory. It was never about the music. I should've seen that."

"Lars isn't perfect," I said. "But he loves music just as much as you. So he likes the spotlight. He wouldn't be the first musician to feel that way. David Lee Roth? Axl Rose? Dee Snider?"

He waved his hand. "All right, all right, I get your point."

I leaned forward and tapped his knee. "Aren't you at least a little proud that he wrote a song that catapulted him into the spotlight?"

Travis choked out a bitter laugh. "That light is fading, Jess. Lars is going down. You should jump off the boat before he pulls you under."

I frowned. "If you're so done with him, then why did you show up to watch him play on Friday night?"

He shook his head. "I wasn't there to see Lars. I had business."

Ashlyn frowned. "You never mentioned going there."

"You know I had that meeting."

"You didn't mention it was at the bar where Lars was playing."

"Does it really matter, Ash?"

She shook her head. "I guess not. Anyway, why don't you tell Jess about the meeting." When he hesitated, Ash leaned forward and squeezed his hand. "It's okay. We can trust Jess."

Travis shrugged. "Sure." He looked at me. "My sister gave me the heads-up that George Havers was going to be there. She said he needed a new guitar player and that she'd introduce us."

"Mind if I ask how and why Britt would know George Havers's whereabouts?"

Ashlyn looked from me to Travis. "Britt's working on a marketing plan to boost George's career. He fired his manager, and she swooped in at just the right time."

None of this made any sense. "Sorry, guys, I'm totally lost here. I thought Britt worked for a marketing company." *Who told me that? Mom, probably.*

"Close. She works for a PR firm," Travis said.

Ashlyn leaned forward. "It's a good job. She has a big office in the city."

Travis waved an arm. "Hit the ground running because she brought Lars in as a client after his big win. Gotta hand it to her. My sister always knew how to work an advantage."

My chest tightened. "Lars is working with Britt too?"

"Yeah." Ashlyn shot me a rueful smile. "Why else would she be here? She's not exactly the sentimental type."

A tiny seed of rage burned in the pit of my stomach. Lars had never mentioned working with Britt. Had it slipped his mind? Probably not. I could give him the benefit of the doubt, especially under the circumstances, but I wouldn't. Not this time. History had taught me that Lars had a habit of keeping things from me, things he knew I wouldn't like. This time felt even worse, because it wasn't the first time Britt had been part of an omission.

I forced a smile. "Smart move for Britt. With a hot new client in tow, she would have a lot of negotiating power. Big client in exchange for a big job. After signing Lars, it would make sense for her to be given the task of bringing in George too."

Travis shook his head. "You sound just like her."

I couldn't bring myself to thank him. Besides, I wasn't sure it was a compliment.

"Britt bragged about how she initiated a meeting with George at his show. Convinced him to give her a shot," Ashlyn explained. The baby began to cry again from down the hallway. Ashlyn put her finger to her lips, then stood and followed the sound, giraffe in hand.

I lowered my voice. "Is that why George showed up this weekend?"

Travis got up and peered down the hallway. The crying had stopped, so he continued into the kitchen. He opened the fridge, pulled out a beer without offering one to me, and returned to his chair, stretching his legs out as he reclined it back. He used the key ring attached to his jeans pocket to pop the cap off the bottle.

He took a long sip before answering. "Like I said, George is on the lookout for a new guitarist, and Britt mentioned me."

Ashlyn returned and sat on the sofa next to Travis's recliner, reaching out for his hand like she used to do. "Britt bragged about

Travis, said he was a master guitar player. To prove it, she showed him Facebook posts of Travis playing. As soon as George saw that, he wanted a meeting."

"Wow." I couldn't hide my surprise. Britt had gone out of her way for someone other than herself?

"Don't be too impressed," Travis said with a subtle shake of his head. "My sister knows from my years of complaints that it's not easy to put together a band that gels. She'd score big brownie points with him if she could help out."

"It's a bit like matchmaking," Ashlyn explained. "Travis has spent the last month learning all of George's music."

"And Paula called on a daily basis, making sure I was practicing," Travis complained.

"Paula?" I asked, confused. "How does she come into this?"

"She's George's handler."

"Say what?"

Ashlyn snorted. "Yeah, guess she took her job title literally."

Travis cringed. "Ewww. That's my cousin, remember?"

"Sorry, hon," Ashlyn said with a giggle.

I bit my lip. "This is getting too complicated."

"And I'm bored with this conversation," Travis said. "You still haven't said why you're here, Jess."

"I'm trying to help Lars."

He scoffed. "Good luck to you. Sounds like you're going to need it." He drank the rest of his beer in one long gulp and slammed down the bottle. The loud bang made me jump. It woke the baby too. With a sigh, Ashlyn scooched forward on the sofa, but he put his hand up. "I'll go. I'm done anyway." Janis wailed. He turned and reached out his hand. Ashlyn took it. "Sorry, Ash."

Her eyes widened, and she gave an almost imperceptible nod. "It's okay. Everything's going to be okay."

He pulled his hair back into a ponytail and plodded down the hall.

When he was gone, Ashlyn turned to me. "You should probably go too, Jess. Travis just isn't himself right now. He's under a lot of pressure. Another time?"

I stood up. "Yeah, no problem, of course."

We walked together to the front door. Ashlyn opened the door and followed me outside. "You understand, right?"

"Not really." *Should I?*

She glanced back inside before silently closing the door behind her. "Here's the thing. This was supposed to be Travis's big shot. Britt had a plan to capitalize on the rivalry between Lars and George. Bring the two together onstage. Make peace. Maybe even sing a few lines from each other's songs. Travis was going to play guitar in the background to keep the show seamless. Bob Strapp screwed everything up."

I flinched. I hadn't expected such a heartless response to a man's murder. Not from Ashlyn, at least.

"Ash?" Travis called from the bedroom, where the baby had only increased its wails. "I think Janis is hungry." There was a pause. "Ash? You there?"

Ashley pulled the door open and took a step inside before turning back. "I gotta run. If I were you, I'd stay out of this mess. You've got enough on your plate. And so do I. So unless you really want to just come by for coffee, it might be better for you to not stop by for a while. Okay?"

My face flushed. "Yeah, I'm sorry."

She held the door. "Don't be. But things have been hard. I get that a guy died, but Travis's dream might be dead now too. This was an opportunity that might not happen again. I've got to go figure out how to pick up the pieces."

I leaned in and gave her a hug. "Of course. Go."

I spun on my heel and got back into the van. It was time to sort out the clues. Rock and roll had never been for the faint of heart. But had I begun to crack open a solid-gold motive for murder?

Chapter Twenty-Five

I sat in my van in Ashlyn and Travis's driveway, now more confused than ever. There was so much to consider. I needed a minute to unravel my thoughts.

To begin with, there was Ashlyn. She'd always been a friend, but her loyalty was with Travis. So I had to take everything she told me with a grain of salt, just in case she was protecting him.

And what about Travis? He was still so angry. Was it enough to drive him to murder?

Then there was Lars. He hadn't mentioned his ties with Britt. Why not? Was it based on some misguided hope of rekindling our doomed high school romance, or could there be something more?

Speaking of romance, what about the twins? Wasn't the spouse always the first suspect? Elle's crocodile tears told me she hadn't exactly been heartbroken after finding Nicky.

Next was George Havers. With his career taking off, why partner with Lars now? And why risk a scandal hooking up with Paula?

That led to Britt. Would she really go out of her way to help her brother? It didn't align with her selfish ways.

On the flip side, Aunt Marnie was hiding something from me. What was her secret, and why wouldn't she tell me?

226

And finally, Bob and Nicky. Someone had killed them; that was the only thing I still knew for sure.

I reached for my phone. Kat picked up on the first ring.

"Remember when we laughed about all the weird stuff we'd probably encounter as innkeepers?"

"Hello to you too," she said. I could hear splashing and laughter in the background. "What's up?"

I pressed two fingers to my forehead. "My brain is on a spin cycle."

"What? Hold on for a sec, Jess." Kat's voice grew muffled. I pressed my phone closer to my ear so I could hear what was going on. She was using her happy-to-see-you voice, normally reserved for puppies with floppy paws and anyone with access to ice cream. "Hey, kid," I heard her say. "Can you try to remember to pick your car up? Two people have slipped on it." *Slipping on a car? What's going on?* There was some shuffling, then Kat saying to someone, "There you go." Another shuffle.

"Sorry, Jess." Kat was back with me, voice now at its regular inside-voice level. She cleared her throat. "Replacing a toy ball with a toy car may not have been my best idea. Anyway, did you say you went to a spin class? That's great, but I thought you were going to see Ashlyn and Travis."

"Shhh. Don't announce it to the world."

She *tsk*ed. "C'mon. You should be proud of yourself. You've been blabbing on and on about taking one of those classes since you came back. I think it's great you're finally doing it."

I raked my hand through my hair in frustration. "Kat, this conversation is a fail. Can you go somewhere quiet so we can talk properly?"

"Not really. Marnie is folding towels in the supply closet, Penny is under siege with new reservations, Paula is using the printer in our office, and your mom caught a camera crew trying to sneak in the back. Did I tell you she was here? Never mind; she's gone now. Took it upon herself to plant a chair next to the camera van to make sure they don't do any more shady stuff."

I looked at my phone to check the time. "How long have I been gone?"

"Hold on, I'm moving into the shade." The background noise faded slightly. "Hello?"

"Still here."

"Good," she said. "Me too. But I need a break. Should we go to the Coffee Haus for a quick catch-up?"

Smart girl. I nodded into the phone. "You mean an executive meeting."

"Yes, I do." Another splash. "Hey, c'mon now, these are my only shoes." Kat muttered a few obscenities under her breath. "Jess, pick me up?"

"On my way."

The phone went dead. I dropped it onto the passenger seat and turned up the radio. Within ten minutes, Kat was seated next to me and we were heading into town.

Our classic hippie-era VW van didn't have air conditioning, but with the windows down, there was a good breeze. However, no matter how many times we'd had it detailed, the earthy undertones of cedarwood and frankincense haunted the interior whenever the fan was at full blast.

We parked in front of the coffee shop a few minutes later. As soon as I opened my door, the scent of fresh-brewed coffee beckoned me, and I took a minute to breathe it in. The high-pitched whir of an espresso bean grinder was music to my ears. I hopped out of the van with a bounce in my step.

The café door was propped open and a gaggle of young women burst out, each holding a frothy concoction topped with whipped cream and chocolate sprinkles. Kat and I stood to the side to let them pass before venturing in.

"Can you get me a large green tea?" Kat said, craning her neck to get a better look at the seating area. She had an inch or two over most of the other patrons. "There's a spot by the window. I'll go snag it." She took off.

I gave a thumbs-up to her receding back, then turned to peruse the impressive menu, which was filled with options for even the pickiest of java junkies.

"Jess," a familiar high-pitched voice said. I looked around. Where was she? A hand shot up from behind the counter, reminding me of a scene from a B-list horror movie.

"Mona?"

Mona Dumbleries, octogenarian, business owner, and coffee aficionado, popped her head up. "Sorry. I'm in the weeds back here. Just grabbing a fresh supply of beans."

She rose with a large bag in each hand, dropping them on the counter simultaneously with a thud. Tall and sturdy, Mona towered over most folks, displaying an energy and vigor mainly reserved for people a few decades younger. She ran her fingers through her white fluffy hair and shot me a hundred-watt smile. "Juicy gossip brings folks out in droves. Warn me next time, would you?"

My eyes widened, and I couldn't help but grin back at her. "Next time there's a murder?"

"A heads-up would give me a chance to prepare," she said with a wink. "I'm swamped."

"I'll keep that in mind." Never one to hold back an opinion, Mona didn't give a hoot what others thought.

A petite young woman with a lightning-blue streak in her hair bounced up next to Mona. "What can I get for you today, Jess?"

I studied the overhead menu. "It all looks good, but I think I'll stick with my regular order. A flat white—"

Mona snapped her fingers. "With oat milk and a sprinkle of cocoa on top."

The barista glanced at Mona, then back at me for confirmation.

"That's the one," I said. "How do you remember that?"

Mona tapped her forehead. "The *New York Times* crossword and a double shot of sudoku every morning keep me sharp."

"Good to know," I said. "And Wordle?"

"That's my after-dinner treat."

"Anything else?" the barista asked me.

"A green tea for my partner in crime, thanks."

Mona scanned the room till she saw Kat and waved enthusiastically. "Glad to see you two are managing okay with everything going on."

Clearly, she'd been updated. The Coffee Haus was the hub of our small community.

"It's been a challenge."

"There's no preparing for murder," Mona said. "All you can do is make sure your guests are well taken care of and hope the police work fast without getting in the way of folks's vacation time."

"We're doing our best. What's the word around here? Any rumors floating around?" More than once in the last two days, I'd wondered whether a death on opening weekend would dampen the local community's enthusiasm about the B and B.

"Why don't you have a seat with Kat?" Mona said. "I'll bring your drinks over when they're ready, and we can chat then. I'm past due for a break anyway."

"Sounds good to me." I looked over my shoulder to find that the line had grown so much it was threatening to spill outside. I paid for the drinks and threaded my way back through the crowd to our table.

It would be good to get Mona's take on what had happened. I was curious to find out what people were saying about the two murders at the Pearl and whether, if at all, Bob and Nicky's deaths might hurt our reputation. Plus, I was also hoping that Mona might have heard whisperings of who might have been involved. While Nicky was from out of town, Bob was local, and no doubt tongues would be wagging about that.

Kat had snapped up a window table overlooking Main Street and didn't see me approach because she was focused on something outside. I slid into the seat across from her. "What's so interesting? Did the mayor decide to hand out autographed photos of himself in the center square again?"

Not even a snicker. Kat was too fixated on whatever had snagged her attention in the first place. "Across the street," she said, tapping the window. "Look who's crushing widowhood."

I followed her gaze and saw Elle and Lila looking anything but mournful. Lila, still wearing the pink dress and matching scarf she'd had on at the beach, was whispering something in Elle's ear, and Elle was laughing. Not exactly the picture of a grieving widow. She pulled out a wad of cash and fanned it out to show her sister. Elle twirled around, then struck a pose, showing off a white linen dress that looked remarkably similar to one recently featured in the window display at the high-end consignment shop in town. Both women did a little dance, then carried on down the sidewalk.

Love and money. It had been only three or four hours since Elle's husband had died. While not everyone grieved the same way, flaunting a mysterious windfall of cash seemed a little off to me. Besides, Fletcher Lake was more than a hop, skip, and jump from Vegas. Where on earth had Elle gotten her hands on all that dough?

231

Two cups slid onto the table, giving me a start. Across from me, Kat's leg jerked, slamming into the underside of the white granite tabletop. *Ouch.*

"I'm sorry, dear." At almost six feet tall, Mona hovered over us like a vision in peach. She wore a calf-length silk cardigan over a light top with matching pants. "Are you okay?"

Kat's face flushed. "Mm-hmm." She rubbed the top of her knee furiously but smiled through the pain.

Mona glanced from Kat to me, her eyes narrowing. "Maybe I should redo this order using strictly decaf. The pair of you are much too jumpy."

I reached out my hands for the coffee. "Don't you dare!"

Kat pulled her steaming cup of tea close, adding, "Keep your paws off my property."

A snort escaped from Mona as I scooched over to make room for her. "Can't blame you given everything that's happened."

I breathed in the not-so-subtle scent of Chanel No. 5 as I snuck a peek back outside. *Shoot.* Elle and Lila had disappeared. Where had the sisters gone with their fistful of money?

"Listen, you two." Mona sniffed, then took a sip of plain black coffee. "What happened at your pretty new bed-and-breakfast is a tragedy. And I may not know a flying fig about the second victim, but I did know Bob Strapp. He was a snake through and through. I'll never understand why he tempted fate by coming back here after what he did. It was a big gamble . . . and a big loss. But you know, that was the story of his life."

Mona is Fletcher Lake's number-one fan. After she lost her husband several years ago, local residents stepped up and helped the grief-stricken firecracker get back on her feet. Mona repaid their kindness by throwing herself into town life, joining every committee under the sun, and rallying to get Fletcher Lake on every top-ten

list this side of NYC. If anyone had a finger on the pulse of this
town, it was our Mona.

Kat gave her a wry smile. "Sheesh, Mona. How do you really feel?"

"If I'd had a pitchfork on hand when he first came back to town,
I would've joined in the chase and poked that son of a gun where the
sun don't shine."

An angry mob? I wasn't a fan of Bob's either, but Mona's description
didn't gel with the vision I held of my hometown.

"Can you rewind a little bit?" I asked. "I think I'm missing something. I mean, we all know that Bob wasn't a town favorite, but I still
don't get why he was considered worse than that grumpy farmer who
doesn't let people take photos of his roadside sunflowers or the town
inspector who insists on everyone redoing their renovation permits
at least three times."

Mona gave me a hard look, as if I'd grown a third eye. "You must
be joking."

"Huh? What are we missing?" I said.

Her eyes narrowed. "You really don't know?"

"Know what?" I threw my hands up in frustration. Kat was
frowning and looking equally confused. At least we were together in
being out of the loop.

Mona folded her arms across her chest and leaned in. "That man
was a no-good cheat. He swindled people out of their savings and
gambled their money away. I'm surprised your aunt didn't physically
block his entry at your pretty pink front entrance."

My stomach roiled. What did Aunt Marnie have to do with it?
I thought back to the argument between her and Bob that Nate had
mentioned. She said it was over parking. Had there been more to it?

Kat snorted with laughter. "Auntie M would be more inclined to
hide her money in a shoebox under a mattress than trust some fast-
talking sleazeball."

"If you say so." Mona sat up and pursed her lips. *Uh-oh*. She knew something about my aunt, and I had a very bad feeling it wasn't anything I'd be happy about.

"Mona, please. What made you think of my aunt?"

Mona squirmed in her seat. She side-eyed Kat, who took the hint and made a zip-the-lip gesture over her mouth. Mona cleared her throat before speaking, then lowered her voice. "It's all very hush-hush. I just assumed Kat would've found out when she was interning or that Marnie, poor thing, would've told you. My mistake."

What was she implying?

Kat leaned forward. "Mona, when I interned at Sanders Investments, there were strict policies and rules. We weren't allowed to share details of anyone's personal finances, even amongst ourselves. And if anyone was caught asking questions about things that didn't concern them, they were fired."

Mona cleared her throat. "I'll tell you this. Up until two years ago, Nigel Sanders used to have a large cappuccino and a slice of my signature lemon loaf every morning at seven thirty sharp. Then one day he switched to a basic drip coffee at six AM. I asked Helga Mortgensen, his secretary, if he was on a diet and if she thought he'd like a morning glory muffin better. If he had been, I figured it would be a good reason to try a new recipe I found in the Food Section of the New York Times. High protein, low fat."

She was stalling. *Why?* Kat shot me an *Is she ever going to land this puppy?* look.

I pressed my lips together and sighed impatiently. "So was Nigel Sanders on a diet?"

Mona lowered her voice still further so that we had to strain to hear her. "Only the financial kind. Apparently, his firm was in deep trouble. Lost most of their clients due to a sudden drop in proceeds after a charlatan pulled the wool over everyone's eyes, including Nigel Sanders himself."

"Are you talking about Bob Strapp?" Kat asked.

Mona met Kat's gaze. "Mm-hmm."

"So you're saying . . ." I couldn't finish my sentence.

Kat stared at me, the color drained from her face. "Jess, that's around the time the firm almost lost its license. The details were never shared, but I remember thinking something fishy was going down. Everyone involved, including some staff members and select clients, agreed to sign nondisclosure agreements before a settlement was reached. I just never made the connection."

"Until now," I concluded.

"Ding, ding, ding!" Mona touched the tip of her nose with her index finger. "Give that girl a prize."

"That could mean that Mr. Sanders had to pay out of pocket for a chunk of the losses that Bob incurred while working for him," Kat explained.

"No one knows for sure," Mona warned. "But there are rumors about who was affected."

My mouth went dry. "Including Aunt Marnie?"

Mona shrugged. "I'm not the one you should be asking."

My cheeks burned. "If she was the victim of some sort of scam, she would've told me." I tried to sound confident, but I doubted my words as soon as they left my mouth. Aunt Marnie was a free spirit, but she was also proud. And could be stubborn. Had there been signs something was wrong but no one noticed?

Since moving home, I'd been so busy with the reno, I barely knew what day of the week it was, never mind if someone was trying to hide a personal crisis.

A red flag went up in my mind. Why hadn't Aunt Marnie gone on a trip for over two years? Ever since she was a teenager, she'd never stayed home for longer than a few months at a time, yet she hadn't been out of state in at least a year. And why was she really working at the B and B? She said she wanted to help out, but was it actually because she was stone cold broke?

When my grandmother passed away, she'd left a considerable sum to both my aunt and my mom. Did Marnie lose the money in an investment scam set up by Bob?

Had we just stumbled on a legit motive for murder for my lovable aunt? I pushed aside all thoughts of Travis, Ashlyn, and even Lars being involved. I had to talk to my aunt and find out the whole truth and nothing but the truth before the police came crashing through her door.

Chapter
Twenty-Six

When Kat and I returned from the café, we found Aunt Marnie chilling with a handful of guests behind the B and B. They were all sitting on Adirondack chairs around the circular brick firepit, which was glowing against the low-lying sun. Nearby speakers played Norah Jones as guests leaned back, listening to Marnie's tales from her days on the road. Marnie reveled in the heyday of her youth and loved sharing stories of her adventures, from backstage to backwoods, where she'd often camped with friends. Next to her lay her tarot deck and a collapsed table, making me wonder if those in attendance were planning to get their cards read.

As Kat and I appeared on the fringes of the group, Marnie stretched out her arms, signaling for us to join them. "Everyone, make room for my beautiful niece Jess and the lovely Kat Miller."

My heart hurt as I looked into her warm face. "Looks inviting, but I actually need to talk to you in private."

Aunt Marnie's smile faltered a little, but she quickly recovered with a gracious nod. "Duty calls, folks. Kat here happens to be an ace at numbers, so feel free to ask any daunting financial questions you may have always wanted to know but were afraid to ask." She got to her feet and offered Kat the chair. "This is a safe space here, and we're all friends, right?"

There was a murmur of agreement from the half dozen or so guests sitting in chairs, sipping on mimosas, beer, or sparkling water.

"I'm inspired by this place and wonder if I could give it a try." The comment came from a trendy woman with a bright-red pixie cut, wearing loose denim overalls and a teal cropped tank top. "Not start a bed-and-breakfast, but maybe an online jewelry business."

Kat nodded as she sat down. "Are you asking me for advice?"

Aunt Marnie eagerly introduced the women to each other. "Kat, this is Phoebe. She designs her own earrings and bracelets using dapping tools and Swarovski crystals. She has a real talent."

Phoebe flushed and bit her lip. "The basics of what I'd need to start out?"

Kat smiled, settling back into the chair. "I may have a few tips and tidbits to share."

Another guest held up a glass to Kat, offering her a drink. Kat shrugged and gave a nod of encouragement. The guest filled the glass and passed it to her. She held it up in a silent *cheers* and then began to think out loud, listing some of the items Phoebe would need to consider. "Raw materials, of course," she began. "Then there's your tools—sounds like you already have that part." She paused and took a sip of wine. "My biggest suggestion? Focus on branding."

The conversation continued as Aunt Marnie and I headed back into the bar area. We sat at a table out of earshot of the rest of the patrons. Nate was off duty, giving us the opportunity to chat without interruption. His backup, a local snowboarder named Craig, gave me a friendly wave from behind the bar.

Aunt Marnie leaned forward. "What's going on, sweetheart? You look grim. Not that I'm blaming you. It's been a tough two days." She snapped her fingers. "Maybe I should make you a lavender sleep spray. My collection of essential oils would even make a white witch green with envy." She wiggled her eyebrows at me as if daring me.

"Thank you, Aunt Marnie, but no, that's not what I wanted to talk to you about."

"Oh? Then what is it? You know you can tell me anything." She patted my arm and gave me an encouraging nod.

I looked her in the eye. "Do you feel the same about me? That you can tell me anything?"

She frowned. "Of course I do, sweetie. You're my favorite niece."

"I'm your only niece, Auntie M." I grinned in spite of myself. That joke never got old.

"Okay, so what are you on about? Tell me."

I swallowed. This was probably the first time in my entire life I'd felt nervous around my aunt. Not a good feeling. "Mona down at the Coffee Haus mentioned you and Bob Strapp may have had history?"

Marnie's breezy attitude shifted, and her body went rigid. An uncharacteristic scowl appeared, making her face droop.

"Mona should stick with sharing recipes, not secrets."

My stomach tensed. "So it's true? You invested money with Bob?"

"Invested? Ha. It was more of a give-and-take situation. I gave him money, and he took it. Left me penniless, that scoundrel."

I lowered my voice. "When was this?"

"A few years ago. I ran into Bob. Bragged he'd been hired by Nigel Sanders and could guarantee I'd make enough money to travel around the world in style for the rest of my life." She rubbed her wrinkled hands over her face. "I thought it might be fun to upgrade from my youth hostel accommodations." With a sigh, she lowered her hands. "In other words, I was greedy. Gave him my whole nest egg."

My mouth dropped open. "But that would mean—"

"I'm broke. The money I got from selling you this house barely covered my debts." Marnie sighed. "Worst part? The shame. I never needed fancy things, and I've been most places at least once. But if your mom ever found out I'd been taken by that slick scumbag, I could never face her again."

"Is that why . . ." I couldn't finish my sentence. I wanted to ask if that was really why she was working here and why she'd suggested she could do twenty-dollar tarot readings for our guests. But a lump had formed in my throat and I had to stop talking.

She shook her head, making her rusty dangling skeleton earrings dance. "Listen, sweetie. You don't need to feel sorry for me. I made my bed and all that. Mona might've done me a favor. I've been putting off telling y'all for too long. Tarot reading and macrame purses aren't going to recover what I lost, but I'll be okay."

"I'm really sorry," I said.

Marnie put up her hand. "Don't be," she said firmly. "I'll survive. I always have. Between my hours here and my crafty wiles, everything is working out just fine."

"What about retirement?" I said.

"Bob took that dream from me . . . ," she started. Then she paused, her eyes filling with tears.

A wallop of shame hit me. How could I have been so self-involved? So caught up in myself that I'd failed to notice her struggles? "I don't know what to say, Aunt Marnie."

Then it dawned on me that I'd been the one to invite that snake, Bob Strapp, here. Guilt overtook shame. "This is all my fault. I brought back the man who took away your dreams."

She waved away my confession. "Don't give that a second thought, sweetie. It's not your fault. I lost some cash, but I'll bounce back. And Bob Strapp got what was coming to him. He got dealt the hand of death. It was written in the cards."

I didn't like the sound of that. "What do you mean?"

"That man shouldn't have come back here. He sealed his fate the moment his ego and greed pushed past any sense of foreboding he surely had. I believe everyone knows on some level when the end is near. He was nervous before he died. I saw fear in his eyes."

My breath caught. "When?"

She smiled, focusing on something beyond me, as she conjured up the memory. "A few hours before he took his last breath. He was jumpy and scared. Didn't like me pestering him about past misdeeds." Her gaze shifted back to me with a focus she normally reserved for crafts. "But they came back to haunt him, didn't they?"

"Was that in the parking lot? Nate saw you."

"You make it sound like I did something wrong. There's no shame in anger, Jess. You should experience the feeling as it emotes from the inside."

Did emoting include the full-body experience, like hitting some-one over the head and leaving him to drown? "Auntie M, can you tell me again what happened with the camera? Who was it that asked you to turn it off?"

"It was that man who dressed like a teen skateboarder. The other one who didn't make it. What was his name?"

"Nicky. His name was Nicky, or Nico—not sure which is right." I paused, almost not wanting to ask. "And he said he was asking on behalf of George Havers, right?"

"That's what this Nicky fellow told me. The Cowboy Crooner, I call him. George, that is." Her eyes sparkled. "Nice voice. Nice as—"

"So let me get this right. Nicky said his boss wanted the camera turned off for privacy reasons."

She nodded.

241

"Did anyone happen to see you talking to him, or better yet, overhear the conversation?"

She shrugged. "Not that I'm aware of, but he seemed to want to be discreet. Or sneaky. Yes, I'd say sneaky was the better word for him. Why?"

"The police might want to verify the request, that's all."

"I don't see why." She shifted in her seat. "I'm not lying."

I didn't doubt her word. But would the police feel the same now that Nicky was dead and my aunt had a solid motive? I got the impression Nicky had been good at foreseeing problems . . . and opportunities. He was sneaky but smart. Preventing a scandal from embarrassing a potential employer would be a great way to prove his worth. I wondered if George had had the foresight to think about cameras when his tongue was halfway down Paula's throat. More importantly, would he tell the police that turning the camera off was his idea? I wasn't sure. What if Nicky was the only one who could have backed up Aunt Marnie's story about the request? Would the police believe her story?

"Who else was a victim of Bob Strapp's?" I asked.

"Gosh, it was so long ago now. I can barely remember my break-fast, and you want me to remember what happened two years ago?"

"It could be important. Everyone in town knew Bob Strapp would be here with Lars. Maybe one of the other people he duped decided it was time for payback."

"His scam did affect quite a few people," she admitted. "But we all signed an NDA in exchange for a nugget of cash to get us through. Hush money, I guess you could call it."

"Any names you can give me might lead to the truth," I said. "It wouldn't just be solving Bob Strapp's murder. There was Nicky too. And the future of the Pearl. It's not exactly a selling point to have two murders take place on opening weekend."

Aunt Marnie nodded. She began rifling through her bag and pulled out a beat-up corduroy hat. *Good Lord.* Did my aunt use a thinking cap?

Instead of putting it on, Auntie M turned it over and read the label stitched to the underside of the lining. She snapped her fingers and showed me the label. *Middlesex and Company*, it read.

"I don't get it," I said.

She gave me a shy grin. "Middlesex. It was a little joke between my neighbor, Joe Hogan, and me. He had a vest made by the same company. Used to tell me we were two of a kind, that we should get rid of the middleman. He'd say it with a wink, that cheeky monkey."

Where was she going with this? Sometimes Auntie M's stories went on a tangent, ending up far from where they started.

"Joe Hogan invested with Bob?" I asked.

"No, he never had a penny to his name."

"Auntie M? The point?"

"Right. We used to go to the same tailor in town, Joe and I. Arty something or other. Bob Strapp wiped out the entire southeast corner of Fletcher Lake commerce. One shop owner told the next shop owner, and so on and so forth. In total, four or five businesses invested in him, and only one or two managed to survive. The others were wiped out. That's why our town is short of a tailor, a hardware store, and a bike shop."

My eyes widened. "Sheesh."

"That's not all," she continued. "At least three of the teachers from your mom's school were taken too. Your mom said if it sounds too good to be true, it probably is. But fool that I was, I rolled my eyes at her and went in with the rest of them. When she finds out—"

"She is going to understand," I tried to reassure her. "Mom loves to dole out advice, but she's not a told-you-so kind of person."

"True. I just wish for once I'd listened to her."

"And I wish I'd listened to my mom when it came to my last boyfriend. But the dimples got me, just like they did the barista at the Wrecking Ball and the stylist at *Good Morning, San Francisco* and who knows how many other women. So here we are, Auntie M, alone but together."

She reached across the table and grabbed my hand. "Have I told you you're my favorite niece?"

I giggled. "Never. But I'm glad you're telling me now."

"I still have two tarot readings to do. That's okay, right?"

"If people want them done, go for it."

"Not without me," a voice chimed in from behind us.

Sarah was flashing a new deck of tarot cards in her hand. "Look what I picked up today at the bookstore. It took me over an hour to decide, but in the end I went with my gut and chose this one." She held the box out to show us.

She grabbed a spare chair from another table and joined us, sliding the deck across the table so Auntie M could take a closer look. "The Rider-Waite set, a classic. And if there's one thing we know, it's listen to your gut."

I stood up. "My gut wants pizza."

Sarah looked up at me. "I know someone who has the same taste in pizza as you and never says no to a slice."

"Gotcha."

I said goodbye and sent Nate a text. I wished pizza were the only thing on my gut's mind, but it was telling me there was more trouble ahead. Only one day left of the weekend. What else could possibly go wrong?

Chapter Twenty-Seven

Nate and I agreed to split a large pizza. I ordered one from our local place, Pie in the Sky, and it was delivered to the front desk twenty minutes later.

I sent a 911 pizza alert to Nate and scurried back to my room. He didn't waste any time, arriving within a few minutes of my text.

Sarah is vegan, and Nate is happy to adhere to a plant-based diet most days too. But pizza is his Achilles' heel, so when it was time to order our favorite treat, everyone knew not to get in our way. No one wanted to join in either. Our favorite combo seemed to repel even the most adventurous of pizza lovers. Pineapple and jalapeños.

My brother wandered into my room and, without a word, threw open the box, bending over it to take in the cheesy goodness. After scarfing down a full slice, he finally acknowledged me. "Hey."

I poured two drinks, and we clinked glasses before I tore off another bite. "Cheers."

Nate and I had come to love the unusual flavor combo thanks to a summer spent up at Sauble Beach in Canada. Mom had rented a lakefront cabin from the cousin of a teacher at school. We had a great time on the shores of Lake Huron, and the pizzeria up there had our favorite-to-be combo on the menu. Each pizza was named after a famous Canadian actor. They called ours the Ryan Reynolds. Sweet and spicy.

It didn't take us long to make a major dent in the food. Nate glanced over at me as I grabbed another slice. "So how's it going, Nancy Drew?"

I grinned at him. "I prefer Veronica Mars."

He smiled back. "Just be glad I didn't say Miss Marple."

A light elbow jab almost knocked his slice onto the floor.

"Hey, watch it, sis."

I took another bite and eyed Nate as I chewed. He was good at keeping secrets. Had he been keeping things from me? He noticed me watching him and wiped the corners of his mouth. "Sauce malfunction?"

I shook my head and narrowed my eyes. "Did you know Aunt Marnie was broke?"

Nate considered the question while taking a drink of soda. "She showers here every morning, has a strict diet of ramen noodles and peanut butter, and hasn't left the country in ages. Shall we say I had an inkling?" He grabbed a nearby napkin and wiped his hands. "Please don't tell me you think that makes our tree-hugging Auntie M a murderous maniac?"

"Have you always been so observant?"

He shrugged. "Bartenders keep watch. It's become a habit."

I brushed my hands off. "Let me ask you this. Who is on your list of suspects for the murders of Bob Strapp and Nicky the Kid?"

He leaned back in his seat and considered the question. "Sarah and I have been talking about that. Bob wasn't a popular guy."

"Did you know he scammed a bunch of people in town?"

He nodded. "Including Auntie M."

My mouth dropped open. "Why didn't you tell me?"

"I only found out today. Sarah and Britt have bonded."

I pretended to gag. Nate held up his hand. "Sarah likes her." There was a note of warning in his voice. "And Britt's a valuable source of information."

He had me there. "Spill, bro."

"Hey, don't tell a bartender to spill. I account for every ounce poured."

I groaned. "Stop stalling. You're holding out on me."

"Maybe. But my intel isn't free."

"Name your terms."

"Paddleboarding with Sarah on your next day off. Take it or leave it."

What the . . . ? "Did she put you up to this?"

"Of course not. But she's my wife, and I want you to make more of an effort to know her."

"Half day, no lunch."

"Half day, picnic lunch," he countered.

"Deal."

He hopped off the sofa and sauntered into the kitchen, where he retrieved two chocolate chip cookies from my stash above the fridge. He tossed me one and popped the other in his mouth. "It's about Britt."

I held my breath.

He plunked himself down beside me. "She told Sarah she's going to be Lars's new manager once all this blows over."

I almost dropped my Coke. Travis had said Britt was doing Lars's PR. Manager was a big jump. "When did that happen?"

"It was all supposed to go down this weekend."

Ex-squeeze me? "What do you mean?"

"Apparently, Britt wants to expand her horizons. She brought George here to get him and Lars onstage together. The idea was to get photos of her orchestrating the truce between the guys. It would elevate her status and draw a lot of press, a perfect way to kick-start a new career for herself."

A million questions came to mind, starting with the most obvious. "What about Bob?"

Nate shrugged. "Bye-bye, Bob. Out with the old, in with the new."

Irritation shot through me. Lars had agreed to play to promote the grand opening of the Pearl. Why did he have to complicate it with drama? "Did she say why they chose to do it here?"

"According to Britt, the TV audience loved Lars's backstory: small-town boy with big-time dreams. She wanted to capitalize on that, then add George into the mix. Britt had asked Paula to do whatever it took to convince him to give it a shot. It hadn't occurred to her that Paula would stoop so low as to use her, quote, 'feminine wiles.' That's why Britt's so mad those two hooked up. It was supposed to be strictly business."

I rubbed my forehead. "None of this makes any sense."

"I hate to say it, but I think it's becoming crystal clear. An argument that goes south between stepson and father, aka singer and manager. Tempers flare. Things probably got heated and went too far."

"Whoa." I held up my hand. "I need a minute to process this." *Why would Lars agree to fire Bob in the first place? And why didn't he mention any of this to me?*

"Think about it, Jess. We all know Bob spent Lars's college fund."

I shook my head. "Lars didn't want to go in the first place. He was relieved to have an excuse not to go."

"But what if Bob did it again? Wouldn't that be reason to ditch him for good?"

Was it possible? If Bob had burned through Lars's money a second time, it would make sense that Lars would pair up with Britt and get rid of the man who'd betrayed him yet again.

I eyed my brother. "Even if what you're saying is true, why would Lars kill Bob? Just fire the man and be done with it."

"I don't know, Jess. People don't always make good decisions. Heat of the moment? Things went too far?"

"What if Britt and Bob got into it?" I asked. "A tug-of-war over Lars. Britt worries Lars will side with Bob and abandon their plan, jeopardizing her career in the process, so she kills Bob. Nicky is a witness, so she kills him too."

He looked doubtful. "Bit of a stretch. Keep in mind both victims died from a blow to the head."

"You may be right, but I guarantee Britt doesn't maintain her rock-hard abs from slouching around. She's super fit. I wouldn't be so fast to discount her strength." Plus I didn't trust Britt. And if anyone was capable of two murders, I could think of no one to better fit the bill.

A knock at the door made me jump.

Nate put his hand protectively over the pizza box. "I'm not sharing our pie."

A snort slipped out. "I think we're safe." It was hard to stay bleak with Nate around. I hustled to the door and yanked it open, assuming it would be Kat, Mom, or Sarah. Wrong on all counts. Lars stood there, shoulders hunched, head down. It was a pared-down version of the Lars I'd become accustomed to this weekend.

A closer look told me he was in rough shape. Bloodshot eyes and serious five o'clock shadow marred his face, and grease stains marked his signature pristine white T-shirt. Even the usual cedarwood smell of his favorite cologne had been pushed out by the stink of stale sweat with a sour undertone.

"I hope you haven't come for a hug." I took a step back and held my nose.

He laughed in spite of himself. "Is it that bad?"

I rubbed the bridge of my nose. "Uh-huh, but at least you're smiling. Pathetic doesn't suit you."

He shook his head and grinned at me. "You're the only person in the world who could make me smile right now, babe. You're like a ray of sunshine on a dark desert highway."

"Oh, puh-lease," Nate called out from the sofa. I ignored my brother's comment and grabbed Lars's elbow. "C'mon in. Nate and I were just finishing some pizza."

Nate wasn't overly pleased by our surprise guest, but manners had been drilled into us by our mom. He reluctantly opened the pizza box and faced it toward Lars. "Slice?"

"No thanks. I can smell pineapple from here."

"There's no accounting for taste," Nate said, looking at me rather than Lars.

I could see where this was headed, and I didn't have the energy to play ref. "Nate has to get going."

Nate cocked his head. "I do?"

I grabbed a plate and put two more slices on it. "Yes." I shoved the food toward him. "Sarah is probably waiting for you at the bar. It's been a long day."

Torn between respecting my request and playing the protective brother, Nate stood up and sauntered to the door. He paused, then used his one-inch height advantage to give Lars a threatening look before glancing back at me. "Sure you don't want me to stick around?"

"I'm good," I said in a firm voice, sounding a little more like my mom than I'd care to admit.

"Sarah and I will come by before we leave for the night. There's that thing she wanted to show you," Nate went on. I didn't bother to respond.

Lars crossed his arms over his chest. "See ya."

"Ciao." Nate glared at him before heading out.

In that moment, I knew Nate didn't believe Lars could be responsible for the death of two men. Nate could play the part, but had he been truly convinced Lars was a murderer, he never would've left me alone with him. It was a reassuring thought.

Once he was out of sight, I focused back on Lars. "Have a seat."

Lars remained standing. "Nah, I'm good. I sat at the cop shop for two hours answering questions. The chairs in that place? Not designed with comfort in mind."

I grabbed the pizza box and shoved it in the fridge. I turned to see Lars watching me, a wistful look on his face. I pushed aside a sense of unease. "What were they asking you?"

He rubbed his hand slowly over his face. It was the first time I noticed how dark the circles under his eyes were. "Not *they*. It was only James—excuse me—Detective Holloway." He made air quotes around the name and rolled his eyes. "That guy hasn't gotten any more likable over the years."

"I get the impression the feeling's mutual," I said. "Old rivalries can spawn deep resentments."

"Yeah, well, his small-town cop routine got old fast. I liked him better as a cocky quarterback."

I poured two cold glasses of water and handed him one. "So when he was more like you."

Lars almost choked on his water trying to stifle a laugh. He wiped the back of his hand across his mouth. "Do you ever get tired of razzing me?"

I raised an eyebrow. "Not really. It keeps your ego in check. Someone's got to do it." I took a sip of my water and set the glass down. "Besides, you should try to stay on his good side."

He groaned. "You're probably right, but he doesn't make it easy. At least, back in the day, his accusations focused on football and not murder." He finished his water and brought his glass to the sink, then turned and met my gaze. "Seriously, how many times do I need to tell him I was at the wrong place at the wrong time?"

"At least twice." I held up two fingers, flopping down onto my big comfy recliner. "Once for each murder."

Lars shook his head. "No, when Bob was killed, I was in my room alone."

"You know that doesn't sound any better, right?"

He sank down onto the love seat across from me. "Look, I get why he's targeting me. Bob and I were done. I was fed up. Fired him an hour before he wound up dead. Then Nicky quit his job to go work for George Havers. And he died too. Like, I get it. It doesn't sound great. But here's the thing: I'm innocent, babe. I promise you. I'm innocent."

"Then why are you keeping secrets?"

He flinched. "What do you mean?"

There was a slow burn in my stomach. I didn't like this game. "For starters, why didn't you mention that Britt is your new manager?"

He closed his eyes and let his head drop. Then, with a sigh, he looked up at me. "I told the detective. I just didn't tell *you*."

Heat rose in my cheeks, and a fresh sense of humiliation set in. "So Britt was here because you two had come up with some elaborate plan to unveil her as your manager in a melodramatic hometown twist."

He shrugged. "The press—and the fans—love drama. On top of that, her idea had the hometown appeal. Plus Britt hated Bob. She wanted to stick it to him here, and I didn't blame her. Bob messed with her family. I needed the publicity, and to be clear, Bob deserved to be fired."

"Why?"

Lars swallowed. "He wiped me out. Again. I'm broke, Jess."

Chapter
Twenty-Eight

Lars leaned back, his head resting on top of the cushions, and stared up at the ceiling. *Defeated.* That's all I could see when I looked at him. He'd spent so long and worked so hard, only to end up right back where he started. On my sofa, in our hometown, without a penny to his name.

But this time, the odds should have been in his favor. He had a hit record. He had a legion of fans. He'd hired a shark, aka Britt Sanders, to help him pick up the pieces and get his career back on track. All was not lost. We just needed to find a killer so he could get back up on his rock star horse and ride into the sunset of champagne and limousines.

A dreadful realization hit me. I owed Britt an apology. She hadn't been interested in him romantically after all. She'd told me that, but I hadn't listened, instead needling her about pursuing Lars because of some pathetic unfulfilled crush. A cartoon image of a giant heel flashed before my eyes. *Yup, that's me.* Then again, her behavior toward me had been no better. Tit for tat? *Yeah, I'm good with that.*

Eventually, Lars sat up and looked me in the eye. Gone was his flashy smile and rock star attitude. The real Lars sat before me. The thoughtful guy I'd first met right after he'd lost his mom, the guy who loved music and dancing and lifting people's spirits. In a quiet voice, he asked, "What am I going to do, Jess?"

That's when I knew I couldn't let him down, that I wasn't going to give up. "You're going to stay calm and focused. We need to find the real killer. It's the only way to prove your innocence."

He slowly straightened. "How are we going to do that?"

I cleared my throat. "Let's work backwards. Nicky was heard bragging that he knew who killed Bob. True or false, in your opinion?"

He shrugged. "It wouldn't surprise me. That guy knew things about everyone. Knowledge was his currency."

I frowned. "Do you think he was killed because of that?"

"Probably. Who else would want him dead? Bob had enemies in town; Nicky didn't."

I shook my head. "Are you forgetting Elle?"

He expression darkened. "I was surprised to see her here."

"Exactly. She said it was to get closure, but we can't be sure that didn't mean *until death do us part*," I said. "So she's on the list."

He rubbed the back of his neck. "You have a list of suspects?"

"Of course. I have a list for everything. So." I rolled my hand, indicating that he should keep going. "Elle?"

He let out a loud breath. "She was angry, all right."

I studied his face. "Angry at Nicky?"

"Sure."

He was being evasive. Never a good sign. "Why?"

He got up and strolled around the room. He stopped in front of a framed photo of Nate and me. We were standing side by side on a beach, the wind blowing my hair into his ear. We were both laughing. "This out west?"

"Yup, Baker Beach. If you look closely, you'll see the Golden Gate Bridge in the background."

255

"Cute."

"Lars, what's going on?" My tone was clipped. "I can't help you unless you're honest with me. And right now, I'm not feeling it."

He replaced the photo and scratched the back of his neck. "Okay, here's the thing. Elle wanted to divorce Nicky. I don't know why exactly, but she did. Bob advised Nicky against it, and she was upset."

"Why did Bob care?"

Lars shoved his hands deep in his pockets and looked at the floor. "Elle comes from money. Bob said not to sign the papers unless she agreed to spousal support."

"*Spousal support?*" I gawked at him. "You've got to be joking."

"I knew you'd react like that. But . . ." He kicked at a speck on the floor. "Like I said, her dad's loaded. If Nicky could score a little off the top, it would take the pressure off to increase his salary." He shrugged. "At least that was Bob's theory."

I glared at Lars. "Seriously?"

"Just let me finish, okay? Elle said she'd petition the court. But Nicky had something on her. Like he did on everyone."

"So Nicky, under advisement from Bob, was going to extort Elle for spousal support in exchange for a divorce? And you supported the idea so you wouldn't have to pay Nicky a living wage?"

"No," he snapped. "When I found out, I told them it was a bad idea. I didn't understand why Bob was being so cheap. I told him to pay Nicky properly. But he dragged his feet. I didn't understand why until I learned Bob had gambled away every cent I had."

"When exactly was that?" I asked.

"A few months ago. I was doing a show in LA at a private party. It turned out to be Britt's PR firm. I hadn't seen Britt in years, so it was nice to see a familiar face, and we got talking. She told me what she did, and I thought I could use someone like her on my side. Bob said no way, that we couldn't afford it. We argued, and I demanded to see the bank records. That's when he admitted he'd lost everything in a bad investment."

This was getting more complicated by the minute. "So you confided in Britt?"

"Yeah, and she's been amazing. But there's been friction. Bob has a rough history with her family, and neither one trusted the other."

"So you decided to go all in with Britt."

"And Paula. It was her idea to bring us all together. Think of it. George, Travis, and me. A new band, a new start. We'd generate a lot of publicity settling our feud and becoming allies. I'd even thought of a killer name: JFO. Joint Forces Operation. You like it?"

I bit my lip. "Sure, but all this—the band, the betrayal, the divorce—it led to Bob's murder. I really don't understand why you didn't just fire Bob then and there."

"Bob had some ammo he threatened to use against me to blow it all up."

"What now?"

Lars licked his lips. "It goes back to the days of *Sing This!*. There was a rumor I cheated. That I shouldn't have won."

"Because you stole Travis's song?"

Lars flinched. "That's not what happened. Travis and I had a deal."

I groaned. "What sort of deal?"

"How do you think Travis paid for that music school of his? It's not from cutting lawns and washing dishes, Jess. I paid him for that song. It belongs to me."

"Travis agreed to let you copy his song?"

"I got on the show with my own music," Lars insisted. "But Bob didn't think my stuff was good enough to win."

"So you okayed using Travis's music."

"I was in it to win, Jess. So yes." His expression hardened. "Travis was never going anywhere anyway. By the time the production started, Bob had already arranged everything with Travis. Did it behind my back. Each of the competitors brought a great song. I had to make sure mine made the cut."

"But it wasn't *your* song."

"You get one shot in life. *Sing This!* was mine."

"I'm not going to argue about this, Lars. Tell me what Bob had on you."

Lars sniffed. "Bob manipulated the voting process on the show."

"But that would be impossible. The vote was done online."

"The thing is, Bob went rogue, took it upon himself to finagle the vote."

"How?"

"He hired a company to set up fake social media accounts and tricked voters into leaving the wrong number on their virtual ballots. Number one was George, number two was me. Bob had them switch the accounts."

"So . . ."

He sighed. "People who thought they were voting for George were actually voting for me."

My mouth dropped open. "George should've won. So you cheated."

"*I* didn't cheat. Bob cheated."

"Oh puh-leeze! You went along with it. Same thing."

He threw his hands up. "Once it was done, it was done. I didn't know he was doing it. George got wind that something had happened and contacted the show."

"Did they know?"

He nodded. "Yes, they found out after the fact, like me. One of the producers got tipped off. But it was after my win had been announced on live TV."

"So what happened?"

"We had a meeting with the execs. They were mad. But it would've made them look bad too. So they told us to keep our mouths shut. Told George he'd been wrong."

I stared at him. "They just let it go?"

"Yup. Bob was slick. The fake sites were only up for an hour at the height of voting. They were gone before people figured it out."

"That's despicable. How could you okay that?"

"I didn't know, babe. I swear."

"But later on, when you did?"

He looked down at the floor. "I got carried away, I'll admit it. I'm not proud of how I won. But George has done well for himself. He was nothing before the show, and he's as popular as me now. Maybe even more."

"That doesn't make it okay." *That snake.* Bob had known the producers wouldn't lose face over the show's outcome. It would make no difference to them who won the title. A win for them lay in the viewership.

Bob, on the other hand . . . Had stealing the win cost Bob his life?

I carried our glasses over to the sink and washed them. Then I looked at my watch. It was time to get back to work. As much prep as we'd done, part of our brand was top-tier customer service; I needed to make sure everyone was taken care of and happy. But I also needed a minute to process what I'd learned, and there was a lot to process. Lars had always taken shortcuts for as long as I'd known him, but this was next level. Was it possible he was guilty after all?

When I turned back to face him, his head was hanging down. He looked up at me with a perfected puppy-dog expression I hadn't see since Duke had chewed up my favorite pair of slippers last Christmas.

"Don't give up on me, babe. I know I've messed up, but you're the only one on my side. I need you to believe me. To believe in me. Please, Jess. You're the only one I trust."

Frustration bloomed inside me. On the one hand, I couldn't ignore his lack of judgment and poor choices. On the other hand, a twinge of sympathy took hold. Was it nostalgia? Maybe. At this point, only one thing was for certain—I had to figure this out. Not because Lars asked for my help but for the sake of justice, and because I needed to ensure the reputation of the B and B wasn't besmirched by an unsolved murder.

I met his gaze. "Okay. I'll do what I can."

Relief swept over his face as he let out a breath and did a silent fist pump in the air.

A ping from my watch interrupted the moment, and a text flashed onto the screen.

Kat: *We've got a problem. I need your help.*

Son of a motherless goat. What now?

Chapter
Twenty-Nine

I texted Kat back, asking her what was wrong. While I waited for her to respond, I turned back to Lars. "Listen, I've got to get back to work. Let's talk later."

"Sure." He was grinning again, almost back to his usual self. It bothered me that he could be so casual about lying and cheating. He might not be a killer, but he'd acted like a jerk. "I'm going to help you because you're in trouble. But don't mistake that as a pass for your behavior. You've used people, including me."

He approached me, reaching out to twirl a lock of my hair in his fingers. "Aw, c'mon, babe. Don't be like that."

I stiffened at his touch. His attention used to give me butterflies. Now it just gave me indigestion. "I guess that's it, huh? Lie, cheat, and steal. Then just pick up and move on?"

Lars dropped his hands to his sides and took a step back. "Get off your high horse. Travis bought a music school with the money I paid him; Britt's got a new career. And what about you? You're using my success to bolster yours too. But guess what? I'm good with it. Happy to help. Maybe you should be thanking me instead of judging me."

"There's a difference between helping out a friend and using someone."

"We're all adults here. No one is being hurt."

I balled my fists up by my sides. I glared at him. "Bob and Nicky are dead! Has it occurred to you that all this deceit is what got them killed? Actions have consequences, Lars. Stop sticking your head up your a—"

The door flew open. Kat stood there, her eyes fixed on Lars. "Time for you to go, Lars."

Lars glanced between us. "Jess." His voice was softer now. "I'm sorry."

Kat pointed to the door. "Enough. Get out."

"I don't have anywhere to go."

"Maybe you should've thought about that before treating people like disposable napkins," said Kat.

"For now, just go back to your room," I told him. "It's probably the best bet."

Kat flashed him a toothy grin. "Plus it'll give you a chance to get used to small quarters. Just in case."

"If I'm in my room alone, there's no one to vouch for me if anything else goes wrong," he said.

For once, he was right. We both looked at Kat expectantly. She stiffened. "Why are you looking at me?"

"Because you light up my life?" I guessed.

She looked less than impressed. "Try again."

"Fine. The truth is, I have to tie up a few loose strings and we're running out of time. If we don't get to the bottom of this soon, a killer might go free."

She clicked her tongue. "What about my problem? Britt stubbed her toe on a lounge chair near the pool and is threatening to sue."

I did my best impression of puppy-dog eyes.

Kat slowly sucked in a breath and glared at me, then with a groan, she added, "I suppose I could text Nate and ask him to personally deliver a Band-Aid. Lord knows how she drools over him; that'd shut her up."

I pulled her into a hug. "Thank you." I drew away and added, "Maybe you and Lars could play that game you both used to love. What was it called? Cards Against People?"

"Cards Against Humanity," they said in unison. Their eyes locked, and for a moment I thought I saw a glimpse of a smile creep onto Kat's face.

"That's the one," I said. "Nate has it behind the bar with the rest of the adult-themed games. Maybe you could ask him to drop it off en route to tend to Britt? You can duke it out in a game and see who comes out on top." I looked at Kat. "Pretty please with a bottle of rosé on top?"

"You owe me big-time," she said. "Like supersized enormous."

I held up two pledge fingers. "Absolutely. Now go," I said with an outstretched arm. "I don't have much time."

Kat shook her head and stomped out, giving me the stink eye as she left. Lars stopped in the doorway. "Thank you," he mouthed at me before exiting. "Kat!" he called down the hallway. "You forgot something. Me!"

I grinned. Lars was going to enjoy this. I strolled back into my living room and sank down on the sofa. I texted Nate, asking him to drop off the card game at Lars's room. He sent back a quick thumbs-up, and I put the phone down. Time to get back to Murderino-ing.

I went over everything Lars had told me and found myself suddenly feeling sorry for him. He lived in the spotlight, but darkness lurked in the shadows of his existence.

Time for a list of my suspects. Travis. Britt. Paula. George. Elle and Lila. Auntie M? And Lars. All of them had legitimate reasons to want Bob and Nicky dead, and I had less than a day to figure it out before most of them left here and likely never came back.

First things first. I made myself a superstrength coffee. If I was going to do this, I needed every ounce of energy I could get my hands on. I shot it back like a cowboy drinks whiskey. Caffeinated and ready to go, I took a deep breath. Time to find a killer.

Chapter Thirty

M y goal was to narrow down my list of suspects until there was only one left standing.

George was my first victim . . . uh, suspect. Learning that George had been robbed of a win on *Sing This!* put him at the top of the list. He must've suspected that Lars or Bob had engineered the results, because he'd petitioned the production team when Lars won. If he knew for sure, I had to assume, he wouldn't be willing to team up with Lars now. Unless he knew *Bob* had rigged the vote and had decided to kill him in revenge. It sounded extreme, but the cash prize had been a hundred thousand dollars, never mind a record deal. Those were big stakes.

George did have an alibi, so either he and Paula had been together that night or he was lying. And if he was lying, then I had to assume Paula had some inkling he'd been involved. And Paula had a motive of her own to kill Bob. Her family had been bilked out of serious coin, so I wasn't willing to rule her out at this point.

Knocking two off the list in one go would certainly speed up the process. With time running out to clear Lars's name, it was best to start there. And to do that, I needed more information.

I made my way out to the bar. Several guests were enjoying the sunset hour, but I didn't see George and Paula among them. Were they back in their room? Had they already left without formally checking out? I heard the smacking of lips coming from a darkened corner of the pool deck. Paula and George's signature sound. I turned to see them in yet another pretzel pose. Sighing, I walked toward them.

There was no need to clear my throat, because I tripped over an abandoned towel and nearly turned their twosome into a threesome. I put my hand out to stop my full weight from bearing down on them. It made contact with George's chest, and the feel of his soft chest hair made my cheeks burn. His muscles tightened and he sat up, nearly toppling Paula over the far side of the lounger made for one.

"Sorry." I extracted my hand from his personal space as my face became even redder. Somehow managing to stand up, I pointed behind me. "I tripped. Over that towel. On the ground there."

His smile made my throat dry up, and I stopped babbling. *Abort mission?* No way I could go from copping a feel to digging for clues.

"Miss Byrne, you're a firecracker. I like that. Paula and I can make room anytime. Right, darlin'?" *Earth, just swallow me now.*

Paula straddled one leg over his, and a scene from an old James Bond movie came to mind. Her eyes were fixed on mine, but she remained quiet.

I took two steps back. "I only wanted to thank you again, George, for stepping up this weekend." There was truth in my words. If he wasn't a murderer, I would definitely add his upbeat tunes to our Saturday night mix.

"I love to perform." He winked at me. I blinked. *Um, ew?*

Paula giggled and tapped his furry chest. "Cut it out," she said. "You're all mine for the next twelve hours."

Twelve hours. She was right. After that, they'd be gone. Her words served as a reminder. It was now or never. The sign above the bar for Nate's daily drink specials caught my eye, giving me an idea. "You two have inspired me to create a couples' package." I looked from George to Paula and back again. "Do you mind if I pick your brains a little bit before you go?"

Paula massaged the back of George's neck. "How sweet," she purred. "Why not? Right, Georgie?"

"No skin off my bones," George said. "Fire away."

"Super." I pulled over a nearby chair. "One thing I've noticed is how well you two have been able to shut out the rest of the world. It's admirable, something a lot of couples want to do."

"Can't argue that," Paula said, smiling. George squeezed her leg and gave me a nod.

It was time to push. "Is there anything in particular about the Pearl that helped you ignore the murder of Bob Strapp? He nearly ruined each of your lives, yet you were able to shut him, and his subsequent murder, out of your consciousness."

George stiffened. "I get the feeling you're fixing to solve a murder, not market your business." He scratched his beard. "Where I'm from, we like to be direct. So if you got something to say, say it."

Fair enough. No going back now. "Okay. Rumor has it that Bob rigged *Sing This!* and you were the real winner."

George's face went beet red. He glared at me. "The producers canned that rumor, and Lars and I have put our rivalry behind us."

"That's right," Paula said. "Bringing George, Lars, and Travis together is a guaranteed win."

I turned to her. "What about you, Paula? Your dad lost his business because of Bob."

The color drained from her face. She looked from me to George and back again. "Why are you bringing up my father? As far as I'm concerned, what happened between him and Bob is ancient history. Dad moved on, went to California, and started fresh. He told me last year he's actually glad Bob wiped him out, because it woke him up and now he's living his best life."

George turned to Paula. "Sounds like your daddy's got gumption."

Paula squeezed his bicep. "You'd like him."

"Betcha I would." He turned to me. "Now let me give you a little piece of advice, Ms. Byrne. If you expect to run a successful business, stirring up old wounds sure as sugar ain't the way to go."

Paula nodded. "It may be time to face reality, Jess. We may never find out who killed Bob. That may not be good for your business, and I'm sorry about that, but it's the truth. I realized this weekend that life's too short to spend worrying about things that are out of your control. Maybe you should go back to posting photos of pretty pink doors and hope for the best."

"If you two are so laid back about everything, then why did you bother to have the cameras shut off? Who cares what other people think?" I asked.

"That was all Nicky," George said. "I suppose he was trying to impress me. I'm in the middle of a divorce, and he probably thought that by helping me be discreet, it would prove his value."

"Convenient that the only person who can dispute your claim is dead, isn't it?" If I believed George, that meant Nicky had lied about George's request and had asked my aunt to turn off the camera for his own reasons. And his most likely reason was to cast suspicion on an oblivious target. Either scenario could be true. What now?

Paula nuzzled George's neck before looking back at me. "If I were you, Jess, I'd mind my own business and stop sticking my nose where it doesn't belong."

"Two men were murdered at my bed-and-breakfast. Their deaths *are* very much my business."

"Play with fire, you get burned."

"You got that right, darlin'." George put his arm around Paula and pulled her close, then turned to me. "Listen, from everything I've heard, Bob got what was coming to him. And that kid, Nicky? He was bragging from sunrise to sunset he knew who done it. Should've held his cards closer to the vest instead of singing like a canary." He stood up. "Why don't I get us a few beers to go? I think I'm ready to head back to our room."

Paula smiled up at him. "Our room. I like the sound of that."

George turned to me. "Here's a piece of advice, Ms. Byrne. 'When people show you who they are, believe them.'"

"Hank Williams?" I guessed.

"Maya Angelou." With that, he scooped up his cowboy hat and put it on as he wandered over to the bar. I tried my best not to gawk, but aside from the hat, all he wore was a tight red, white, and blue Speedo, or as Kat called them, a banana hammock.

Paula leaned back in the lounger and studied me. "The police seem to think Lars is the only one with a real motive."

"That's what everyone thinks, but he's known Bob most of his life and forgiven him for all his mistakes. Why would he kill him now?"

She shrugged. "Maybe because Bob gambled all his money away? Again. Lars was so broke he hadn't paid Nicky in weeks. That's why Nicky quit and came crawling to George."

What Lars had told me confirmed what she'd said, but none of it was public knowledge. I frowned. "How do you know that?"

She rolled her eyes. "I work for Britt, remember? I read all her emails, I'm privy to all her private chats. Lars begged her to help him get back on his feet. She's got a soft spot for him and saw it as a good opportunity to expand her career."

"Yeah, I'm aware of that."

"Then you should know this link-up of George, Lars, and Travis has been in the works for months; we just hadn't figured out where the show would take place. Your email gave us the perfect venue to fit with the hometown narrative. Bob was warming up to the idea too. He just didn't know it meant the end of the line for his career."

"So . . ."

"So I would assume that Bob didn't take the news very well, and things went south."

Everything Paula said made sense. It was another strike against Lars but it could implicate Britt just as easily. She'd banked on making a big splash with her two new stars. If Bob held her up and Lars backed out of the deal, she could have been in serious trouble.

Before I could say anything else, George returned. He ducked his head under the umbrella. "Ready to go back to our room and chill out before I play my last set?"

"You couldn't stop me if you tried," Paula cooed, pulling him down and giving him a wet kiss before turning to me. "I'm going to put a *Do Not Disturb* sign on our door. That means leave us alone, okay? We've answered all your questions and have nothing more to say. I don't want to hear from you again."

And then they were gone, leaving me standing alone under the umbrella and wondering if Paula had just reinforced a solid motive for Lars to kill Bob. Could I have been wrong? Was the most obvious answer the right one? Could Lars be a murderer? Maybe it was time I considered that possibility. For real this time.

I turned to see Sarah rush inside. *Where is she going?* I looked at my watch. Almost nine o'clock. Yoga time. She must be running in to change. I tapped my lip. This could be the opportunity I needed to question one last suspect.

If I was lucky, Britt would be there early, rolling out her mat for the inaugural moonlight yoga session. According to Auntie M and Sarah, a full moon was expected tonight. Maybe I could harness the energy of the lunar cycle to find the truth.

Chapter Thirty-One

I hustled over to the gazebo. As I'd hoped, I arrived to find Britt alone. She was already practicing yoga on her mat, holding still in a move Sarah called the warrior pose. Left leg bent, right leg stretched out behind, and both arms held above her head. As darkness blanketed the sky, I wondered if this was really such a good idea.

Before I could decide, Britt turned and saw me. She greeted me with an exaggerated eye roll and a groan.

"Hey," I said with an awkward wave.

"What do you want? Sarah told me to meet her here. We're doing a class." Britt was dressed in full Lululemon gear: black yoga leggings and a cropped teal tank top revealing an impressive core. Without waiting for an answer, she lifted her back leg so she was balanced on one foot. She bent her torso forward with arms stretched out in front so she was parallel with the floor. She held the pose for a good thirty seconds before lowering her raised leg, standing upright, and dropping her arms back to her sides. She looked annoyed to see I hadn't left. "Why are you still here?"

I rolled my shoulders back, summoning my courage. "Can I ask you something?"

She fanned her hands out and took a deep breath. "I'd rather you didn't. I'm trying to focus here, and your presence casts negative energy my way."

I ignored her comment. "Why did you come here?"

She pointed a finger at the sky. "Something about the full moon and the movement of air, I think. Although it's starting to feel a little stuffy, if you ask me."

I gritted my teeth. "I mean, why did you come this weekend? If you wanted to set up a meet-and-greet between George and Travis, why not set it up in the city? It's been bothering me all weekend."

"Don't forget, Lars is my client too. Getting them all together makes for great publicity."

"But why here? Why not in the city with more press around to pick up the story?"

She reached down, grabbed her left toe, and stretched her leg out in front of her, bending forward, showing serious balance and flexibility. She spoke into her knee. "It just worked out that way."

I waited until she'd completed the stretch and was standing back up to her full height. "You don't have an answer, do you? If I really want to know, should I ask Paula? She does most of your work, doesn't she?"

Britt grabbed her right toe and tried to repeat what she'd done on the other side, but she lost her balance before she could complete the stretch. With a huff, she dropped her foot and put her hands on her hips. "I want you to go away, so I will ignore that comment. However, as it happens, Paula thought this would make for a better angle. People love hometown stories, she said. Watching people's dreams come true. I agreed, yet look what happened. A nightmare, with *you* smack in the middle of it."

"News flash: you're not who I was hoping to see this weekend either."

273

She held her hands up and took a step toward me. "Can you leave now?"

"My place, remember? And I'm trying to figure out what happened to Bob and Nicky. So if you'd like me to leave, tell me what you think happened."

A cold, hard laugh escaped her lips. "You disrespect me at every turn, and then you want me to trust you? I don't think so, Jess the Mess. I don't play that way."

"It's not a game, Britt. Two men are dead."

Her eyes flashed with anger, and she began stalking toward me like a cat approaching its prey. I retreated backward, tripping on a built-in bench. I landed with a thud, and before I knew it, Britt was standing over me, a wicked grin on her face.

"Look who's finally down for the count," she said. "Little Miss Perfect."

I scrambled to my feet. "Cut it out."

"I am so sick and tired of your act," she practically spat at me. "So desperate to please. Do you know what it's like to struggle, Jess? To have your father nearly lose everything, your uncle abandon his family, and your mother blame you? Do you even know what Bob Strapp did to my family?"

I glared at her. "You obviously want to tell me, so please, go ahead."

"Let's see, where to start? Oh, right. After Lars and I became friends"—she held up her hands and made air quotes around *friends*— "Bob pressured Lars into asking me to put a good word in with my dad. He'd only ever had short-term work, but after my pestering, Dad gave him a chance. At the beginning, it was all rainbows and roses. Bob was good at numbers and had a head for business. My dad even trained him as a portfolio manager and introduced him around town as an up-and-coming investment shark." She balled her hands so tightly her knuckles turned white. "Bob used the connection to pull in lots of new clients. And then he bet on high-risk stocks behind my father's back and lost everyone's money. Every. Last. Dollar. Do you know what it's like, Jess, the guilt I felt for bringing him in?"

I bit my lip. "Why wasn't Bob arrested or fined or whatever happens when investment people screw up?"

Her lip curled. "Grow up, Jess. He somehow convinced the Securities and Exchange Commission that it was a rookie mistake. He got a slap on the wrist, lost his job. Boohoo. No charges were laid. But my dad knew, I knew, even Lars knew it was greed, pure and simple. Bob gambled, lost, and moved on. I had to grovel just to get my dad to look at me again."

Daddy's girl was no longer the apple of his eye. That must've stung. Especially when the person responsible never had to pay. At least, not until this weekend. "I'm sorry, Britt."

Her eyes went glassy. "When I ran into Lars at my company party and he and Bob were on the outs, I knew it was my chance."

My heart skipped a beat. "Chance for what?"

Her eyes narrowed. "To get back at Bob while kick-starting a new career. All in one go. But when Bob found out last night, he and Lars got into a huge fight. He actually told Lars he'd sue him if he tried to leave."

I swallowed. "Is that why you killed him?"

"Is that a joke?" she balked.

A twig snapped in the dark, and I turned around to see Sarah rushing forward, a yoga mat tucked under her arm. "Sorry about that, Britt." She hopped up onto the gazebo and took a moment to catch her breath. Her eyes lit up when she noticed I was there too. "Are you going to join our sesh, sis? That would be super dope. You two could finally get past your differences. I may have mentioned it's a full moon tonight? Good timing. It represents transformation."

The wind picked up, and a lone coyote howled in the distance. "Sorry, Sarah, I have to go."

Britt shot me a wicked grin. "Nice chatting with you, Jess."

I raced back to the bar in record time. All I could think about was finding Kat.

As I rushed through the back entrance, I saw George setting up to play and Nate chatting with a small group at the bar. He quirked an eyebrow at me. I sped past him, through the pool area, and into the lobby. Kat wasn't there, so I pulled up my phone and started to type.

Me: *Where are you?*

Duke approached and rubbed my leg. "I know, you must be hungry." He barked his response. My phone pinged.

Kat: *Minor mishap in guest suite. Cleaning up some broken glass.*

Me: *Come find me when you're done. I'll be in my room.*

She replied with a thumbs-up, and I headed back to my place with Duke. I had a feeling this was going to be a long night.

Once inside, I fed Duke, then dropped my phone on the kitchen counter and stretched out on the couch. As the adrenaline rush slowed, I realized how utterly exhausted I felt. This sleuthing stuff wasn't for the faint of heart. I closed my eyes and waited for Kat to arrive.

I woke with a start in the pitch-black with my favorite faux-fur throw covering me. *What happened?* Feeling discombobulated, I threw off the blanket. *What time is it? Where's Kat?*

I rubbed my eyes and stretched my arms over my head. A sliver of light caught my eye. *Oh no.* I ran to the window. The blackout blinds had been drawn. I pulled them up. A sinking feeling hit me. It wasn't dark anymore. The sun made me squint as I looked up at the bright blue sky.

I ran to the counter and grabbed my phone. The time said eight fifteen AM. *No, no, no!* I must've slept through the night.

Duke sauntered over to me and stretched.

"Thanks a lot, pal."

He barked and wagged his tail.

"Glad someone's feeling good. Now c'mon, let's go."

I threw my shoes on, grabbed my phone, and ran out the door. Duke followed me.

I reached the lobby in no time. Kat's shiny black hair was barely visible over the snug wicker lounge chair. She was stretched out, her long legs propped up on the coffee table, and I guessed she was riffling through the latest *Style at Home* magazine. Light jazz music was playing faintly in the back ground and I slowed my pace, allowing the soft lighting and the comforting sound of Diana Krall's voice to help calm my racing heart. I saw there were two more people chilling in the lobby, huddled together on the sofa nearby. Beads of sweat collected on my forehead, and I wiped them away as I gave a small wave to the couple who'd taken a weekend away from the kids.

"Hey, sleepyhead," Kat said, drawing my attention back to her. Her eyes grew wide at my disheveled appearance. "You okay?"

Frustration stirred inside me. "What happened? You were supposed to come to my apartment last night."

"When I got there, you were out cold. I couldn't bring myself to wake you up, so I covered you with a blanket and pulled the blinds. Everything okay?"

"Can we chat for a minute privately?"

Kat held her hands up. "Lars is fine. George stopped by his room last night, and they talked. Is that what you're worried about?"

Before I could answer, the twins entered the lobby, looking remarkably unscathed and cheery after the weekend's events. Elle wore a light-yellow jumpsuit with her hair pulled back. Lila, still rocking the pink neck scarf, had matched it with a floral sundress. I tried to look cheery. "How are you two managing?"

Elle gave us a tentative smile. "Hey, I'm sorry about yesterday. Finding Nico like that was just such a terrible shock. I couldn't process it."

"Please don't apologize. I should be the one saying sorry." I approached the twosome and lowered my voice. "I don't think I've had the chance to properly say that yet."

"Thanks," Elle said. "Now that he's gone, I feel like I can finally admit the truth. He wasn't a good husband, and I didn't love him anymore. I came here for closure." She massaged her neck. "Hadn't expected it to be so literal."

Lila rubbed her sister's arm. "Elle felt like she had to put on a show yesterday."

Elle crossed her arms tightly. "When I saw his body, after the initial shock, I wanted to cry, but the tears wouldn't come."

"Sounds like there was a lot of history."

Lila shrugged. "You can't get blood from a stone, or tears in your case, Elle. You spent far too long crying over that man. There was nothing left."

"You know, I'm feeling a weird sense of calm. With Nico gone, there are no more games. The pain he inflicted on me is over." Elle sat back and took a deep breath. She peered at me. "You must think I'm a monster."

I shook my head. "His death is a tragedy, but maybe it'll help set you free."

Lila lowered her voice. "I know we shouldn't speak ill of the dead, but I'm relieved he's finally out of your life for good, Elle." She reached down and picked up her designer purse, then held out a hand and pulled Elle up. "Shall we?"

Elle nodded. Lila unzipped her bag and dug through it, pulling her phone out. "We got some great shots." She pulled up her photo icon and showed me half a dozen. Each one was gorgeous. "I'll put them up on Instagram and tag you."

"That would be great," I said. "Thank you."

Elle pulled two matching carry-on suitcases up to the reception desk. With a final look out at the pool, she linked her arm in Lila's. "Did I ever tell you I'm the luckiest sister in the world? I don't know what I would've done without you."

"I'm always here for you," Lila said.

Elle rested her head on her sister's shoulder with a sigh. "Guess that's what twins are for."

Lila put her phone back in her purse, then placed the beautiful bag on top of the luggage. "Remember, today's a new day. Let's go home and make a fresh start." She stretched her arms out over her head. "Time to hit the road."

Elle perked up. "Let's do it. I called Detective Holloway, and he said we're free to leave."

"All right, I'll check you out," Kat said.

Duke galloped over and stuck his nose inside the purse, which was now at doggy eye level. I rounded the reception desk. "I'm sorry. I haven't fed him breakfast yet." I snapped my fingers. "Duke, get out of there."

His muzzle was now fully inside, and I felt my face flush. "Duke, stop it."

Lila grinned. "I tend to keep a stash of beef jerky in there. Guess I'm not the only one who appreciates it after all."

Duke ignored my commands. I grabbed his collar and pulled. His head popped out. With it came a ball. A red rubber ball.

Kat's mouth dropped open. "You've got to be kidding me. It's that kid's lost ball. I spent an hour looking for that thing."

Lila's face flushed. "That's odd. How did that get in there?"

Kat shook her head. "Poolside, my bet. His mom and I combed the whole pool area. Now I know why we couldn't find it." She called Duke over, and he dropped it in her hand. She gave him a pat. "Good boy." She turned to Lila. "Mind if I take this? It must've bounced into your bag."

"Maybe next time bring a smaller purse," Elle said, grabbing Lila's hand.

They walked a few steps before Lila turned around and looked at Kat and me. "You two are amazing, by the way. Following your dreams, doing it your way. The Pearl is going to be a huge success."

Kat and I looked at each other, beaming. "Thanks," I said.

"Go big or go home, right?" Kat said.

"A hundred percent," Elle said. "It's time to start fresh. And with the money I got from the sale of Nicky's guitar, I might even get myself a matching purse."

Lila and Elle linked arms and strolled out of the lobby without another look back.

"I like those two," Kat said.

"They're cute," I agreed.

"Want to fill me in now? You seemed a little spun when you got here."

I took a deep breath. "What would you say if I told you I confronted Britt last night and she didn't deny killing Bob?"

Her wary expression wasn't what I'd expected. "Jess, that's not the same thing as a confession." She began to bounce the red ball in her hand. "I think you want it to be her. That doesn't make it so."

I walked over to the coffee table and picked up two empty mugs. "I know it sounds shady. But Britt's name comes up at every turn."

"So she knows the people involved," Kat said. "Don't we all? Small town equals big gossip. But there's a difference between mean-girl antics and murder. Jess, I don't see it." Kat tossed the ball up and down in her hand. "Have you seen the mom and red-ball son? I have to return this."

"Hold on." Kat had dismissed my theory, but I wasn't so ready to let it go. "What about Britt's family? Her dad almost lost his business because of her championing Bob. That's a lot of Gucci purses that Britt didn't get."

"Okay, I'll admit you have a point," Kat said. "I asked Judy Sheehan at the bank. She wouldn't tell me much but did admit Bob cost several clients a lot of money. Apparently, there were at least a dozen victims."

"That's probably why Britt's working so hard now," I said. "She can't rely on daddy's money. And a lot of other people affected were here this weekend too. Paula? And Travis?"

"*And* Aunt Marnie," Kat said with a warning tone. "Maybe it's time to let this drop."

"Auntie M doesn't have it in her," I said. "And Paula's dad landed on his feet out in California. Travis is still on my list, though. He was here Friday night and has no alibi for when Nicky was killed."

"Then again, he's a new dad with a good business," Kat reasoned. "And he's likely linking up with George Havers. Would he risk all that?"

I shrugged. "In the heat of the moment, he may have lost his temper. If they'd gotten into an argument, it's possible."

"I could see it if the victim had been Lars, maybe." She paused. "Have you even discussed any of this with James? Remember, he's the real detective."

"He thinks I'm on Team Lars. That all I want to do is help Lars avoid being arrested."

"Isn't that part of it?"

"Maybe it was at first," I admitted. "But at this point, I just want to know the truth. Everything I've learned reminds me he's not the guy for me, never really was. But I'm still not convinced he's guilty of murder."

"Then pick up the phone and call James. Tell him your theory. It's now or never."

"You think he'll listen to me?"

"I think it's worth a shot. If nothing else, you can feel better knowing you did everything in your power to help, right?"

"I guess." I knew she was right, but I still wasn't rushing to call.

"Good. You do that while I try to find the owners of this ball. I'd better grab a handful of corkscrews from the supply closet too. None of the picnic baskets have one. Big oversight. When I get back, let's make cappuccinos and work on our Instagram posts. Hashtag *nomoremurder*, hashtag *makeitadoubleshot*."

I froze. "What did you say?"

"Hashtag . . ."

"No, not that. The thing about the corkscrews."

"I'll grab some. Don't worry. I forgot to put them in the picnic baskets when I made them up last week."

"Are you sure?"

"Yeah, the couple from the beach the other day alerted me to it. I checked the rest of them, and they were all a corkscrew shy. What's wrong?"

My body began to tingle. "Kat, we need James."

"*You* need James. I've got my eye on—"

"I'm not kidding." I grabbed my phone, then snatched a business card he'd left on the reception desk. Kat stood frozen, her face going pale.

James picked up right away. "Holloway here."

I sucked in my breath. "It's Jess. Come to the Pearl right away. I know who the killer is."

Chapter
Thirty-Two

There was no time to wait for James. I had to act now or the killers would walk. I rushed out the front door, Kat at my heels.

"Where are we going?" she demanded.

"To stop them before they leave."

I sprinted toward the white SUV as the twins loaded their bags into the back.

"Elle! Lila!"

The twins exchanged a look before turning to face us. Elle cleared her throat. "Did we forget something?"

Lila opened the passenger side door and threw her oversized purse onto the seat. "Sorry, Jess. We've got to run. Elle, get into the car."

Elle's eyes were wide. She swallowed.

I stood my ground, edging closer to Lila. "Wait."

Lila glared at me. "We've done enough of that. It's time for us to go. Elle, now."

"Not until you've answered my questions."

Lila stiffened. "Why should we?"

Kat approached us. She had at least three inches on the rest of us. "Because we won't move until you do, that's why. Now listen up." She turned to me. "Go ahead."

I shot her a grateful look, then focused back on the twins. "Where were you when Bob Strapp was killed?"

Elle licked her lips. Lila held up her hand to stop her from answering. "We were having drinks at the firepit behind the bar. You can ask Nate."

I looked from Lila to Elle. "Were you both at the bar at the same time?"

Elle shifted her focus down to her shoes. Lila met my gaze and narrowed her eyes. "Why are you asking?"

Kat step forward. "Why aren't you answering?"

Lila huffed. "We took turns, okay?"

I drew in a long, slow breath. "And when Nicky was killed?"

"Nico!" Elle snapped, raising her eyes to meet mine. The hair on the back of my neck stood up.

Lila latched onto her sister's arm. "His name was Nico. Elle and I were at the beach. We were having a picnic and a swim."

Elle pointed at me. "With one of your signature baskets."

Lila nodded. "You can check your records. We signed it out." With a dismissive wave, she pivoted away from me.

"Last question." I waited until she'd turned her head and caught my eye. "How did you open the wine? I don't remember seeing your purse there, Lila."

She blinked. Then glanced at her sister and blinked again before looking back at me. "The opener from the picnic basket. I wouldn't bring my designer purse to the beach. I left it in our room."

Kat's eyes widened and she gasped, finally recognizing what had dawned on me a few minutes earlier. "That's impossible. None of the baskets had a corkscrew."

"Ours had one," Elle insisted.

I turned to Kat. "What did James instruct the officers to look for at the beach?" I paused to give Elle a pointed look.

"Something sharp and narrow." Kat looked from me to Lila to Elle. "An item that would puncture his temple."

The faint sound of sirens blared in the distance. In a flash, Lila opened the driver's door of the SUV and hopped inside. "Elle, hurry!"

Elle did as she was told, but as Lila reached over and grabbed her door to close it, Kat lunged forward and stopped her.

"Let go!" Lila demanded.

Kat gripped the door, her whole body shaking as she struggled. "We have a strict policy." She gasped for breath. "No murderers allowed."

James's car flew into the parking lot, its single red siren still squealing. The car screeched to a stop and he leapt out. "What's going on here?"

My stomach flip-flopped, and I pointed at the SUV. "Two sisters, two murderers."

With James's arrival, Lila abandoned her attempt to flee. Kat took a step back and rested her hands on her waist while she caught her breath.

Elle slowly got out of the SUV. She was shaking. "That's not true. I saw Nico kill Bob." Her eyes filled with tears. "Then he tried to kill Lila. I had to save my sister before he got her too."

Lila quietly exited the driver's seat, her head hanging down.

James held up his hand. "I'm going to need everyone to rewind a few steps so I can catch up."

Lila walked over to her sister, and they stood side by side, holding hands. "My sister's telling the truth. Nico tried to strangle me. Look." With her free hand, she pulled off her perfect peach-colored scarf. Ugly red-and-purple bruising encircled her neck. I gasped.

James approached her and bent down as she raised her chin to let him examine the injury. "You'll need a doctor to look at that, assess the injuries."

She nodded. "Yeah, no problem."

Kat moved closer. "What happened?"

Elle wiped a tear from her eye. "Let *me* explain. Please."

No one said a word, including Lila. Elle took a deep breath. "I saw Nico the night of the concert. He was sneaking around the back of the B and B. I thought it would be the perfect opportunity for me to talk to him alone. I'd received a notification from my lawyer an hour earlier that he'd received the divorce papers from his lawyer. And I was glad, really, that Lila had finally convinced me to leave him. I just wanted the opportunity to explain. You know, closure."

Lila gave her a reassuring nod. Elle continued. "Anyway, like I said, I saw Nico duck behind the building, so I followed him." She licked her lips. "When I got closer, I realized someone else was there waiting for him. Bob. The two of them began to argue. I felt awkward watching them, so I hid behind a tree. Bob said something about it being Nico's fault that Lars had fired him, that he'd been the one to tip Lars off about some missing money. Nico denied it, but Bob wouldn't listen. He said he was going to blacklist Nico so he'd never have a shot at making it in the business. They were in each other's face, and then Nico reached down and grabbed a rock. Bob laughed. Then Nico hit him on the head and Bob keeled over. Nico hit him again and again. I ran to see if I could stop the fight, but it was too late. Bob was on the ground by then. His head was a mess and his eyes were open, and I knew . . . I knew Nico had killed him."

For a minute, no one said anything.

"What did Nico do when he saw you?" James finally asked.

Elle's breathing quickened. She glanced at her sister, who nodded, before turning back to James. "Nico begged me to keep quiet. And . . . and . . . I was in shock. I know it was wrong, but . . ."

Lila squeezed her sister's hand, then took over. "My sister was terrified. She agreed to keep his secret. Can you blame her?"

"Why didn't you tell me the truth when I interviewed you the next day?" James asked.

Elle shook her head. "I don't know. I was scared, I was confused. Nico started talking about marital privilege and how I wouldn't be allowed to testify against him—"

James interrupted her. "Not true."

Elle shrugged. "I didn't know that, so I promised not to say anything. He said he'd sign the divorce papers and never contact me again if I stayed silent. I thought I could live with myself, but that night I confessed everything to Lila."

Lila took over. "I should've called the police then. That's on me, and I know it. But Elle wanted to give Nico one last chance to do the right thing, warn him she couldn't keep his secret and he should turn himself in."

Elle nodded. "I hoped he'd confess, tell the police he'd killed Bob during a heated argument. It never even occurred to me that he'd try to . . ." She paused, then took a deep breath. "I never thought he'd try to kill me instead."

"Wait," I interrupted. "So Nicky attacked Lila thinking she was . . . ?"

Elle jabbed herself in the chest. "Me." She glanced at her sister. "Lila almost died because I wasn't brave enough to call the police the night I watched my husband kill another person."

Elle began to cry in earnest now. Lila pulled her close. "Nico told Elle to meet him at the secret beach. I didn't want Elle to go alone, so I grabbed the picnic basket and went to the meeting spot early. She was still in the shower, so I left her a note in our room." She brought her hand up to her neck and began to massage it. "It sounds silly now, but I thought after she spoke with him, she and I could stay by the water and decompress. Unfortunately, Nico must've seen me and mistaken me for Elle. I'd just opened the bottle of wine with the opener in my purse when he snuck up behind me and . . ." She closed her eyes. "And tried to kill me."

Elle pulled away from her sister. "I got there and found Nico on top on Lila. He was so focused on strangling her he didn't hear me come up from behind him. I grabbed the corkscrew and rammed it into the side of his head as hard as I could."

"Elle saved my life." Lila shook her head. "We took the bloody clothes she was wearing and stuffed them into my purse. Luckily, she had a bikini on underneath."

"We hid Lila's purse in the bushes and dragged Nico's body near the water. Then we threw the corkscrew into the lake," Elle said.

"Afterwards we washed off and ran," Lila said. "Then we just waited."

Everyone was silent for a minute. Even James.

Then Kat said, "A little convenient, isn't it? With Nico gone, he can't defend himself."

James cleared his throat. "Too bad I hadn't gotten confirmation a day earlier. I may have been able to prove Nico killed Bob without your help."

Lila's and Elle's eyes both widened. "How?" they said in unison.

He looked from one to the other. "A little thing called DNA." He turned to me. "Remember the piece of fabric we found on the fence? Turns out it was a match for a hoodie I found in Nico's room. And it had Bob's blood on it. He must've caught the fabric on the fence after he killed Bob. I'm not saying it would make solving the crime a slam dunk, but that fabric certainly warranted further investigation."

The twins clung to each other as James pulled out his phone and called for backup. "Does that mean you believe us?" Elle asked.

James looked from Elle to Lila and back again. "I'm not making any promises, but if a doctor agrees the bruising on Lila's neck was from an attempted strangulation, we can talk. For now, I need to take you to the station for questioning."

Both twins nodded and were escorted away in silence. There was nothing left to say.

Chapter
Thirty-Three

An hour later, Kat and I were sitting in the lobby with Duke at our feet, waiting for . . . I'm not sure what we were waiting for.

I could feel Kat's eyes on me. "Must you stare? It's freaking me out."

She narrowed her eyes. "I can't figure it out. How did you know?"

I grinned at her. "The ball."

"The ball? What ball? Cinderella's ball? Lucille Ball?"

"The kid's red bouncy ball, you goof. It must've bounced into Lila's purse when he was playing with it at the pool. Remember the strap almost took out his mom when she was chasing him? That was the same day Nicky was killed."

"I'm still lost."

"Seeing the ball in her purse today triggered a memory." I tapped the side of my head. "When the twins checked in, I couldn't help but notice Lila's designer purse. You know me and purses." Kat nodded. "That purse was Lila's lifeline. Working twelve-hour shifts as a nurse, it makes sense. Like my mom would say, she kept everything in it but the kitchen sink."

Kat waved her hand in a get-on-with-it motion.

"At check-in, I asked for a credit card. Elle had to dig through Lila's purse to find her wallet. She pulled out half the contents in order to locate it, including a corkscrew."

Kat sat back and groaned. "I think I'm starting to get it."

"It's the only way she could've opened the wine she was carrying, since we forgot to provide corkscrews in the picnic baskets. But when Lila and Elle showed up and pretended to see Nicky's body for the first time, there was no purse. Just the picnic basket and the open bottle of wine."

Kat nodded as she followed my reasoning. "The only way they could've opened the wine was with a tool they had on hand."

"Exactly." I gave her a thumbs-up. "That red ball, like Elle's wallet, had gotten lost in the purse. Lila didn't even notice it. As soon as Duke pulled it out, it reminded me of all the other things she'd been carrying when they'd arrived, including a corkscrew. My only question is why Duke grabbed the kid's ball in the first place."

"Uh, that's my doing," Kat said. "Yesterday, I told him to find the ball. He searched the pool area with no luck. I guess he remembered his task and sniffed the ball out today."

I glanced at the slobbery sleuth, who was currently lying upside down with his tongue hanging out. "That's my boy."

There was a screech of tires in the parking lot. Kat and I exchanged a look of unease. *What now?* Before we had the chance to check it out, my mom rushed into the reception area. She dropped down next to me and began to examine me closely. "Helen called me. Filled me in. Are you okay, Jessica?"

I was about to answer when she engulfed me in a hug. Barely able to breathe, I wheezed out an answer. "I'm good, Mom."

"What a relief." She pulled me even closer and squeezed me like a lemon. We stayed like that for a minute. "You sure you're not hurt?"

"Not yet," I squeaked, trying to catch my breath.

She stroked my hair. "Thank goodness." She let go and slid in beside me on the sofa, effectively shooing Kat out of her seat. "In that case, I guess there's no reason to put it off."

I scrunched up my nose. "What's that?"

"That cameraman out front, Rick, is owed an interview. He's sort of grown on me since I spent so much time guarding him. His job isn't easy. He's really got to hustle to make enough money for his children's education. He's got three boys all under the age of six."

"Sure, Mom." It was easier to get it done then argue.

"Great. C'mon, hon. No time to lose."

My shoulders slumped. "Now?"

She stood up and pulled me to my feet. "I already spoke to Lars. He'll be there with you."

Kat stiffened. "Is that a good idea?"

I held up my hand. "It'll be fine, Kat. Don't worry." I turned back. "Okay, Momager, lead the way."

Mom led me outside and pointed to where Lars was standing, dressed in a fresh-pressed T-shirt, jeans, and a bright smile. He was chatting quietly with the cameraman. "What's up, sunshine? Look at my girl here, Rick. Saves the day and still looks gorgeous."

Rick barely looked at me before turning on the camera. "Can I roll?"

Lars turned to me. "Sorry, babe. Apparently, other crews are on their way. He did what we asked, so he deserves his exclusive. Right?"

I waved to Rick. "Do you really need me? Wouldn't it be better with just Lars?"

"No way," Rick said. "Hot girlfriend breaks the case, reunites with hometown hero. It's golden."

My mouth dropped open. "We're not—"

Lars grabbed my hand. "We're not going to keep you in suspense. Hit it, Rick."

I was caught off guard, and a red dot on the camera began to flash. "Hey, Lars, got a sec?" Rick asked.

Lars smiled. "Of course."

"Is it true your manager was killed this weekend?"

Lars stopped smiling and nodded. "While I can't go into the details, I can tell you a tragedy occurred, resulting in the death of Bob Strapp, my stepdad and former manager. We'd recently parted ways professionally, but he was and always will be my stepdad."

"Can you tell us what happened?"

"Like I said, not yet, but this beautiful woman is the reason I can still smile in the face of tragedy."

Wait, what? I felt my face flush.

Rick pressed on. "Back in the arms of your first love, Lars?"

Lars tapped his chest with an open palm. "Home is where the heart is, isn't that what they say?"

The camera turned toward me. From behind the lens, Rick boomed, "Lars, can you introduce us?"

Lars took a step back and fanned out his arm. "This is Jessica Byrne, owner of the Pearl Bed-and-Breakfast right here in my hometown of Fletcher Lake, New York. If you're looking for the best place to stay when you're visiting the Hudson Valley, this is it."

"Jessica," Rick said. "Are you thrilled to have your man back home?"

I looked at Lars's grin and couldn't help but smile back. But out of the corner of my eye, I saw another face. James. He watched quietly as the camera rolled.

"Lars and I have history. But I'm sure Lars will tell you that's all it is, folks. Just history. He's still the most eligible bachelor in rock. Right, Lars?"

Lars's smile faltered for just a second. He followed where my gaze had strayed and stiffened as he and James locked eyes. A beat passed before he rubbed his forehead and widened his grin, focusing back on me. "You got it, babe." He then turned back to the camera. "I couldn't settle down just yet, right?"

"Okay, thanks, Lars. You heard it here first. For more exclusive content, go to our website."

The red dot shut off and Rick shook Lars's hand, then gave me a dismissive wave and left.

"That's it?" I asked.

Lars looked down at me. The smile faded, but just a bit. "It doesn't take much. As long as he's the first to make the headlines, with a live view, he did his job." He glanced over at James, then back at me. "So, guess I'm not keeping your number on speed dial?"

I reached out and squeezed his arm. "We can't go back, Lars. Too much has happened."

"Okay." He pulled me into a hug, then stood back and ran a hand through his hair. "Yeah, I get it. I better go find Britt, then. She doesn't want to stick around."

"You okay?"

"You know me—I'll be fine. I have a songwriting session booked for next week in New York with Travis and George." He paused. "If you change your mind before that, let me know." Before I could say anything else, he spun on his heel and walked away.

I heard some shuffling behind me and turned to see Kat approaching. She locked arms with me and led me back to reception. We plunked down on the sofa together, and she studied my face. "You okay?"

"Yeah, it's just weird, you know?"

"That about covers this whole weekend."

"Can I borrow one of our *Do Not Disturb* signs? I'm not ready to adult anymore. I see a big bag of Doritos and a lot of Netflix in the next twelve hours."

"Not so fast. I thought you and—"

I shook my head. "Whatever you have in mind, I'm not up for it."

She held her hands up. "Not me. I have a bottle of rosé chilling. I've got number crunching to catch up on."

I groaned. "Then who are you planning to stick me with? Mom? Nate?"

Before Kat answered, James strolled in, his eyes locked on mine. "Hey."

My face flushed all over again. "Oh. Hi."

The right side of his mouth curved up. "Kat mentioned there's a new breakfast place in town. Wondered if you'd want to go check it out with me."

"What about . . . the case?" I cleared my throat. "*Your* case."

He rubbed his jaw. "The canaries are no longer singing. Elle and Lila lawyered up and refuse to say anything else until their attorney arrives from New York. Should give us just enough time for brunch, I'd guess."

I looked at Kat. *Is he asking me out?* She tilted her head, one eyebrow raised.

I smiled at James. "Okay."

He nodded. "Good."

"Good," I repeated. "Can you give me a few minutes to get ready?"

"I'll wait out front." He glanced at Kat. "I'll see you around."

"Sounds that way," she said with a wink.

He turned and shot me a smoking-hot smile before walking out. Once out of earshot, I turned to Kat. "What just happened?"

"I think you got yourself a hot date, babe."

Whoa. I guess I did. With my innkeeper duties done and the murders solved, I was officially and unofficially off duty. I promised to call Kat later and headed back to my room. It was time to hang up my sleuth hat and grab my heels.

Acknowledgments

It is a dream come true to have the privilege of publishing a book I've come to love. A huge thank you must first go out to the readers who have given my book a chance. I hope you enjoy getting to know Jess, Kat, and the rest of the gang who make up this story.

I'm so grateful to Carol Woien, my agent, and Dawn Dowdle, of the Blue Ridge Literary Agency, who have believed in me from the start—thank you.

I bow down to my editor extraordinaire, Terri Bischoff, who made this book so much better. And to the entire team at Crooked Lane—thank you. You are the dream team.

The writing community I've come to know and love is talented, supportive, funny, and a delight to be around. I have to say an extra big thank you to a few who have gone out of their way to help me succeed: Melodie Campbell, Des P Ryan, Joan O'Callaghan, Brian Henry, Hannah Mary McKinnon, Olivia Blacke, Janet Bolin, and Vicki Delany.

Cheryl Freedman, thank you for giving my novel the help it needed to get noticed. I learned so much from you.

Acknowledgments

I have to thank Karen Kilgariff and Georgia Hardstark for starting *My Favorite Murder* and giving us murderinos something to look forward to every week.

I'd be remiss to not thank the "jerks" AKA my besties—c'mon, you know I had to! And to my dad, my sister and brother-in-law, and to the best beta readers around, my mom and my Aunt Stella—love you guys!

Finally, to Troy, my amazing husband, whose unwavering support has kept me going. And to Scarlett and Remy, who are my everything. I love you.

Dream big, laugh hard, and never give up!